# The Resurrection: A Criminal Investigation...

**The Resurrection: A Criminal Investigation of the Mysterious Disappearance of the Body of the Crucified Criminal Jesus of Nazareth**

**By**

## Dr. Rocco Leonard Martino

**BlueNose Press, Inc.**
**Wayne, Pennsylvania**

Published by BlueNose Press

ISBN-10: 0983564973
ISBN-13: 9780983564973



**Please visit: www.roccoleonardmartino.com**

Published by:

***BlueNose Press, Inc.***
***www.bluenosepress.com***

*Published in the United States of America*
*Published July, 2013*

## Novels by Dr. Rocco Leonard Martino

*9-11-11: The Tenth Anniversary Attack*
*The Plot to Cancel Christmas*

## Nonfiction Books by Dr. Rocco Leonard Martino

*Applied Operational Planning*

*Allocating and Scheduling Resources*

*Computer-R-Age with Webster V. Allen*

*Critical Path Networks*

*Decision Patterns*

*Decision Tables* with Staff of MDI

*Dynamic Costing*

*Finding the Critical Path*

*Heat Transfer in Slip Flow*

*IMPACT 70s* with John Gentile

*Information Management*

*Integrated Manufacturing Systems*

*Management Information Systems*

*MIS Methodology*

*Personnel Management Systems*

*Project Management*

*Resources Management*

*UNIVAC Operations Manual*

*People, Machines, and Politics of the Cyber Age Creation*

## Reviews of
## *The Resurrection: A Criminal Investigation . . .*

"So yesterday I finally had time to pick up your book and the only problem was I couldn't stop reading it. Congratulations and thanks for my wonderful experience. You really captured the essence of our faith in a manner easy for all to follow. Your book is an excellent tool for the Year of Faith.......Your summary of leadership was also right on target!"

***-Tim Flanagan, Founder and Chair, Catholic Leadership Institute***

"This book brings commonality to theology."

***-Dr. Patrick McCarthy, KMOb***

"Dr. Martino paints Tribune Quintus as a savvy detective assigned by the Roman Emperor to undertake seriously the apparent disappearance of the body of the crucified criminal Jesus of Nazareth. Filled with tension and mysterious details, the book locks our attention. I found it hard to put the book aside....the story finally shines into the face, and the soul, of us readers an important serious question....does that reveal the crucified Criminal Jesus of Nazareth as ALIVE? And if so, how important is that to all of us?....The novel, breathless at times, rings with the Good News of the Risen Jesus."

***-Fr. George Aschenbrenner, SJ, Jesuit Center, Wernersville, Pennsylvania; Rector Emeritus, Scranton University***

"Throughout history many have attempted, well intentioned or otherwise, to augment or rewrite the gospel record of the life, death and resurrection of Jesus Christ: Gnostics in the early centuries of Christianity and modern movie producers being two examples. In most cases artistic license, or worse deliberate theological distortion, trumped truth and accuracy. A clear exception is "The Resurrection: A Criminal Investigation..." Faith is not being challenged; it is enhanced. Doctor Martino has expertly crafted an imaginary scenario of the events not recorded in Scripture of the happenings surrounding the death and resurrection of Jesus. The story is not only plausible but compelling. The characters with familiar names are vividly portrayed. The reader easily is carried back two thousand years to contemplate, through the eyes of a Roman Tribune, the Paschal Mystery, and become better for the experience."

***-Paul Peterson, Professor of Theology, Archdiocese of Philadelphia***

"Believe it! For 99 cents, I was able to read, perhaps, one of the most important books I will ever read! Once I started, I couldn't stop until finished, less than a day! For me personally, it seemed to give me what I had been searching for all my life!....This is a must-read for anybody who would like to learn how the investigation of an individual should be conducted...before...they were crucified....Thank you Dr. Martino for satisfying my personal need for closure...and for justice to prevail, at least legally..."

***-Glenda A. Bixler, Editor, GABixlerReviews***

"I am reading your book myself and find it thoroughly gripping and very well researched....your book is a real page turner....it is a deeply inspirational work."

***-Gerard O'Sullivan, PhD, Vice President for Academic Affairs, Neumann University***

"A vivid portrayal of the most time-less events of our salvation history... the empty tomb elicits gripping attention, lingering wonderment and thanksgiving."

***-Dr. Robert Capizzi, FACP, FASCO, Co-Founder, President, Chief Medical Officer, CharlestonPharma, LLC***

"I wanted to let you know that I just finished your latest book, The Resurrection. I thought it would be a fitting read for Holy Week. Thank you for writing it! Even though I'm a believer, it always helps to have my beliefs reinforced, and your wonderful book certainly did that for me. I enjoyed your creative approach and liked the way you brought the characters to life. Every doubter of Christ's life, death and resurrection should read this book."

***-Stafford Worley, Co-Founder, Worens Group***

"THE RESURRECTION. What a marvelous experience. Congratulations! I thoroughly enjoyed it. You really integrated everything in a most engaging way."

***-Rev. Fr. Dominic Maruca, S.J., Professor Emeritus, Pontifical Gregorian University of Rome***

"Leaving to others the subtleties of biblical criticism, Dr. Martino leads us through an engaging series of interviews conducted by a persistent but sensitive Roman tribune seeking the answer to why the tomb of Jesus was empty. The author gives expression to his vivid faith and his taste for logic and reasoning, treating us to a couple of imaginative surprises at the end."

***-Peter Kearney, Biblical Scholar***

"I read your book, 'Resurrection', and it is the best yet. It's fascinating to see how one uses logic to arrive at the same conclusions that the rest of us arrive at by faith."

***-Dr. Stephen Schuster, University of Pennsylvania Health Systems.***

"I enjoyed reading it very much. The way the author told the story kept my interest in the factual details of what really happened to our crucified Lord. I learned so much of why Jesus was unjustly murdered. Reading your book strengthens me in my own fundamental faith and beliefs in the agony and suffering of Jesus."

***-John Snyder, S.J.***

"…just as Mel Gibson's movie The Passion has forever changed how I feel about the ministry and painful death of Christ…The Resurrection has changed how I…feel about the politics behind Christ's conviction to death…I really enjoyed this…and foresee a film version…"

***-James Longon, Entrepreneur***

"I must congratulate you on your page-turner THE RESURRECTION. It is fascinating, beautifully written and – well brilliant! I enjoyed every minute of it. It deserves a wide readership…a potent force for evangelization. Thanks for writing it…"

***-Patricia Lynch***

# Dedication and Acknowledgements

I wrote this book when our son Paul challenged me to write a book - fiction or non-fiction - that would critically examine the story of the Resurrection of Jesus. Was it reality or a myth? This miracle is the foundation of the Christian religion. In this book, through the eyes of a skeptical Roman Tribune, I have attempted to pursue an investigation along the lines of a detective mystery. The evidence is presented for the reader by the Tribune just as he presented it to the Emperor Tiberius. Draw your own conclusions.

Before beginning to write this book, I completed extensive research on the First Century using numerous sources. These included the text and commentaries of the Bible; the books and writings of Pope Benedict XVI, especially his books on 'Jesus of Nazareth', on Paul, and on the Apostles; the books of Father Raymond E. Brown, S.S., Father Gerald O'Collins, S.J., and Father Frederick J. Cwiekowski, S.S.; and various anthologies, encyclopedia, and commentaries.

My sincerest thanks to Sister Joan Dugan, S.S.J. and Ashley Pavone who were meticulous in smoothing my word flow and in checking my logic and clarity. My thanks also to Adrienne Holcombe for typing the original manuscript.

This book is dedicated to the three ladies who motivated and supported me throughout my life. Barbara is my wife of over fifty-one years, my best friend, the mother of our children, and an unbelievable buttress of strength when I am weary. Josephine my mother never left me even though she departed this world when I was eight years old. Her 'presence' during my toughest exams, if not all my exams, was key to whatever success I achieved. The Virgin Mary, mother of Jesus, mother of God, and mother of us all, was often there when I cried for help, especially on the multiple occasions when I came so close to death. Thank you dear ladies.

Dr. Rocco Leonard Martino
Villanova, Pennsylvania
January, 2013

# Table of Contents

**The Resurrection: A Criminal Investigation of the Mysterious Disappearance of the Body of the Crucified Criminal Jesus of Nazareth**

# Chapter One
# Capri

"Execute them all!" The Emperor Tiberius was angry. The news from Judea was ridiculous. What was that fool Pontius Pilate up to? What incredible nonsense in that last dispatch from Judea. The carpenter son of a virgin had risen from the dead after being crucified. Impossible! What fools would believe a fairy tale like that? The criminal was really innocent? Who would murder an innocent man? Was this an execution for state reasons or for private gain? How could Pontius Pilate allow such a mess to happen? Worse still, how could it now come to his attention? There must be a situation brewing. The followers of this risen criminal could be a threat to Pax Romana - the peace of Rome. Nonsense! He would send Tribune Quintus to find out what had really taken place. His orders would be to investigate what happened, determine the best interests of Rome, and act accordingly. If need be, he could execute the whole lot; all the followers of the criminal, and even Pontius Pilate. "Send for Tribune Quintus!" he roared to his aide.

Some days later in his palace high on the bluffs of Capri, looking to the Northeast, Emperor Tiberius paced impatiently. He had summoned the Tribune of his Praetorian, Quintus Gaius Caesar, to report immediately. As he paced back and forth between the conference room and the terrace that overlooked the sea and the route from Rome, Tiberius continually tapped a rolled papyrus against his right leg. He was frustrated. With all his power as the Emperor of the

Roman Empire, he seemed unable to control that idiot, Pontius Pilate. Pontius Pilate was certainly a problem ever since he was appointed as Governor of Judea in the twelfth year of the reign of Tiberius (26 AD). He stirred up a host of trouble with the Jews in his early years mainly because of his complete ignorance of their religion. Since then, he had behaved satisfactorily by keeping everything under control. Judea had been relatively free of major problems until this latest series of dispatches from Pontius Pilate, which indicated trouble over some executed criminal; a carpenter from Nazareth named Jesus. Pontius Pilate was a weak, vacillating idiot. If he had any courage or command ability he would be in battle somewhere. He was good enough for Judea, a place no one wanted to rule over, but not good enough for any better assignment. Tiberius growled inwardly. Little troubles become big troubles quickly if not handled correctly. It appeared that Pontius Pilate had not handled this one right. A new problem had to be solved. But first, Tiberius needed the facts. That is why he had summoned Quintus.

Tiberius was Rome's Emperor and greatest general prior to that. He was a vigorous man, disposed to immediate action, smashing problems as they occurred. In his later years, and especially after becoming Emperor, he had learned to bide his time, to strategize each move before acting. While he detested administration, he was determined to exercise control of everything about him without becoming so engrossed in details as to become tied down. First and foremost, Tiberius sought freedom, and complete control over that freedom.

In his 76th year of life, approaching his twentieth anniversary as Emperor, Tiberius was very physically fit. He was lean and muscular, exercising daily, mostly in simulated combat with his troop of trainers. Of late his whiskers had become silver colored, but his step was springy and rapid, more especially when he was angry.

As Tiberius stared into the gloom of approaching nightfall, he saw in the distance a squadron of five galleys moving rapidly toward the landing dock of his palace here on the Island of Capri. His impatience eased a little: soon he would be able to take some action. He knew he could rely on Tribune Quintus.

Ruling the Empire of Rome from Capri had mixed blessings. The Emperor had built a magnificent palace on the northeast ridge of

Capri, looking north to Naples and Rome. He had retired to this estate in the twelfth year of his reign (26 AD), when he felt his power was complete and he could rule at a distance. The views were magnificent, but more importantly he was separated by distance from the pettiness of Rome, and the continual threat of assassination. The day-to-day trappings of governing had always been a burden since becoming Emperor as a result of the death of Augustus Caesar in the 785th year from the Founding of Rome (14 AD). Almost immediately Tiberius had appointed his close friend and confidant, Lucius Aelius Sejanus as Prefect of the Praetorian. Tiberius consolidated his power the following year with the transfer of elections from the Popular Assemblies of the People to the Senate. With the control of the Praetorian in his hands through Sejanus, his personal and direct control was complete. He then worked to bolster the strength of his support. With the construction of the Castra Praetoria completed in the eighth year of the reign of Tiberius (22 AD), and centralization of the Praetorian into a single barrack, the power of the Praetorian was secure and complete. Through them, Tiberius had absolute control of everything. Then he could and did move his residence to Capri, but left the actual government in place in Rome.

Tiberius never wanted to be Emperor. He was happiest leading troops into battle, and relishing in victory over the vanquished. He approached government in the same way. Just as in the field of battle, he prepared his strategy, picked his commanders, and executed his plans. Hence his strategy was to consolidate power, appoint those through whom to exercise that power, and then to leave Rome and do as he wanted. Against the advice of many, he left Rome to find peace in an idyllic refuge free of the squalor and continual pettiness of those seeking favors and power. In Capri, he would govern the affairs of the far-flung provinces. He had placed the head of the Praetorian, Sejanus, in charge of day- to- day affairs as he left Rome.

All was well until the seventeenth year of his reign (31 AD) when Tiberius discovered that Sejanus was seeking to overthrow him and assume the position of Emperor for himself. Tiberius learned Sejanus had actually been instrumental in having Tiberius' son, Drusus Julius Caesar, murdered in the ninth year of his reign (23 AD). Carefully orchestrating his control over events, Tiberius had

Sejanus arrested and executed. Tiberius soon appointed Naevius Cordus Sutorius Macro as Prefect of the Praetorian, but without control over Rome's day-to-day activities. That Tiberius now reserved for himself. He had then appointed Quintus Gaius Caesar as Deputy Prefect of the Praetorian. Though he mostly trusted Macro, he placed unlimited trust in Quintus.

Quintus was the only man in Rome that the Emperor fully trusted. He was the son of his first wife, born some years after their divorce, yet rumor had it that the Emperor was also his father. Quintus was certainly favored by Tiberius. Tiberius smiled at the thought; only he knew the truth. Perhaps, he mused, Quintus might even succeed him.

Quintus had distinguished himself in battle over the years. He had even served in Judea as a Centurion in the early days of Pontius Pilate's term. That experience would certainly help with this assignment.

Tiberius walked to the balcony once more. His impatience was rewarded. The galley was getting closer. He looked at the sky and saw dusk approaching. It would be a race but he knew that his orders would be followed. The galley would dock even if the sun had set.

Tiberius abruptly turned and walked toward the entrance of the meeting hall bellowing for the guard. When he appeared, Tiberius gave the orders for extensive torches to be lit at the dock and on the path from the dock to the palace. He also ordered that a chariot wait at the dock to bring Quintus to him as quickly as possible following the anchoring of the galley.

Tiberius walked rapidly to his accustomed place at the head of the meeting table. And in a vile frame of mind, he threw himself in the chair and began to unroll the papyrus, reading it again and muttering his displeasure as he waited for the arrival of Quintus. The problem of Pontius Pilate sprang to his mind; venting his anger and impatience he tapped the papyrus roll against his leg as repeatedly.

* * *

Aboard the bireme galley, Quintus stood on the command deck with the Captain. In the distance he saw torches as they were being lit, outlining the path upward to the palace. It was quickly getting dark; it would be a race to reach the dock before the sun set totally and the darkness was complete. The Ship Master had ordered steady high speed cadence on the drum. The 120 rowers on deck rowed to the beat of the drum, with cracks of the master's whip punctuating drum beats. Occasionally there was a cry of pain from a rower, but this caused no pause in the steady rowing. The single sail was full, adding speed to that of the rowers.

Quintus was born to be in command. Standing taller than most Romans, he was fair-skinned and remarkably handsome, with the clean cut features he inherited from his mother, one of the noted beauties of Rome. In battle he had distinguished himself because of his strength and fearlessness. His promotions had been rapid, and now he was deemed one of the small handful of ultra powerful men in Rome. He was repeatedly called upon by the Emperor for special assignments. His normal duties now were Deputy Commander of the Praetorian Guard, the resident Legion that was the central power of the Emperor. Through the Guard, Tiberius controlled everything, including the Senate. So long as he controlled the Praetorian, he controlled Rome. The Commander of the Guard was personally indebted to Tiberius, and completely loyal to him. The power of the Emperor within the Empire was secure. The only mar on this could be revolts or unrest with any of the conquered people.

Quintus turned to the Captain, "Will you dock tonight or in the morning?"

"Tribune, the Emperor's orders were explicit. I was commanded to deliver you to him as quickly as possible. We will dock tonight!" exclaimed the Captain, ending the discussion.

With that, the Captain signaled the Shipmaster to increase the beat by raising his hand twice. Almost immediately, the drum beat increased in tempo from high speed to ramming speed, the fastest rowing speed possible in the high speed bireme galley. The row master strode back and forth cracking his whip even more furiously on the backs of any rower who did not respond as rapidly as needed. The rowers met the beat, and the galley seemed to leap forward. Quintus and the Captain had to reach out for support to maintain their balance.

As they sped toward the dock, the Captain told Quintus that a cohort of one hundred soldiers would be assigned to him. While

Quintus met with Emperor, the cohort would be boarded on the five-ship squadron, which would also be provisioned for a long voyage. When he asked their destination, the Captain said he wasn't quite sure. His orders were to go wherever Quintus commanded him, and to ensure his safety at all times.

Quintus wondered. Could be it Egypt, or to the west and Iberia? He knew he would be told soon by the Emperor. He truly admired Tiberius, one of the greatest generals Rome had ever had. Quintus knew Tiberius favored him, and that rumors circulated that he had fathered Quintus. Quintus disregarded those rumors as jealousy for the fact that he had found favor with Tiberius. He assumed the rumors had their source in the fact that his mother, Vipsania Agrippina, had once been married to Tiberius.

The galley rapidly approached the torchlight landing dock as the sun set. The drum beat slowed and then stopped, the rowers lifted their oars and the galley glided to a stop at the dock, pulled in by the slaves on the dock using the lines thrown from the galley. A chariot was there waiting. On landing, Quintus jumped on the dock and strode rapidly to the chariot alone, leaving his cohort of soldiers to follow. Once on the chariot, Quintus gave the driver orders to proceed. At the snap of the whip they took off at a furious pace up the torch-lit path to the top of the bluff.

* * *

After the heart-stopping ride, the chariot screeched into the courtyard of the palace, coming to an immediate halt. Quintus jumped off and followed the waiting escort into the Emperor's Council Room of the upper level of the Palace. Quintus entered, strolled rapidly to the Emperor's chair and saluted, "Sire, I am here and ready to do your bidding!" He remained standing. The Emperor rose from his chair, grasped Quintus by the arm, and welcomed him. "I am pleased you came so quickly, Quintus." He smiled at Quintus, then released his arm, motioned to the chairs, and sat down. Brusquely he handed the papyrus roll to Quintus and commanded, "Read this dispatch from Pontius Pilate!"

Quintus looked at the Emperor and realized how disturbed he was. It wasn't so much what he said as how he said it. His immediate guess was that there was a problem revealed in the dispatch from Pontius Pilate. He caught the roll, and sat in a chair facing the Emperor.

Quintus unrolled the papyrus and read quickly. He could not control the puzzled look on his face. When he stopped reading, he stared at the roll in his hands for a minute and rolled it up again, looked directly at the Emperor and said, "Sire, I can understand that you must be disturbed by this dispatch. I know Pontius Pilate. I served in his Legion in Judea some years ago. He is not a resolute man. He seeks power ruthlessly while appearing to be everyone's friend. He is weak and vacillating. I would not trust anything he says, but you can trust that he will do anything you ask as Emperor because he fears you. With others, he acts to keep support for himself. In his weakness, he tries to please everyone and ends up pleasing no one."

He stopped, paused for a moment and then abruptly changed the subject. "This dispatch just doesn't make sense. He says that he has condemned to death a man in whom he found no fault, but he still executed him as a criminal. Rome does not execute innocent people and then tell the world that they are innocent. We execute criminals, even if innocent, as a lesson for others. This man Jesus, a carpenter from Nazareth, must have been a threat to Pilate even if he had not been guilty of sedition against Rome. Pontius Pilate should have so stated."

Then looking directly at the Emperor he quietly added, "Why don't you replace Pontius Pilate?"

Tiberius looked at him and chuckled, "All in good time Quintus, all in good time. For now I have a bigger problem." And with that he handed Quintus another papyrus roll. "Now read this one. It just arrived this afternoon. I summoned you when I received the first papyrus two days ago. Now your mission has become more critical. Read this and then I will explain."

Quintus unrolled the second papyrus. He began to read and he could not control the look of surprise and dismay across his features. He finished with a gasp, and turned to the Emperor, "I understand."

Tiberius grunted and continued, "The body of this criminal has disappeared and Pilate thinks he may have killed a god. That is impossible. Gods cannot be killed. They are immortal. If Pontius

Pilate would do his job as governor, he would discover who made off with the body and who is spreading the false rumors. This is a criminal investigation. Pontius Pilate seems incapable of discovering who did it." With a note of exasperation in his voice he added, "He even had a sign placed over the criminal on the cross labeling him as 'Jesus of Nazareth, King of the Jews.'"

"Sire, replace him!"

The Emperor gazed thoughtfully at Quintus. He waited for a moment before replying, "Quintus you were born to command. You understand completely. But as I said, 'All in good time.' What is required first is an investigation. Replacing Pontius Pilate now will give credence to rumors." Tiberius stopped, and seemed to smile sardonically before continuing, "I knew that Sejanus had plotted against me and had even been instrumental in the murder of my son Drusus. It took me years to regain control and have Sejanus executed, even though I am Emperor. Quintus, you will learn that the exercise of power must be done gently so that when strong steps are taken it is obvious to everyone that it is the right thing to do. Theoretically as Emperor I can have the head of the Praetorian executed but if I don't have the support of the Praetorian, then they may assassinate me. Here it is obvious that Pontius Pilate is not an effective Governor and that he must be replaced without causing greater harm. Leaving him in place for a short period of time will not do as much harm as replacing him hurriedly and increasing the unrest. That unrest is what really concerns me. We have to nip that unrest in the bud now before it becomes serious. The Jews of Judea are an intelligent hard-working people. They will always fight for their freedom. We give them more latitude than most conquered people, but periodically we have to show our power. Pontius Pilate has been ruthless in dealing with them, more than required. For whatever reason, he has acted strangely. There must be some unrest. Whatever we do, we must quell that unrest that I sense, and which Pontius Pilate hints at." Looking directly at Quintus, he added, "More can be achieved in a short period of time by sending a Legate to gather all the facts so my actions will not only be effective, but will have wide support." Tiberius chuckled. "Now I sound like Pontius Pilate." The chuckle gave way to a benevolent smile.

He continued, "I tell you this because I see in so much of myself in you. I want to teach you how to govern. You have proven yourself a leader in all you do in battle, and as a Tribune what you do beyond battle. You know how to command and lead. You have shown that. You are one of the most powerful leaders in the entire Empire. Someday you may even lead the Empire. But leadership is much more than just issuing orders. True leadership is the ability to decide and give the commands that are best and right for the situation at hand. But most important of all, leadership depends on having everyone follow these commands because they accept them, believe in the leader, and are prepared to do what he commands. It is this ability to direct others and to have them follow because they respect and believe in you, that makes a great leader. Forcing people to do your bidding because they fear you is a sham. Using your power to enforce bad decisions is also a sham. Making decisions out of fear, haste, or expediency is also a sham. Leadership is knowing what has to be done, making all the decisions to do it, and getting those you command to follow you. That is the essence of a leader."

The Emperor added, "Pontius Pilate does not have that kind of ability. You do!"

Tiberius stopped, looking intently at Quintus. Throughout all this, Quintus sat quietly with his mind in turmoil. He knew that Tiberius favored him and he began to wonder if the rumors were true and he was the Emperor's son. The next words from the Emperor did not really surprise him, but it was not what he expected.

The Emperor gazed thoughtfully at Quintus. "I rule. Pontius Pilate plays at it." Then looking earnestly at Quintus, Tiberius added, "Quintus, I want you to go to Judea as quickly as possible and begin a criminal investigation of the disappearance of the body of Jesus of Nazareth. Investigate everything. Interview everybody. Uncover all the facts about this man, Jesus, and the circumstances associated with his trial and execution. In particular, check on the disappearance of His body. Make sure He actually died on the cross. Make sure there is no alternative way out of the tomb other than the entrance sealed with a large stone that covers the entire entrance."

Quintus could not restrain himself from asking, even though he was sure he knew the answer, "Sire, why send me? Why is this situation so important to you at this time?"

Tiberius swirled the wine in his goblet. Looking directly at Quintus, he smiled, raised his goblet in a half toast in his direction, and said, "Because I trust you, and because you are a leader." Pausing to sip his wine, he continued, "As for your second question, Judea is one of the most challenging provinces or sub-provinces in the Empire. The people are highly intelligent, and want their freedom. Governing there requires great finesse and diplomacy. If we succeed, the people become a potent bulwark against the barbarians to the East of them. Otherwise, the always present threat of insurrection can ignite into a major problem." He stopped and his face scowled. He almost spat out the next words. "That cursed place is like a unlit pile of tinder, requiring only a spark to ignite." He paused again, staring thoughtfully into the distance, before looking at Quintus, then went on, "I can't really explain why, but my gut tells me there is more here than meets the eye. This whole situation doesn't smell right to me. The man executed may or may not have been a criminal, but He certainly had a following from the reports I received over the past few months. Pontius Pilate may be a fool, but he is a crafty bastard who will do whatever it takes to save his own skin and further his career. Something about this man Jesus scared him. If something is brewing at this end of our Empire, it must be crushed before it has momentum. We have to nip it in the bud. That is why I must also send someone with the authority to take over if necessary. You have the authority to depose Pontius Pilate on the spot. If you have to arrest and execute the leaders of the Jews, do so. I would rather you did not; I would much rather do it calmly and slowly," Tiberius added as he nodded slowly to Quintus, "But if immediate action is needed, take it."

Quintus was puzzled. "Sire," he asked, "what of the Jews. Did Pontius Pilate provide any information about the reaction of the Jewish people?"

Tiberius smiled. "Quintus you have put your finger on the problem." Taking a sip of wine, he added, "There is no mention of reaction from the people, only from their leaders, especially the High Priest, Caiaphas."

Both men remained silent for a moment. Quintus quietly observed, "Then Pontius Pilate is helping the High Priest to maintain his power. This Jesus must have been a threat to that power base and

Pontius Pilate decided to side with them. He may even have sided against the will of the people themselves."

"Exactly" said the Emperor. That's why you must go and find out what and why it all happened. The Jewish people can be a bulwark of strength for us if they are on our side. The High Priest will always be on his own side whatever that may be. We can never count on him."

The Emperor paused, took another sip of wine, and then continued, "Quintus you may not need it, but let me give you a reminder on handling this diplomatically. Trust no one. Assassins are everywhere. That is the easiest way for many people to solve a political problem." Looking earnestly again at Quintus, he added softly and calmly, "You will be a problem for some of these people. You will be a real threat. The possibility of assassination is real." Here Tiberius stopped, looking intently at Quintus for a few seconds, and then turning away, sipped his goblet, and abruptly changed the subject.

"Quintus, be a blood hound on this. Find the criminals behind the theft of the body and execute them. Make them an example, bringing fear to any others who would break our laws. Uncover all the true facts. Chase every lead to its end and document them fully. Try and keep the Jewish people on our side. I will send my personal scribe, Marcus, with you. He will make notes of all your meetings, transcribe them into a full report, and prepare dispatches for me. He is fluent in Hebrew, Aramaic, Greek and Latin. You speak some Aramaic and Hebrew I am told."

"Yes, Sire. I learned both while I served in Judea," replied Quintus. "I will also recruit from the resident Roman Legion there. Many Legionaries are native people who have joined our Legions."

"Good. That solves the language problem to some extent. I like your idea of finding and using soldiers to help who also speak some Aramaic. I asked for a Centurion and a cohort of one hundred soldiers who spoke the language to be assigned to you. Check on that." Tiberius took another sip from his goblet and continued regarding the dispatches and report, "You can deliver your final report when you return. Send the dispatches as you proceed," then he added as a quiet postscript, "Do this as quickly as you can." Tiberius stopped and handed Quintus a small roll of papyrus. He continued, "I have prepared a command papyrus for you to show to anyone you choose to prove that you have my complete authority. Your requests are commands from me." With that Tiberius handed Quintus a small papyrus. The Emperor stood. Quintus rose immediately since no one sat while the Emperor stood.

Tiberius walked over to Quintus and took him by the arm, "Come let us have supper. In the morning at first light, you leave."

* * *

The dinner was a great success. They dined alone in the great hall with a blazing fire and musicians playing the latest popular music in Rome. The two men spoke of the campaigns they had fought, what the strategy had been, and why they had won them all. They spoke of the provinces and the governors. A number of times Tiberius smiled crookedly, raised his wine goblet, toasted Quintus, and asked, "Do you want that province?" Then he would laugh, and add, "But perhaps the best province is Rome itself." After which he once said in a very dour way, "If you want it."

Occasionally Tiberius would gaze into the fire and ask for news of Quintus' mother, Vipsania Agrippina. Quintus was certain Tiberius still loved her even though he had divorced her to marry Julia, whom he had since divorced for infidelity.

Quintus noticed the guards everywhere. He asked Tiberius the reason. Tiberius muttered, "Assassins are everywhere. Even here. I must be protected."

Quintus began to understand.

After dinner, Tiberius again raised the issue of unrest in Judea, "If they are a threat, Quintus, we must crush them." As he said this, Tiberius raised his right hand and raising it, clenched his fist. Again he said, "Crush them." Then he relaxed his hand, clamped it on Quintus' shoulder, and said, "Goodnight, Quintus. I will be with you in the morning when you leave."

With that, Tiberius strode into his bedchamber, with Quintus calling after him, "Good night, Sire."

Quintus retired to his bedchamber. Sleep eluded him as he kept pacing the room, thoughts of his mission circling in his brain.

Was this Jesus a criminal or not? Was He a threat to the public order or were there other considerations leading Pontius Pilate to have Jesus crucified? Why did Pontius Pilate place that idiotic sign over his head on the cross? Was he trying to call attention to this man, or was he trying to mitigate the crime he had committed by having an innocent man murdered? Quintus shrugged. As distasteful as it was to his sense of honor, it was done all the time. Murder was the easiest way to solve a political problem. Quintus could understand that, even though he would challenge its use as a lasting solution.

The missing body bothered him; Why? How?

Most disturbing of all was the reference to 'killing a god.' Was Pontius Pilate insane or was that what really happened...killing a god!

Then there was the unrest. What caused it? Was it potentially a conflagration requiring intervention from Rome? Could it be handled locally? Most importantly, could it be handled discreetly without creating even more unrest?

The ramifications of his mission circled in his thoughts until, with a major effort, he stilled the cycle. There was no point now in anticipating what he would find. His mission was clear:

I. Find out what exactly happened to the body.
II. Determine the political and power situation in Judea. This would require exhaustive examination of the relationship of the Jews, the Jewish leaders, King Herod, and the followers of Jesus to each other and to Rome.
III. Uncover the reasons for the current unrest, and unearth all factors in the life of Jesus and the actions of his followers, both as real and potential threats to Pax Romana.

The project was clear in his mind and he was anxious to get started. First, however, he had to get to Judea. Despite the lateness of the hour, Quintus summoned the Captain from the galley.

When the Captain arrived, he and Quintus planned the voyage. They consulted members of Tiberius' household for suggestions of places to stop for supplies on the way. In one session with the Chief Steward, the name of Saul, a tentmaker in Tarsus, was mentioned as a possible source of information. There wasn't much additional information beyond the mention of his name. Since Tarsus was a convenient port for supplies towards the end of their voyage, the men decided to add Tarsus as the last stop before Caesarea in Judea, their final destination by sea. Quintus would travel to Jerusalem by chariot from there.

* * *

The next morning, the five fast bireme galleys were ready to leave. The cohort of one hundred soldiers and a Centurion had already embarked. The cohort was divided into twenty soldiers in each galley. The Centurion, Aurelius Antonius, was on the lead galley with Quintus. He and twenty-seven of the cohort spoke Aramaic. Also with Quintus was his scribe slave, Marcus, who would record notes of everything Quintus discovered in a report to the Emperor. Marcus spoke Greek, Aramaic, and Hebrew, as well as Latin. Although Quintus had been taught to read and write, it was best to leave the tedium of writing to a slave. A sixth smaller galley with dispatches for Pontius Pilate and Roman garrisons along the journey had already left for Judea.

The Emperor rode down to the dock with Tiberius. As the first light of day pierced the gloom, Quintus saluted the Emperor and they both grasped arms. The Emperor quietly spoke, "May the gods be with you, Quintus."

Quintus stood totally erect, and looking directly into the Emperor's eyes, said quietly to the Emperor, "Sire, I will not fail you. I will find out what really happened, and report directly back to you." With a final salute, he boarded the command galley and strode to the command deck. He nodded to the Captain and said, "Set sail!"

The Captain motioned to the ship commander; the rumble of the drum began to beat, and the row master began snapping his whip on the backs of the rowers. The oars erupted in and out of the water. The galley began to move to the cadence of the drum as the squadron of galleys set out for Judea.

The Emperor stood at the dock and watched until the galleys were almost out of sight. Then he turned, mounted the chariot and gave the order to proceed to the palace. As he rode, he kept opening and closing his fist. His whole life had been devoted to crushing opposition. He knew Quintus would provide him with the necessary information for an effective decision. What a problem to have as he approached the twentieth anniversary of his reign. (34 AD)

"Go faster!" he commanded the chariot driver.

## The Resurrection: A Criminal Investigation of the Mysterious Disappearance of the Body of the Crucified Criminal Jesus of Nazareth

# Chapter Two
# Saul of Tarsus

The voyage was long. The five galleys proceeded as a squadron with the galley of Quintus in the lead. The four supporting galleys would change position, depending on what kind of attack might come from pirates or enemies of the Empire. The bireme was the fastest galley available to the navy of the Roman Empire. It was estimated that the trip to Judea would take three to four weeks. In order to reach Judea as rapidly as possible, they would travel to Caesarea in Judea and from there proceed by chariot to Jerusalem. The dispatches sent by the Emperor would arrive at each port before them with the assurance of support of the Roman garrisons at each stop.

During the voyage, Quintus planned the approach in his mind that he would take in completing his investigation. In order to solve the mystery, he had to resolve six fundamental issues:

I. Was Jesus truly dead when placed in the tomb? Had He been placed in the tomb alive, either conscious or unconscious? Had Jesus walked out of the tomb?

II. Was His body stolen or not stolen from the tomb; and if stolen, by whom?

III. Could Jesus have been a god and actually risen from the dead?

IV. Was Jesus a criminal or an innocent man? If He was innocent, why was he executed?

V. How could the strange irresolute behavior of Pontius Pilate be explained? Was he a pawn influenced by other forces? If so, by what or whom? Was it Jesus, the followers of Jesus, the Jews, or whom? To what extent, then, was Pontius Pilate compromised as an effective Proconsul of Judea?

VI. Was Jesus a threat to Rome in His lifetime, or now, after His execution? Were his followers organized to become a revolutionary group against Rome? Were his followers coalescing into a sect that could become a thorn in the side of Rome? If so, then Quintus had to advise Tiberius how to crush it.

He went over and over all aspects of the assignment from the Emperor and determined that these were the salient points that needed to be covered. As he continuously recounted the elements of his assignment, he mentally nodded to himself at each point. He finally had Marcus commit his thoughts to words as the beginning of his report to the Emperor.

He was anxious to begin, but the trip was long and arduous. There were many storms, but they finally passed the rough waters south of the Grecian Islands. They stopped three times for food and water supplies, each stop-short and very business-like. The rowers were driven to their limit in the press for speed. They were replaced by fresh slaves as needed during their supply stops. The strong winds of late spring's stormy season gave the ships some respite when it filled their sails.

Soon they came to the coast of Cilicia and headed directly for the port of Tarsus as Quintus and the Captain had planned. During the voyage, the Centurion told them that he had just returned to Rome from Judea and he knew that there was a zealous enemy of the followers of Jesus who lived in Tarsus, a tent maker named Saul. He was a highly educated man and a Pharisee. It would be worth while speaking to him. This confirmed what Quintus had learned in Capri, and it reinforced his decision to use the port time in Tarsus to seek out this Saul and speak with him.

The five galleys landed at Tarsus. The Centurion immediately secured horses from the Roman garrison there for Quintus, ten guards and himself. When the horses arrived at the dock, they mounted and went in search of Saul. The Centurion Aurelius

Antonius asked directions from persons along the way, and led Quintus and the troop. The journey was short. Soon they rode into a small courtyard adjoining a large building. There they saw a man sewing together pieces of canvas stretched on frames that were placed just inside the building entrance. He worked quickly and seemingly without effort, moving along the edge of two sections, holding them together with one hand while he used a long needle to sew them together. He was thin, of moderate height and had an upright bearing, closer to that of a soldier than of a workman. He had a light brown beard and a high forehead, with his hair growing towards the back of his head. He seemed to have a spring in his step and in his movements as he worked. He stopped, still grasping the canvas sections with one hand, needle in the air in the other hand as he saw the troop enter the courtyard. He directed a quizzical look at the entire troop and then directed his attention to Quintus as he saw the tunic and emblems of rank belonging to a Tribune. A puzzled look came over his face, with no shred of fear whatsoever. He put his needle down, laid the canvas sections back on their frames, and let the sewn section drop to the ground. Then he stood erect looking directly at Quintus waiting for someone from the troop to speak.

As Quintus rode up, he too was puzzled. This man had no fear and had the bearing of one used to command. If he had not seen him sewing the pieces of canvas together to form a tent, he would have sworn the man was a soldier, perhaps a Centurion or even a Tribune. He seemed more like a soldier or statesman, out of place as a tentmaker.

Quintus waved the Centurion Aurelius away and rode directly up to the man. He stopped in front of him, and, leaning forward asked in his halting Hebrew, “Are you Saul the tentmaker?”

The man looked up in surprise, a smile tugged at his lips, and amusement seemed to ignite his features. In a firm voice, he answered in Greek, “Tribune, yes I am.” Then he added in Hebrew, “Where did you learn Hebrew? Are you not a Tribune?" Then Saul looked more closely at the insignia on the tunic, "You are more than just a Tribune. What are the extra badges of rank you have?"

Quintus was surprised. This was no ordinary tent maker. He had immediately identified his uniform and emblems as that of a Tribune and he spoke flawless Greek. He also had a commanding presence and had spoken as if he was his equal. Quintus smiled. He would be able to converse easily with this articulate and strong person. He decided to speak only in Greek. He beckoned Marcus, the scribe, and told him to take notes of the conversation. Marcus immediately took a clay tablet from his pouch and a stylus to make notes of the conversation. As he spoke to Marcus in Latin, he noticed the quick uptake of Saul's face. Quintus immediately discovered that Saul understood Latin as well. Saul was indeed a learned man.

Quintus dismounted and strode over to where Saul stood. "You are right, Saul. I am Co-Prefect of the Praetorian, second only to Naevius Sutorius Macro, the Prefect. I am here to find out about Jesus of Nazareth, and why His death is so important to so many people."

Then with a smile he added, "I see you speak Latin as well as Greek. Where did you learn all this? Surely not while mending tents."

Saul laughed. "You are right, Tribune. I am impressed with your rank. If I am not mistaken, you are one of the most powerful men in the entire Roman Empire. This mission of yours must be very important for you to come all this way to talk to a lowly tentmaker." Here Saul even grinned a little. He certainly had a sense of humor to go with his perceptive mind. As the grin changed to a slight smile, he continued, factually, with no hint of assumed pride, "I am a Pharisee. I studied in Jerusalem with the great Rabbi Gamaliel, and am well versed in the faith of the chosen people of God. I am a Roman citizen, and take pride in my ability to speak Latin. Greek is my normal language, except in the work of the Temple, when it is Hebrew. Someday I hope to travel to Rome, but for now, I have much work to do here as a Pharisee and as a tentmaker. I am a tentmaker as a means of earning my daily bread."

This confirmed Quintus' opinions about the education of Saul. The quick and factual summary confirmed his command capability. He was certainly learned; not pompous. He could be relied on for some good testimony, but it would be of his choosing. Quintus had to be wary of the questions he posed and the answers returned. Abruptly Quintus said, "I have been told you knew this man, Jesus of Nazareth. What can you tell me about His life, death, and reputation?"

Saul's face clouded over and he spat on the ground, "That scoundrel blasphemed! He misled many with His magic and trickery. He deserved to be put to death! I am commissioned by the Sanhedrin, the priests of the Temple, to search out all His followers, arrest them, and have them admit their errors, and recant. If they do not, then to have them stoned."

Saul paused. After a long sigh, he continued, "I do not condone stoning, but it is necessary to stop this evil from spreading. This false teaching must be stamped out even if it means death for those who refuse to give up their false beliefs." Looking directly at Quintus, he continued, "I was instrumental in having one of his followers stoned recently. His name was Stephen. I did not throw any stones, but I guarded the robes of those who did." Once again Saul stopped, now gazing into the dirt at their feet as if reliving that vision, "It was difficult for me." Then he stopped, seemed to breathe a little harder, and looked up at Quintus. Quintus saw emotion in Saul's eyes; a look of concern yet one of great strength.

In a firm voice, Saul went on, "In fact, I always do what I believe is right. I am a trained Pharisee who believes in the law. Now my commission from the Temple is to find and root out all believers of the false teachings of Jesus, especially in Damascus. I depart in a few days when I finish my assignment on this tent."

Saul stopped and with a quizzical look on his face, asked Quintus, "Why did you come to see me? Surely you seek more than my opinion of the false teachings of Jesus of Nazareth? What can I tell you that you don't know about that group of misguided and misled rabble?"

Quintus was surprised at the strength of the man he was facing. He saw before him an articulate, strong-willed and learned zealot, a man dedicated to upholding the law as he knew it. What the Centurion had told him was true, but the depth of the emotion in Saul of Tarsus surprised him. "What kind of man was Jesus?"

Saul's brow wrinkled, while he replied, "I never met him. I was never in the same place at the same time when Jesus was. I saw and met many who knew him, people he cured of illness, people he spoke to, people he dined with, and people in whose homes he stayed. I have spoken with many of his followers, and heard them tell stories of what he did and said." Here Saul stopped, pausing in deep thought. Then he shrugged his shoulders, and continued.

"I don't believe it, but in their eyes he was a great man. They called him 'Master' and looked upon him as the Messiah." Saul showed some confusion. Once again he shrugged, shook his head a little, and went on.

"They spoke of him in awe. He always communicated gently, preaching constantly speaking of the kingdom of God, curing people and telling stories that exhorted them to do what is right. They always understood the point of his stories, simple folk tales that spoke of doing good for the sake of good. He rebelled against our rules by healing on the Sabbath."

Now Saul's eyes brightened as he felt on safe ground, the ground of his rules, "He even dared to associate with tax collectors, publicans, sinners and even prostitutes. He stopped us from stoning one lady by asking the one without sin from the crowd to throw the first stone," and again Saul paused.

"And yet, He blasphemed! He claimed he was the son of God. He even said, and many who heard him told me, 'Before Abraham was, I am!'" Saul spat to give emphasis to his words, "He blasphemed!" Saul stopped, waiting for a reaction from Quintus.

Quintus had remained silent throughout. He wanted to hear everything Saul had to say. He decided to ask about a troubling fact from the dispatches of Pontius Pilate.

"Do you know anything about this claim that he was 'King of the Jews?'"

Saul looked at him and said with a note of derision in his voice, "I am told he claimed to be the Messiah. Sheer nonsense! The Messiah will not come as a beggar, but as a King, - an Emperor! - full of authority. The Messiah will lead us to greatness. Our people will be free with the Messiah as their leader."

As he said this, Saul's face brightened, his eyes sparkled, and he seemed to swell and grow in stature. Quintus knew that Saul was zealous in his belief, and let his zeal fuel his actions. After speaking, Saul stared into the distance and quietly continued, "This Jesus could not be the Messiah. He was too kind, too tolerant, too accepting of the frailty of the human spirit. If it wasn't for his blasphemy, I might even have become his friend." Saul let a long sigh escape from his lips and then added, strongly, and yet with sorrow in his voice:

"He blasphemed! He deserved to die!"

Quintus was puzzled. He could sense that Saul had mixed thoughts about this Jesus of Nazareth. Quintus sensed an admiration for the man, even in the midst of the diatribe. For Quintus, however, it was mystifying. He was not interested in the religious beliefs of Jesus, but in his crimes and political impact of his teaching. He probed that point with Saul.

"My good man, I am not interested so much in whom Jesus was or what Jesus said," Quintus began, "but rather in what crimes he committed. He was condemned to death by the Roman Governor and executed by Roman soldiers. What Roman law did he violate? Did he preach sedition? Did he threaten Roman control of Judea? Did he speak against the Emperor? Did he steal? Did he murder? Did he rape? What was he guilty of? Why did Pontius Pilate condemn him to death?"

Saul started to reply, but Quintus held up his hand, and continued, "But did he *die*? His body has disappeared from the tomb. Did he walk out, or was his body stolen? If so, by whom, and how?"

Saul held up his arms, "Hold! Hold! That's a whole battery of questions. I don't think he was guilty of breaking any Roman law. Nothing I have heard gives that indication. The only laws he broke were in Jewish religious law. He blasphemed before Caiaphas, the High Priest, and before the Sanhedrin, the council of the High Priests and leaders of our Church, acting as a Court. There, under questioning by Caiaphas, the High Priest, he claimed to be the Son of God. As Jews, we believe in only one God. Jesus spoke as if He was a part of that one God. That was blasphemy," Saul paused, "All his good work means nothing if he is a blasphemer."

Saul stopped, looking thoughtfully at Quintus, and then continued, "There is yet another factor to be considered. You are a man of command. You know that authority cannot be divided," Saul stared at the ground and in a voice not as strong as before, went on, "I think Caiaphas saw Jesus as a threat to his power as High Priest. He had to be rid of him. What better way than to have him crucified by the Roman authorities? He provoked Pontius Pilate into the execution," He stopped. Then looking up directly at Quintus, added,

"In regards to the missing body, I know nothing. I heard about the disappearance of the body. I too am mystified. His followers must have stolen it, and there are rumors that they did, but I find that hard to believe. They were a group of frightened people without the necessary courage. They had the most to gain, but I can't see them overpowering the guards, stealing the body, and then keeping it a secret." Saul looked at the ground in thought and then continued, "But it is hard to imagine anyone else even considering it. Why steal a body and say nothing about it?" Here Saul stopped. He stared at Quintus intently. Quintus stared back and remained silent, waiting for Saul to vent and give his complete opinions.

Finally Saul added, looking directly at Quintus, "In summary, Jesus broke no Roman Law. I don't know why His body disappeared. Someone stole it but I can't imagine who…" he continued, "I imagine that is why Pontius Pilate washed his hands of the whole matter."

Before Saul could continue, Quintus interrupted, "What do you mean 'wash his hands?' We know nothing of that from his dispatches to Rome."

"Can I assume you know nothing of the actual details of the trial and execution?"

"Yes. Please assume I know nothing and tell me everything you know."

Saul looked at him quizzically, and then began, "The Nazarene was arrested by the Temple guards and taken to the High Priest, Caiaphas. Jesus blasphemed, and Caiaphas rent His garments. By his blasphemy, Jesus deserved to die. Caiaphas then sent him to Pilate. When Pilate discovered he was a Galilean, and remembering that King Herod of Galilee was in Jerusalem for Passover, he sent Jesus to Herod. Jesus refused to say anything during this interrogation by Herod. Then Herod sent the blasphemer back to Pontius Pilate."

Here Saul stopped, and then added, "These are the essential facts." He gazed into the distance as if Quintus was not even there, then he continued, still staring, in a subdued quiet voice, "I can just imagine the scene. Once again, I wasn't there, but had detailed reports. Jesus politely answered the questions of Pontius Pilate. Pontius Pilate had already been informed that Jesus had not challenged the power of Rome and in fact had repeatedly, even when directly questioned, admonished all: to 'Render unto Caesar that which is Caesar's; render unto God that which is God's.'"

Saul stopped and looked directly at Quintus, "The man was not preaching sedition. He was exhorting all who listened and heard him, to obey the laws of God and to follow the paths of righteousness."

"I am a Pharisee. We believe firmly in the law. Our lives are essentially directed by 613 rules handed down to us by our prophets, from the time of Moses, and in the writings of our great prophets such as Isaiah, Ezekiel, and Elias. We call that the Mitzvot, or the Mosaic Law. It has been codified from the Torah. Jesus did not rigidly follow Mitzvot. He was a threat to our system of rules which regulate every aspect of our lives. The Mitzvot was developed over centuries. He had no right to challenge these laws and even to flaunt his disregard."

Quintus interjected, "What kind of laws?"

Saul looked at him frankly and said, "Look at the dietary laws for example, what we can eat and cannot eat, and that we observe the Sabbath and cease all work on that holy day. Jesus ignored that rule and even cured people on the Sabbath, supporting the idea that it was wrong to let the letter of the law interfere with the observance of the spirit of the law. In fact they affect every aspect of daily life. For us, there is no separation of our religion from our government. The two are linked. When the Romans came as conquerors and occupiers, they brought their law which we obey; but we still have our laws."

Quintus was a little surprised. So the Jewish religion was intertwined with their concept of government. He thought for a moment and then stated, "So Jesus did nothing wrong to challenge Roman law but did ignore some of your rules of behavior. What crime is that? Suppose I live in Jerusalem and do not follow all your numerous rules or laws. Does that make me a criminal in your eyes?"

Saul averted his gaze, staring at the ground, he said, "You are not circumcised. You are a Gentile, a pagan and not one of the chosen people."

Quintus was a taken aback. He had been told of the rigid attitude of the Jews and here he was directly encountering it for the first time. He shrugged and pointedly asked Saul, "Let's go back to my question about Pontius Pilate washing his hands. Please tell me about that."

“When Jesus was returned to Pontius Pilate by Herod, Pontius Pilate continued his interrogation and then announced he had found no fault in Jesus. He then had him severely chastised or whipped. When they brought Jesus back, it was clear that he had been nearly beaten to the point of death, Jesus stood before him, dripping his blood and that is when Pontius Pilate called for a basin and had water poured over his hands as he explained, ‘I am free of the blood of this just man.’ Then he gave the crowd a choice of freeing Jesus or a condemned murderer, Barabbas. The people chose Barabbas, and insisted that Jesus be crucified. Caiaphas undoubtedly engineered the appearance and control of the crowd, filling it with supporters of Barabbas. They would certainly choose freedom for Barabbas and demand death for Jesus. It was the supporters of Barabbas and not the Jewish people who condemned Jesus."

Saul stopped. His face showed that he had sunken deeper into thought and introspection. Then his face cleared and he seemed to become resolute, “At the time, I was convinced Jesus was a blasphemer and had to die. But I am plagued by the memories of all the good he did. I wonder if he knew what he was doing when he blasphemed. Did he truly understand that he was claiming to be God? Did he truly understand that he was claiming to be the Messiah who would lead all our people to victory over all our enemies?”

Saul paused, then looked directly at Quintus, "Was he a fool, a man who sought importance, a man who would die in agony rather than admit he was a fraud? Or was he really the Messiah, really the Son of God, and actually the sacrificial lamb to be slaughtered for all? After all, it was a fitting day - the day of Preparation for the Passover. Tribune, you must know that we slaughter the lambs on the afternoon of the Day of Preparation." Here Saul stopped and gazed unswervingly at Quintus, awaiting his reply.

Quintus suddenly understood the dilemma. Jesus had become a threat to the status quo and was rapidly gaining the support of the people because of his good will with the poor and outcast, and because he cared for the people, especially the sick and maimed. He decided on a different tactic to his questions.

"Saul, did Jesus do anything to challenge the power of the Pharisees?”

"Yes. He was always telling stories that made us look bad. He always called us 'Whitened Sepulchres,'" in deep thought, Saul continued, "He even challenged our worship process in the Temple, overturning the tables and money changers and whipping them."

Quintus laughed. "What do you mean money changers in the Temple? Are not your Temples places of worship to the gods?"

"Tribune, we have a single Temple. We believe in but one God. There are sacrifices performed as acts of penance and reverence. The animals to be slaughtered must be brought to the Temple for sacrifice. As a convenience, we have money changers who will provide animals for sacrifice, and all for a small fee."

Quintus immediately grasped the situation, "So Jesus was a threat to the profits generated by this 'convenience?'" Quintus continued, "Who is the greatest beneficiary of this practice?"

"Why, the Sanhedrin, the council of the chief Priests and the High Priest of the Temple."

"And who was the High Priest?" asked Quintus.

"Caiaphas is the current high Priest," Saul replied, "And he is the son-in-law of Annas, the former High Priest. He was also a leading member of the Sanhedrin."

Quintus began to see the pieces falling into place. Jesus was a threat to the status quo; a threat to the income of the High Priest and his associates; and a potential threat to Rome as he gained more and more support.

"Tell me, Saul, was there widespread support for Jesus amongst the Jewish people?"

"On the first day of the week in which he was crucified, Jesus entered Jerusalem for the first time riding a donkey. He was greeted exuberantly by the people. Wherever he went, there were crowds of people who wanted to crown him King."

"So Jesus was popular with the people, and not the High Priest and Pharisees."

"Yes."

"So, the High Priest may have connived with King Herod to convince Pontius Pilate that he should have Jesus crucified. Is that right?"

Saul positioned himself so that he was staring eye to eye with Quintus and then said with intensity, "Jesus blasphemed. He had to die, whether by stoning or crucifixion. Caiaphas thought it best to have him executed because of the popular following that Jesus had developed. It was best for one person to die than to place the entire nation in peril. It was imperative that Jesus be executed by Rome before he became more of a problem."

Quintus was beginning to see that the Roman concept of government and that of the Jews was different. With the Jews, religion and government were solidly connected. In Rome, they were separate. He would have to follow this element of the case thoroughly to understand why Jesus was crucified when he was deemed innocent of crime by the Procurator. He probed further with Saul, "Is there anything else you can tell me, especially in regards to Pontius Pilate's decision?"

"I think Pontius Pilate made a terrible mistake in executing Jesus. Pilate became a pawn in the hands of Caiaphas and Herod. He probably thought he was buying peace in a province of Rome but in reality he was not exercising the power of Rome and the power of his office. As a Pharisee, that was a good thing. As of now we have a friend as governor," again Saul paused, "but as a Roman citizen, I wonder if it was right for Pilate to associate Rome with such a misdirection of justice. No wonder he washed his hands. But to no avail! It was he who sentenced Jesus to die."

Quintus found the facts enlightening and was beginning to recognize the political intrigue of the execution of Jesus of Nazareth. His initial supposition that Jesus was a criminal was being challenged. It was beginning to appear that he was more a victim rather than a criminal. The Pharisees, as Saul stated, were incensed at a challenge to the status quo and especially to the violation of the numerous rules. The High Priest, Caiaphas, saw Jesus as a threat to his power, influence, and income and had to have him neutralized. The Sanhedrin connected government and religion as one. Hence any attack on the status quo was an act against their government. That could cause trouble, perhaps even a popular uprising. The triumphant entry into Jerusalem by Jesus must have severely frightened the Sanhedrin and the High Priest. Pontius Pilate feared a popular uprising and followed the premise of squelching any potential leader for the Jewish people by siding with the nominal leaders. He was actually dependent upon the good will of these leaders to maintain peace. Quintus mentally laughed. Pontius Pilate would fit well in the conniving cadre of Roman senators. Principle had been sacrificed for expediency. If this information was correct, Jesus was not a criminal and His execution had been a fraud and in itself was a crime. This stop in Tarsus and his meeting with Saul would be very helpful in guiding him in his investigation for the Emperor. He decided to close the meeting with a final question of Saul.

"Is there anything else you can tell me that will help my understanding of what happened?"

Saul looked to the ground and then looked up, "I think I have told you everything I know. I could go on and on and it would only be a reinforcement of what I know."

"What about the disappearance of the body of Jesus?"

Saul raised his head toward him, "I wondered if you were going to ask about that again. I repeat, I do not know. He was certainly dead when he was placed in the tomb. Three days later, the tomb was empty. Guards were posted in front of his tomb by Pilate upon the request of Caiaphas who feared some problem with the body. Jesus had foretold his death and his rising from the dead on the third day. Caiaphas wanted to make sure Jesus' followers did not steal his body and circulate stories that he had risen from the dead. So he asked Pontius Pilate to post Roman guards at the tomb."

Saul stared with fixed eyes at Quintus, "No one rises from the dead. The body must have been stolen."

Quintus persisted, "What about the guards?"

"I have heard two sides of the story. One side says they fell asleep and when they woke up, the stone was rolled aside and the tomb was empty. The other side claims that a bright light blinded them, the stone suddenly rolled to the side breaking the Roman seal of Pontius Pilate, and Jesus left the tomb as a shining blob of light, walking right through them."

"What happened to the guards?"

"They knew Pontius Pilate would have them executed for dereliction of duty. They went to Caiaphas for support. He gave them money to circulate stories that the body had been stolen. Some guards, however, told the true story, and told of the bribery. Pontius Pilate was furious! He had the guards arrested and tortured, in an attempt to get to the truth. They confessed to a man of their intrigue with Caiaphas, and were executed, even though they claimed to the very end that an unearthly force had moved the stone away and that Jesus of Nazareth had risen and walked right past them."

Saul laughed, "His followers have even insisted that they spoke to him. I do not believe it. They are cowering cowards, hiding together in rooms hidden from the general public." He stopped, looked down, and suddenly just raised his head and added, "But it doesn't make sense! His body must have been stolen and his disciples are the likely criminals, although they lacked the courage to do it."

Quintus looked steadily at Saul for a moment, and then abruptly asked him, "Tell me, Saul, what do you really think happened?"

Saul's gaze pierced Quintus' eyes with his own, as he paused in deep thought for a while, looked up and stated directly and forcibly, "Tribune, for the third and last time, let me tell you I think that somehow or other His body was stolen. The problem with that notion is that his disciples were too cowardly to do it; but the guards went to their deaths claiming the body was not stolen, that they were not asleep, and that the body walked out of the tomb. I just don't believe it." In a note of exasperation, Saul virtually shouted, "I don't know!"

Saul then stood and ended the conversation. Taking a deep breath, he regained his complete composure. "With your permission, Tribune, if you have nothing further to ask of me, I have to get back to work," said Saul, "I must finish this tent and be on the road to Damascus as quickly as possible. I hope to leave in the next few days. There are followers of Jesus in Damascus whom I must apprehend, arrest, and bring to the High Priest in Jerusalem." Quintus stood and parted from Saul, "Thank you. I am going to Jerusalem where I will seek more facts and the opinions of others." With that, he strode to his horse, mounted it, signaled the other mounted soldiers to follow, and left.

The troop rode back to the galley, dismounted and left the horses to the garrison. They went on board the galley and Quintus ordered the Captain to be ready to sail as soon as he had completed his dispatch for Capri. He and Marcus then went into the small enclosed space set up for Quintus on the command deck. "Marcus," Quintus said, "read me your notes from this meeting with the tentmaker, and use another tablet to take down the notes I dictate.

Then transcribe both. Do my notes first. These notes I dictate shall form a dispatch for the Emperor. The document of our conversation, enhanced with my notes will form the report I will give the Emperor upon our return."

"Yes, Tribune," said Marcus, who immediately started reading his notes from the meeting. When Marcus finished, Quintus dictated a summary for the Emperor. Then this was copied by Marcus to be retained by Quintus for security in the event the dispatch did not reach Capri. When completed, Quintus read the dispatch very carefully.

"Marcus," he called, "I have a small addition to make in the dispatch. When you are ready, I will dictate."

"I am ready now, Tribune."

"Then add the following: *'Sire, you were right to have qualms about this man, Jesus. Saul the tentmaker is an educated man, a zealot for his beliefs. He has acted as a dedicated adversary of those who followed this Jesus. But now he seems to be wavering, almost to the point of admiration for Jesus. That is a straw in the wind of the dangerous influence which the sect of Jesus has on people. If this is or can be a threat to Rome, then I will determine how it can be crushed. Sire, you were right to send me now. I will not fail you.'*"

When Marcus completed the addition to both copies, Quintus signed both, and gave one copy to the Captain to have it dispatched immediately to the Emperor in Capri.

Shortly after, the rowing drum began to beat its cadence; the oars were lowered into the water. With the sail set, they moved forward to the beat of the drum and the snap of the lash. They left Tarsus for Caesarea where chariots and horses awaited them for the final leg of the journey to Jerusalem.

During the voyage, Marcus transcribed all his notes into a full report which he then showed to Quintus who made some minor corrections. This again was copied. He then affixed his signature to both, one copy to be dispatched to Capri immediately upon their arrival at Caesarea, and the other to be retained until the end of the entire voyage for delivery to the Emperor.

Throughout the short journey to Caesarea, Quintus continued to ponder the strange story of Jesus of Nazareth. For a carpenter, he had certainly stirred a large number of people into having strong feelings.

Quintus wasn't sure where the whole investigation was going, but if Saul's facts were correct, Jesus was not a criminal in Roman law. He should not have been crucified. But that still didn't solve the dilemma of the missing body. Who stole it, and how?

And Saul. What an enigma that man was – so zealous, so brilliant, and so confused about Jesus – but he seemed to be fighting an internal battle between his 'Pharisaic' training and his personal recognition of the complex nature of the criminal Jesus of Nazareth. Or was it the 'demi-god' in the body of a man named Jesus of Nazareth? If Jesus could have that kind of effect on a zealot like Saul, what was his effect on true disciples? Quintus was beginning to truly appreciate the genius of Tiberius and the sense of foreboding that led him to initiate this investigation. Quintus was beginning to relish the nature and importance of this assignment. If indeed he did succeed Tiberius as Emperor (as he believed Tiberius wanted to have happen), then this problem must be resolved before it became a threat to the Empire.

**The Resurrection: A Criminal Investigation of the Mysterious Disappearance of the Body of the Crucified Criminal Jesus of Nazareth**

# Chapter Three
# Jerusalem - the Garrison

Jerusalem was a bustling city. The chariot ride from Caesarea had been swift. On their arrival in Caesarea, Tiberius had instructed Aurelius to have the soldiers disembark and proceed in an orderly fashion to Jerusalem. There they were to report to the Tribune in command of the Legion station. Further instructions would await them. Quintus bade Marcus to stay with him.

Upon arrival in Jerusalem, Quintus proceeded directly to the Proconsul's House. He learned Pontius Pilate was in Damascus, meeting with his superior, the Governor of the Province of Syria. Quintus was actually pleased at this delay in meeting with Pilate. It would give him time to gain valuable background information. Quintus sought out the Tribune of the Roman Garrison, Lucius Arconius. He was escorted into a sumptuous meeting room hung with tapestries, and carpeted with large, thick rugs, obviously the Governor's meeting room. Lucius sat in a chair at a small table off to the side of an elevated platform with a large and ornate chair. The room reminded him of a throne room, more suitable for an Emperor than for a Proconsul in a remote province of the Empire. But then again, the thought flashed through Quintus' mind: a Governor in a distant Province was almost an Emperor in that local area. Tiberius' appellation of Pontius Pilate as a pompous idiot came into his mind. The evidence of 'pompous' was now right in front of him. The rest was to be determined.

The two men saluted. While they were of equal rank, it was obvious to Lucius, and to anyone who saw the badges on Quintus' tunic, that Quintus was the superior officer. Lucius took caution in how he handled this important representative of the Emperor. He actually remembered Quintus when they were both stationed in Judea. Lucius had been his Commander. Quintus had established himself as a fearless, resourceful, and brilliant leader with his men and with his superiors. Lucius had been highly impressed with his ability and character. He was not surprised to see Quintus now as the deputy commander of the Praetorian. Certainly Quintus was a powerful man in Rome. But what was he doing here? Lucius asked him.

Quintus was surprised. He had assumed Lucius would have seen the Emperor's dispatches sent to Pontius Pilate. Apparently they had never arrived or Pontius Pilate had not shared the information with Lucius. He would clear that up when he met with Pontius Pilate. He told Lucius about the mission and showed the Emperor's command papyrus for co-operation. Lucius stiffened a little as he saw the importance of the mission. In his mind he wondered why he had not been told of this visit.

"Thank you, Quintus. I understand and see the importance of this mission. How can I help, subject of course to the Proconsul's approval?" Here he stopped, and with a somewhat rueful smile, added, "Which I am sure will happen when he sees your document." Lucius even laughed at that sally.

Quintus was pleased. Lucius was going to be no problem.

"Lucius, the Emperor wants to know who stole the body of this criminal carpenter Jesus of Nazareth. And he wants me to find out all the circumstances of his sentence of execution, the reasons why the Proconsul 'washed his hands' of the matter, and why Pontius Pilate placed the sign ‘Jesus of Nazareth, King of the Jews' on his cross." Then he added, “And Lucius, the Emperor wants to know if there is any threat to Rome due to unrest here in Judea resulting from the Jews or the followers of the criminal Jesus."

Lucius did not appear perturbed in any way, "We don't know what happened to the body," Lucius stated, "the tomb is empty." He shrugged and continued, "We arrested and tortured the guards. They claimed a ghostly figure, emitting a brilliant light, emerged from the tomb, and walked right through them. They kept to their stories even until death," Then he emphasized, "all of them, all sixteen!" He stopped as if witnessing the scene again in his mind. With slight sarcasm, he added, "The Governor thinks this Jesus was a god and rose from the dead."

"What do you think, Lucius?" asked Quintus.

"I don't know, Quintus. That could be. There were certainly strange things that happened surrounding the death of the criminal." Lucius stopped again deep in thought, "I was not in favor with what the Governor decided about the execution, but it was not my prerogative to have an opinion."

"What is your opinion, then, Lucius?" Quintus asked.

"The High Priest manipulated the Proconsul into executing Jesus and eliminating a problem for the priests and the Temple. Jesus was a religious problem, not a political problem. We should have made the High Priest Caiaphas handle the matter himself."

"What about the unrest?" Quintus asked.

"In my opinion, Quintus, there is none at this time. The seeds are there for problems in the future, but I am not sure when that future may be. The Jews certainly resent us. The sect of Jesus' followers ignores us," Again Lucius shrugged. "Frankly I am happy to see you here, happy to see your mission launched. It is needed."

Quintus was pleased to some extent, but not totally. The situation was being defined more clearly by Lucius, but the mystery of the missing body, and the strange actions of Pontius Pilate still had to be investigated thoroughly.

Quintus decided to continue his conversation with Lucius after he had more information. He decided to switch to logistics.

"Lucius," he began, "I have to do a great deal of investigation. I need resources. I need men who speak the local language to search out all those who know anything about this. That includes the followers of Jesus, and general people in the area. I am told he cured people of disease. I want to speak to them. I want to speak to people who heard him preach. I will, of course, speak to the High Priest and the Governor. But I need troops to help me. The Emperor sent a cohort and a Centurion, Aurelius Antonius, with me as guards during the trip and to help in the investigation. Aurelius and 27 of them speak Aramaic. Only a handful speak Hebrew, and not even very well."

Quintus saw the wary worrisome look on Lucius' face. Quintus quickly added, "I know you have many duties for your men. I won't ask you for more troops, but a trade, one-for-one, and only while I am here, of the men I brought for your men who speak Aramaic or Hebrew." Lucius relaxed and readily agreed. This would be accomplished as soon as they arrived.

He then asked Lucius to provide a list of all those who had been involved in any way with the life, execution or burial of Jesus of Nazareth. Two Centurions were identified, Sutonius, who had a slave cured by Jesus; and Longinus, who had commanded the troop at the execution of Jesus. Longinus had also been the one who insured that Jesus had been dead on the cross by piercing his side with a lance. The garrison commander identified eleven other soldiers who had witnessed and reported curious activity on the part of Jesus while he was alive.

He then asked Lucius to assign both Centurions to work with him during his time in Jerusalem, and to make the eleven soldiers available as he might need them. Quintus decided to interview both Centurions and the soldiers; the Centurions separately and then the soldiers as a group with the Centurions present.

He met first with Sutonius. He decided to conduct the interview in a small sitting room seated behind a desk with Sutonius standing before him. Marcus was also present across from Quintus, off to the side so he was behind and out of direct view of whomever Quintus was interviewing. Quintus wore his full tunic for the occasion. Sutonius entered the room, and saluted Quintus, who acknowledged the salute and immediately began the interrogation.

"Centurion," he said quite formally, "I have heard that your favorite slave was quite ill, but you asked this Jesus to cure him and he did. Is that true?"

"Yes, Tribune," Sutonius answered in a very quiet voice. Then he added, with full feeling, "I was patrolling in Capernaum when I learned that my most valuable servant was ill and near death. I had heard that Jesus had a reputation of curing people so I went to some Jews whom I knew and asked them to approach Jesus about the matter." He seemed almost to be reliving the episode as he told the story to Quintus. Then he continued, "My intermediaries came back and told me Jesus had agreed to come to my house to heal my servant." The Centurion stopped, and with what seemed a note of embarrassment, the Centurion added with deep sensitivity,

"I sent back word that I was grateful but unworthy to have him come to my home." Again the Centurion stopped, then went on, "Word came back that Jesus had praised me for my faith and that my servant would be healed - instantly! I noted the time out of habit and later learned that my servant had been healed at the exact time Jesus had said he would be. "

Quintus thought for a moment, "Do you think Jesus healed your servant?"

"Yes. I firmly believe that my servant was healed, a servant I believed to be on the point of death and who now lives because of the intervention of Jesus of Nazareth."

Quintus drummed his fingers on the table top. Something strange was going on here. He decided to proceed sternly with the Centurion. In a commanding voice, looking directly at Sutonius, he briskly said, "You violated a basic rule. You are here as part of an occupation force in a conquered area. It is your task to keep the peace by observing what is happening, by stopping disturbances, and by arresting any who break our laws. In particular, you are here to protect the interests of Rome." Here, Quintus slammed his fist upon the desk and began to speak louder, "And you dared to be a supplicant, asking a favor of conquered people. How dare you! How dare you violate the most important aspect of being in command! We do not ask conquered people; we command them!" Quintus stopped. He let his anger leave him. He had to remember he was on a mission of unearthing the facts and not one of command. If he had been in command of Sutonius, he would have had him flogged. He wondered why the commander had not done so. He would find out. In the meantime he decided to uncover any additional facts that would be useful in his investigation. In a quieter tone, still one full of sternness, he asked Sutonius, "Did this change your opinion of this criminal Jesus?"

"Tribune," answered Sutonius in a firm voice, "you are right that I may have violated the spirit of our law, but I was careful not to violate the principle. I did not contact Jesus directly." At this,

Quintus snorted, but still continued to look at Sutonius, and said nothing. Sutonius continued, "And I did not ask on behalf of myself, but on behalf of a valuable slave. I explained this to the commander of our garrison who was equally upset and gave me a stern reprimand." At this point, Sutonius' back straightened, "Since then, I avoided any direct or indirect contact with the criminal, Jesus of Nazareth, or with any other Jews."

Quintus now understood and decided to be lenient as well, "Very well, Centurion, I will accept your apology and of all those involved with your error. Is there anything else you can add from your knowledge of the activities of the executed criminal Jesus of Nazareth?"

Sutonius stood for a moment. Quintus could imagine the rapid circulation of thoughts in the mind of the Centurion. "Tribune, I know we executed Jesus of Nazareth as a criminal," Sutonius continued in a sympathetic tone, "I found it difficult to mock him while he was in our custody before his execution. I saw him beaten to the point of death. I saw him mocked with a crown of thorns with blood streaming down his face. I was not there at the execution site, but I heard of all the strange things that happened afterwards. I am a simple Roman soldier. I know how to fight in battle, and I know how to kill the enemy. In carrying out my duties I have killed many in battle or in command of the executions of criminals. I know our Prefect, Pontius Pilate, condemned Jesus of Nazareth to death and I can accept that since he is in command here. But I cannot overcome the sense that there was something different about this man, Jesus of Nazareth. We executed him as a criminal, but I wonder what he really was. Was he really a man or a god disguised as a man?"

Looking directly at Quintus, the Centurion Sutonius proceeded, "Tribune, our commander told me that you are here to investigate all aspects of the life and death of Jesus of Nazareth, and the mysterious disappearance of the body of this executed criminal. I am ordered to help you to the extent I can, and this I do willingly as a soldier and as a person."

Quintus nodded and said nothing. Sutonius then asked, "Is there anything further you need?"

"No. You are dismissed." Sutonius saluted and left. As he left, Quintus said to Marcus, "Read back his testimony and take my notes as we go. Collect all these notes into a single dispatch for the Emperor when I have completed them all."

The process continued until it was complete. Then Quintus summoned the second Centurion, Longinus. The same process was used in that interview as had been used with Sutonius.

*   *   *

Longinus was the Centurion who had been in charge of the execution troop from the garrison. As with Sutonius, Quintus sat behind the desk with Longinus standing before him, and Marcus off to the side, behind Longinus. The story he told was short and very informative. “I was assigned to implement the execution order of the carpenter Jesus of Nazareth. Pontius Pilate had ordered him to be scourged before he finally gave the order for crucifixion. Had he died during whipping, the execution order would have been unnecessary. I believe the Prefect wanted that to happen since he gave no instructions that the scourging was not to cause death. Jesus was tied to the whipping post and scourged until my men were exhausted. He still lived. Since he had claimed to be King of the Jews, I decided to give my men some time for levity in mocking him. They placed a piece of purple cloth over his shoulders as a robe and then hammered a crown of thorns into his head. Then as he sat, barely alive, my soldiers saluted him in mockery, as the King of the Jews. This went on until he was summoned once again before the Prefect, Pontius Pilate. Then the order for execution was given and I directed my troop to carry it out.”

"Was there anything different about this execution than with others you commanded?” asked Quintus.

“Yes Tribune,” replied Longinus. “Jesus of Nazareth offered no resistance to what we did. When, as usual, he was ordered to carry his own cross, he could not. When he was given assistance by a bystander at our command, he obeyed. When we nailed him to the cross, he gave no cries of pain and did not resist us in any way. And when we raised the cross and he hung there in agony, he did not blame us or curse us as other criminals have done. Rather he prayed to his father to forgive us since we did not know what we did. I understand enough Aramaic to know that is what he said. He also conversed with the criminals on either side and with his mother Maryam at the foot of his cross." As Longinus continued at great length with the facts of the execution, Quintus could see the deep effects from his time with Jesus affecting the Centurion. He could well understand the impact, but decided to let the Centurion continue without interruption.

"At the ninth hour, he finally died with a quiet statement: 'It is finished.'"

"How do you know he was truly dead?" Asked Quintus.

The Centurion once again paused and struggled to continue. His face held the deep anguish of spirit as he said, "I pierced His side with a lance and blood and water came out, so I knew he was dead. My mission was accomplished. We did not break his legs, since it was unnecessary."

Quintus had been deeply affected by the recitation and the manner in which Jesus of Nazareth had been executed. It was not the actions of the Roman soldiers that moved him but the actions of the criminal. Quintus was inured to brutality, and to blood and death. But those he had killed or executed normally resisted or cursed him. To hear that while being executed the criminal Jesus of Nazareth had prayed for the executioners was highly unusual. He decided to probe further, "Centurion, what happened next?"

"In the usual fashion, Tribune, my men cast lots for the seamless garment of the criminal. I also allowed his relatives and followers to claim the body when I was assured that proper burial had been arranged. Normally we just let the bodies hang until they are devoured by animals or rot on the cross. But in deference to the Jewish custom of their Sabbath, we allowed the burial to proceed."

"And how was that done?" interjected Quintus.

"The tomb was nearby. A new one which belonged to a member of their religious council, the Sanhedrin. He was called Joseph of Arimathea, a friend of the family of the criminal. At the tomb, the body was dressed with spices, wrapped in a burial cloth and placed in the tomb with the burial cloth over the face of the body. Then the burial stone was rolled into place in front of the tomb by a number of His followers, aided by my soldiers. The stone was very heavy and difficult to move in place. Then I affixed the seal as ordered by the Prefect."

"And what was on the seal?"

"It read, 'All those who tamper with the seal or the grave will be subject to execution as ordered by the Prefect.' Then I left with my soldiers."

"Was there anything special that happened when the criminal died?" Quintus asked.

"Yes, Tribune," said Longinus, "almost immediately the skies darkened and thunder roared, but there was no rain. I was told that graves opened, and the dead walked. The Jews told me that the Veil of the Temple was torn apart."

"Was a guard posted at the tomb?"

"Yes, Tribune, but those guards were posted there by the Proconsul, but not until the next day; and only when the High Priest approached him to do it as a provision against the body being stolen. The Proconsul is mandated to preserve order. The High Priest convinced him it was necessary." The Centurion remained rigidly at attention before Quintus.

In the silence that followed, Quintus carefully digested what he had heard. Then looking directly at the Centurion asked, "Do you have any personal feelings apart from exercising your duty?" asked Quintus.

"Yes, Tribune," replied Longinus. "I always thought the rumors I heard of the miracles of this man Jesus were some form of trickery. On more than one occasion I heard that he had raised or called people from the dead. I know of a fellow Centurion whose servant was cured by this man Jesus. I always attributed these stories of 'cures' to hysteria and trickery, but did not believe it. I truly believed, as I always did and do, that in carrying out the execution of a criminal and enemy of Rome I am carrying out my duty. A criminal or enemy of Rome deserves the fate meted out to him. I never feel remorse. In this case, even with the beating and the crowning of thorns of Jesus of Nazareth, I felt I was carrying out my duty as a soldier. But as I watched him die, heard him pray for us, and saw the heavens move in anger; that is when I began to doubt. Now I am not so sure he was a criminal. The stories circulated of his resurrection from the dead seem to be more and more credible to me than the stories circulated by the Temple authorities that his disciples stole his body. The teachings of Jesus were for truth, for the dignity of all people, and for love of one another. I find it hard to believe that any followers of his would steal his body and then circulate the story that he had risen from the dead."

Quintus kept a straight face, but he was greatly disturbed. Tiberius was right. Something very out of the ordinary had occurred here. This was a Centurion before him. This was a man who had carried out many executions and who was now telling him that the disappearance of the body of the criminal may have been a true resurrection from the dead. He decided to be stern to gauge the reaction.

Emphatically he lashed out, "Centurion, you are a Roman soldier. Are you a believer in this Jewish Sect? Are you no longer a believer in our Roman gods? In fact, what do you believe?"

Drawing himself even more erect, Longinus looked directly at Quintus, "Tribune, I am a firm believer in the gods of Rome. I am a firm believer in the laws of Rome. I am a firm believer in the policy of our occupation that we work in a cooperative atmosphere with the religious beliefs of our conquered people. I am not a follower in the belief of the Jews as I understand it, and as I have seen it practiced in the Temple and in my duties as part of the occupation garrison," Here the Centurion took in a deep breath, "but I do believe there is something radically different about this man, Jesus of Nazareth. I am leaning more and more toward the opinion that this man was not a criminal, but only a political pawn between the religious forces of the Jewish people. I believe he was caught in a power struggle between what he was preaching and the status quo. He was a threat to the religious leaders of the Jews, and they engineered his execution by us."

The centurion paused, somewhat lost in deep thought, and continued, "He may have even been a god. As time goes on, I am attracted more and more to what he had preached. Upon my retirement as a soldier in a few short years, I may even become a follower of his beliefs. I truly believe that none of his teachings are detrimental to Rome. Some of our soldiers even reported to me that he continually preached and said, 'Render unto Caesar that which is Caesar's, and to God that which is God's.'"

"What about the Roman gods?"

"Tribune, I have always kept a separation between my duties as a soldier and our religion of many gods. I know the Jews believe in one god rather than many; I further accept Jesus of Nazareth believed in a singular god. I am beginning to wonder if he was man and part of that god at the same time."

Quintus sat back. This was a Roman soldier telling him there was a possibility that Jesus of Nazareth had not been a criminal and that he had risen from the dead, and that he might have been a god. Quintus was silent.

"Thank you Centurion. You are dismissed."Longinus saluted and then left.

* * *

That night, Quintus sat running over in his mind the testimony of both Centurions. He had Marcus transcribe his notes and read them to him. The dispatches to Capri were completed, and he signed them. They would go with the dispatch of his findings in the interview with all the eleven troops and the two centurions which he scheduled for the next day. Once that was completed, it was imperative that he interview Pontius Pilate, the High Priest Caiaphas, both the followers and enemies of the criminal Jesus, and perhaps even his mother, Maryam. It would be an exhausting process, but it had to be done. He also had to visit the execution site and the tomb. Quintus shuffled these requirements in his mind and estimated he would be able to return to Capri, and then to Rome, in another month.

He slept badly. His dreams were a confusing quilt of voices and images clamoring for his attention, with opposing views of whom and what this criminal Jesus was. Quintus woke twice before finally falling into a deep troubled sleep.

* * *

.

The next morning, he met with the group of eleven and the two centurions in a large room. Again Marcus sat out of view behind all of them. They all stood as Quintus sat at a small table in the front of the room.

As each entered, he saluted, identified himself, and stood. They finally assembled into two small lines in front of Quintus. The two centurions were in the back rank.

The entire morning was spent in discussing the teachings and supposed miracles of the criminal Jesus. All had some knowledge, but it was a confusing set of unconnected facts, memories, and opinions, except for one thing, and that soon became very clear. Contrary to what Saul had stated, the followers of Jesus were no longer in the shadows. Immediately before the execution, and for some time afterward, they had grouped in remote places, hiding and afraid. But now they were everywhere, openly and actively proclaiming the teachings of Jesus. Furthermore, they were loudly proclaiming that he had risen from the dead. The whole demeanor of the followers of Jesus had changed. Suddenly they were everywhere. Their fear was gone. In fact, they seemed to fear nothing. He decided to ask Longinus, who had caught his attention as a thoughtful, well-adjusted person not given to impulsive change, to explain what had happened.

Quintus stood and addressed the group, "I thank you all for this information you have provided, but I am interested in the change in demeanor in the closest disciples of Jesus." Turning to Longinus, he added, "Centurion Longinus, would you please tell us all your assessment of the when and why of that change."

Longinus began, "It seems to have started on the Jewish feast they call Pentecost. The streets were full of people going about their shopping, visiting and parading, many of them visitors from different parts of Judea and the Empire. Most of them were Jews, believers in their one God."

"It was the first day of the week. Many witnesses give testimony that there was a roar in the sky, like thunder, but there was no lightning, no clouds, and the sun shone brightly. I was on duty patrolling with my troop that day in Jerusalem and heard it myself. I thought it very strange. Almost immediately the followers of Jesus appeared in the squares and market places proclaiming the teachings of Jesus loudly and powerfully. Their leader, Simon Bar Jonah, whom Jesus had called Peter, was understood by everyone, no matter what their native language. I saw the phenomenon myself, and heard Peter speak in Latin, a language I know he did not speak."

Looking directly at Quintus, Longinus continued, “Tribune, I found it hard to believe that I heard Peter speak in Latin, and at the same time, no matter what the language of the others, each heard their own language and understood completely, even as Peter spoke. I thought it so strange that I verified this by questioning people in the square one-on-one." Longinus paused for a moment, and then went on, "Tribune, I verified that Peter spoke only Aramaic and Hebrew; yet I heard him speak Latin and others heard him speak simultaneously in their own language." After a short pause as he searched his memory, he was reaching the end of his thoughts, "The same was true of the other followers of Jesus, who were also out speaking that day. Furthermore, all were without fear of any kind."

Longinus concluded, "I do not know how this trick was performed, or whether it was some miracle of this group. They claimed Jesus had sent the Holy Spirit upon them. I believe something happened that changed them, took away their fear, and gave them this gift of language."

Quintus too found it hard to believe, even after hearing the same thing from so many, even from the Roman Centurion.

Looking directly at the Centurion, Quintus asked once more, “Longinus, did he really speak Latin?”

“What? Yes, Tribune.”

Quintus said, “And everyone else with their different languages said they heard their own language.”

“Yes, Tribune.”

Quintus sat silently, and everyone, too, remained silent. All were apparently recounting their experiences with the man Jesus and with Peter. Quintus asked again, “What you are saying is that everyone heard Peter and his associates speak their language, all at the same time, and they all spoke different languages. Is that true?”

“Yes, Tribune,” Then he added for emphasis, “Many of my soldiers who were around the city that day can tell you the same thing. They will also tell you that the people who were preaching did so in a manner that everyone understood and were no longer afraid. When we approached the speakers, they did not turn to run or hide, but stood there resolutely and continued to speak. They were not intimidated or fearful of our presence. I tested this by galloping up to one of them, and then stopping before knocking him down. He continued to speak as if I was not there. Something changed them. I believe we could have killed them on the spot and they still would have continued to speak."

Quintus closed the discussion with, "Let us accept this as a fact and move on." He paused for a moment, and then continued.

"I am going to call an end to this meeting now. I want all of you, together with the Centurion Aurelius who accompanied me, to spend the rest of the day and even the evening in the city. Approach Jews that you know, and even those you don't know if they look like followers of Jesus, and ask for information on these supposed miracles, his teachings, and try and get the names of people he cured. Try to talk to them and come back with as much information as you can."

Turning to Aurelius, he added, "Centurion, take with you any of our men who speak Aramaic or Hebrew. Have them join this group."

Then turning to Longinus and Sutonius, he proceeded, "The same for you. Ask Lucius if he would assign anyone in these barracks who speaks Aramaic or Hebrew to join you. I myself will tour the city alone out of uniform. Longinus, I would appreciate you going with me, also out of uniform. I wish to learn without attracting attention. This meeting is over and we will meet again after breakfast in the morning. Meeting adjourned."

Quintus went in search of civilian clothing.

* * *

Quintus joined Longinus a few minutes later. Both wore common robes and headgear. Close scrutiny would show they were not natives, but casual observers in the street would accept them as inhabitants or more probably as visitors.

Quintus' objective was to get a sense of the people and the environment. He had been stationed there years before so he was no stranger to the noise, smells, and confusion that seemed to be everywhere. And yet there seemed to be a sense of purpose as the people moved. If not stopped in conversation, they walked firmly and did not shuffle. They did not give the impression of a beaten and subdued people. They had spirit. Even when they stood and talked, it was animated.

Between his memory and help from Longinus, they found their way to the Temple. It was crowded. People were moving in and out. They walked into the portal and found the money changers at work exchanging sacrificial animals for money. Quintus could understand why Jesus would be upset at this system of generating profit out of religious belief.

Beggars were all about, some blind and lame, or pretending to be. They had pitiable looks on their faces, some crying out, 'Mercy.' One came running up to them and shoved his dish into their faces while he rolled his eyes and looked at the sky, moaning all the while.

Quintus threw some coins in his dish, took Longinus by the arm, and hurried along. "Take me to the execution area and the tomb," he commanded.

Longinus led him through the city to the outer area to the place of skulls, Golgotha. It was outside the gate and on a rise he saw three posts rising from the ground. "These are the crucifixion poles," Longinus said, "we can nail the criminal to the crossbeam, raise it, and then nail his feet to the riser, just above the foot post. Or we can take the pole out, nail the criminal and it together, and raise the pole in its hole. The first way is easier on us. It really does not matter to the criminal. Most of them faint or die from the pain when we nail their hands to the cross piece. Besides, most of them have been scourged and are almost dead when they get here."

"How was Jesus?" asked Quintus.

Longinus drew a deep breath, eyes fixed on Quintus, and said very softly, "Different! He did not curse us, but prayed for us. He was alert until the very end. He must have been in great pain but he did not show it. He was weak, weak from the beating and from loss of blood." Very softly he added, "He was the bravest man I ever saw. He endured the pain, ridicule, and torment as if he were achieving some goal. Maybe what they were saying is true, that he died for all our sins."

Quintus was shaken. Brusquely he said, "Let's find the tomb."

After a few minutes, they came to an open hole in a hill. A very large somewhat flat stone stood upright to the left of the tomb opening, on a skid path. Three or four men would be needed to roll it to close the hole. On its side was the remnant of a seal. From what was left, Quintus could see it was an official one. It was probably the seal Pontius Pilate had ordered his soldiers to affix to the closed tomb.

"Are there any torches?" Quintus asked.

"I ordered a detail to bring us torches about this time. They should be here shortly," Longinus explained.

They sat for a few minutes. Quintus looked all about him. The tomb was built into a hill side. No one could approach on top without the risk of falling from a height. The hill continued for some distance on either side of the tomb, which was probably a cave excavated only a minor amount. The only accessible ground was in the front, where Quintus was told the guard had been placed. He turned to Longinus. "How many were in the guard?" He asked.

"Sixteen so far as I know to ensure that at least four, if not eight, were awake and on duty at all times," He answered.

Quintus nodded. It was just as he would have done. For the next few minutes until the torches arrived, he just stood and pondered the whole situation.

As soon as the soldiers arrived with the torches, they were lit, and Quintus entered the tomb with Longinus. There was a shelf opposite the doorway, obviously for the body. It was empty.

They examined the entire interior very carefully, holding their torches close to the walls everywhere. There were no possible exits other than the frontal hole that would be completely covered by the large rock.

The two Roman soldiers looked at each other, shrugged, and walked out into the open. They extinguished their torches, gave them to the soldiers who had brought them, and stood for a while observing and taking in the whole area. Finally Quintus said to Longinus, "Somehow or other the body went out the front door. It's the only way."

Longinus nodded. Then he said with a note of awe in his voice, "How? Was he carried or did he walk!? I know he was dead when he was put there!" After a moment he added, "Did the guards lie even as they were tortured and dying? Would they?"

Both men looked at each other. The mystery was deepening. In his heart Quintus had a sinking feeling that the corpse had not been stolen. Yet Jesus had died!

The two men walked back to the barracks lost in their own mind. Along the way, they saw a boy with two baskets, one of bread and one of fish. They stopped and asked in Aramaic if he had ever encountered Jesus of Nazareth. The boy's eyes widened and he began to shake. Longinus calmed him and asked why he was so disturbed. Haltingly the boy told his story.

He had been out in the countryside when he saw this huge crowd - thousands of people. He had five loaves of bread and two fish with him. One of the men with the leader, a man he called 'Master,' had purchased the bread and fishes from him. The 'Master' raised his arms to the sky, praised God, and blessed the food. Then this small amount of food was passed around to feed the multitude of thousands. When all had eaten their fill, twelve baskets of crumbs were collected. The boy had stood and watched the whole situation. He didn't know how the trick was done, but he wanted to find out. He learned that the name of the Master was Jesus, and that he was a carpenter from Nazareth. Still shaking a little, the boy went his way.

Now fully mystified, the two men resumed their walk to the barracks, each rapt in thoughts, seeking an explanation. They discussed the possibilities all the way to the barracks. Did the people have food with them that they then ate? But if they just followed Jesus, how did they come to bring food with them? Perhaps some did. But all? It was possible that nothing unusual had happened, that the people had food with them, and shared it so all ate their fill. It was possible, but highly improbable. They just didn't believe it was so. The gods must have been involved somehow in all of this. It was not natural.

On their arrival back to the barracks, they parted. Quintus checked and learned his men had arrived and were bivouacked. The reassignments had been made. He met with Lucius for a few minutes and arranged to have the cohort assigned to him, including the men temporarily transferred from Lucius, plus the three Centurions to meet with him in the morning. Then he went to dinner with Lucius, where they reminisced about their times together.

In his quarters that night, Quintus reviewed in his mind how his task had taken on new dimensions after only one day in Jerusalem. First the missing body, and then the generation of food...what next?

**The Resurrection: A Criminal Investigation of the Mysterious Disappearance of the Body of the Crucified Criminal Jesus of Nazareth**

# Chapter Four
# Jerusalem - The Miracles

The next morning Quintus met on the barracks parade grounds with the three Centurions and the mixed cohort of Legionaries from his Rome-based group and those from Jerusalem that spoke Aramaic, Hebrew or both. The three Centurions and thirty-eight of the soldiers were fluent. He divided them into fifteen uneven groups, five assigned to each Centurion, making sure that each group had at least two who spoke Aramaic. The eleven from Jerusalem were assigned to individual groups. In that fashion he hoped to maximize their ability to report back to him with worthwhile information and with subjects for him to interview. When all the organization was complete, he addressed them.

“Legionaries of Rome," he began, "the objective of all this organization into groups is to have you go and discover everything you can about this executed criminal, Jesus of Nazareth. We will meet here every evening for your reports. That will continue until the investigation is complete. I will be the sole judge as to when that event will occur. Until then, you will discover anything and everything you can."

Quintus continued, "As you know, Centurion Longinus was in charge of the execution. The groups of Legionaries assigned to him are to scour the city for information about the reaction of the people to this execution, both before and after. In particular, they are to investigate the disappearance of the body from the tomb. Any rumor of noise coming from the tomb area or suspicious figures lurking there are to be investigated. Your assignment is to track down any lead whatsoever associated with the execution, burial, and theft of the body from the tomb." Then Quintus paused to give further emphasis to his next words, "You are to listen carefully for words or hints toward unrest. Do these followers of Jesus pose any threat to Rome, now or in future?" Then he stopped and scanned the faces of Longinus and all the Legionaries in his group, "Are there any questions?" After a short pause during which no questions were asked, Quintus added, "Very well."

Turning to Sutonius and his group, Quintus began, "Centurion Sutonius had a favored and valuable servant cured of illness by Jesus of Nazareth. He is aware of the reputation for miracles claimed by that executed criminal. His groups will scour Jerusalem and all the areas visited by Jesus and His followers and create a list of the supposed miracles." Once again he stopped to scan the faces of Sutonius and the Legionaries assigned to him, "Are there any questions?" After a short pause during which again no questions were asked, Quintus added, "Very well."

Then he turned to Aurelius and his group, "Centurion Aurelius who came from Rome with me, is to investigate the teachings of this man Jesus. His groups too are to seek out the followers of Jesus and interview them with regard to what was preached, how it was presented, and what the outcome was. If you encounter word of a miracle, gather the information, but make sure you share it with Centurion Sutonius or with Centurion Longinus if it concerns the execution or the tomb." Then looking at all the men, he added, "All of you are to work together, share information, consolidate it with your Centurions, and report to me each day." Quintus paused for a moment.

"Are there any questions?" There were none.

"Then, may the gods favor your search. Come back at any time with anything that will pinpoint who stole the body of the executed criminal, the carpenter, Jesus of Nazareth. Then we can establish 'why' and 'what' the future may bring." With that Quintus saluted the Centurions and the soldiers. They returned the salute, and then began leaving the parade ground in their groups, on foot or mounted, to begin the investigation.

* * *

Each day Quintus inquired if Pontius Pilate had returned. Finally he was told Pilate would be back at the beginning of the following week. Quintus intensified the search effort to get a significant portion of it done, if not totally completed, before the Proconsul returned.

He toured the city himself, dressed as a native, accompanied by Marcus. Everything he heard was confirmed in the reports he received each evening. By the third day, Sutonius and his groups had established a significant amount of information about the supposed miracles of Jesus of Nazareth, some thirty-seven in number. With the help of Marcus, a list was created. This list was then assembled into the approximate sequence in which they occurred and short explanatory comments were added to each. The results of this effort were as follows:

I. Jesus changed water into wine at a wedding feast in Cana. When the wine ran out, at the request of His mother, Jesus told the wine steward to fill the jars with water. It became the best wine of the day.

II. A royal official named Joseph went to Cana, begging for Jesus to cure his son who was on the verge of death in Capernaum. Jesus told him the son was cured. The official verified the boy was cured at the exact time he had been told.

III. While Jesus was preaching in a synagogue in Capernaum, a man possessed of demons cried out, "What do you want with us, Jesus of Nazareth? Have you come to destroy us? I know who you are - the Holy One of God!" Jesus commanded the spirit to be quiet. Then Jesus said sternly, "Come out of him!" The impure spirit shook the man violently and came out of him with a shriek. The man was cured before the congregation.

IV. From the synagogue in Capernaum, Jesus went to the home of Simon bar Jonah, whom He called Peter. Peter's mother-in-law was ill with a high fever. After being asked to help her, Jesus bade the fever leave her, and she was cured.

V. That evening in Capernaum many people who suffered from various diseases and disabilities were brought to Jesus. He cured them all.

VI. One day, Jesus asked Peter if He could use one of his boats as a platform to address the people who followed him to the Sea of Galilee, also known as the Lake of Gennesaret. Afterwards, He instructed Peter to move his boat to a deeper part of the lake. Peter protested that nothing had been caught, but still did as Jesus asked. The boat almost sank from all the fish caught. The same occurred with another of Peters' boats that also came out to that location.

VII. After preaching to a multitude on a hillside, a leper approached Jesus and asked to be cured. Jesus cured him.

VIII. In Capernaum, the Centurion Sutonius, learning that a favorite servant was extremely ill, asked a Jewish friend to approach Jesus about the illness. Jesus cured the servant. Sutonius verified that the cure occurred at the hour Jesus had told the Jewish friend that it would be done.

IX. Jesus was still in Capernaum in a house surrounded by a crowd. A paralyzed man on a mat was lowered from the roof into the house by his friends. Jesus first told him he was absolved of his sins, stating he wanted to prove he had the authority to forgive sins. Then he cured him.

X. One Sabbath, Jesus was preaching in the synagogue. A man with a withered hand was there. Jesus asked if it was lawful to do a good deed on the Sabbath. When all remained silent, Jesus called the man forward, had him hold up his withered hand, and made it whole.

XI. Jesus was followed by a large crowd of disciples at the town of Nain when he encountered a cortege carrying a dead young child, who was the son of a widow. Taking pity on her plight and sadness, he restored the dead boy to life.

XII. Jesus and his disciples were in a boat on the Sea of Galilee when a frightening storm arose while Jesus slept. The disciples woke him in fear; and Jesus calmed the stormy seas.

XIII. Jesus and His disciples encountered a wild man in the area of Gerasene. The evil spirits in the man spoke to Jesus, giving his name as Legion, and begging Jesus to cast them into a nearby large herd of pigs. He did so, and the herd of one hundred rushed into the lake and drowned. The man and a companion, who was also possessed, were cured.

XIV. A woman had been suffering from internal bleeding for twelve years. She knew that by touching Jesus' cloak she would be cured. When she did, his power entered and cured her body. Despite the crowd, he felt the power surge, and turned to her with His blessing.

XV. The leader of the synagogue in Capernaum, Jairus by name, came to Jesus to beg for a cure for his young daughter, a child of twelve, who was on the verge of death. With the crowd following, Jesus went to Jairus' home, but was told the child had died before arriving. At the home, Jesus told the crowd she was not dead but asleep. The crowd jeered that the child was dead. Jesus went into the child's room, accompanied only by Peter, James, John, and the parents of the child. There he took her by the hand and brought her back to life.

XVI. Shortly afterward, two blind men followed Jesus asking for mercy. Jesus asked if they believed he had the power to cure them. They replied, "Yes." Then he touched their eyes, and said their faith had cured them. Instantly they could see. He asked them to be silent about it, but they were not. The news spread throughout the region.

XVII. Almost immediately after curing the two blind men, a mute man possessed by a demon was cured. He spoke to the amazement of the crowd.

XVIII. Jesus encountered a man who had been crippled for thirty-eight years. He commanded him to pick up his pallet and walk. He did. This was on the Sabbath, which caused difficulty with the Pharisees.

XIX. A large crowd of about five thousand men and their families were following Jesus when it came time for a meal. One of his disciples found a boy with five small barley loaves and two small fish. Jesus blessed these, and distributed the food for all to take as much as they wanted. After all had been totally fed, twelve baskets of crumbs were collected. The people were amazed.

XX. Jesus' disciples were out in a boat in the middle of the lake when a ferocious storm came up. Jesus came down from a nearby mountain and walked over the water to them. Peter, seeing Jesus walk on the water, cried out that he wanted to join Jesus. Jesus invited him to do so. Partway to Jesus, Peter grew fearful, and began to sink. Jesus touched his hand and Peter again stood on the water. They both then walked into the boat, and the seas became calm.

XXI. Afterwards, Jesus and his disciples landed their boat on the shore of the town of Gennesaret. Recognizing Jesus, the townspeople brought their sick and crippled to them. Jesus cured them all, including those who touched his cloak.

XXII. In the region of Tyre, a Gentile woman of Syrophoenician origin came and begged Jesus to cure her daughter of an unclean spirit. Despite being a Gentile, he cured the daughter in her home. When the woman went home, she found her child well, with the demon gone.

XXIII. Jesus left Tyre and proceeded to Decapolis where a man who was deaf and dumb was brought to him. Jesus cured him completely.

XXIV. A crowd of four thousand men with their families followed Jesus for three days. Jesus was determined to feed them so they could return to their homes safely. There were only seven barley loaves and a few small fish. He blessed the food, and distributed it until everyone had eaten their fill. Seven baskets of crumbs were collected. This was the second time Jesus had fed a large multitude with only a small amount of food which he magnified multi-fold.

XXV. In Bethsaida, on the north side of the Sea of Galilee, Jesus completely cured a blind man of his infirmity.

XXVI. Jesus then saw a man who had been blind since birth. He tested the faith of the man by having him bathe in the pool of Siloam. When the man did this, he was cured and could see. The Pharisees disputed this as a true miracle, even questioning the parents of the man. They verified he had been born blind since birth. The Pharisees still refused to acknowledge the miracle cure. Jesus was then reputed to have said something like, 'For judgment I have come into this world, so that the bli nd will see and those who see will become blind.'

XXVII. In company with Peter, James, and John, Jesus was implored by a man to remove a demon from his son. He had previously asked other disciples of Jesus to cure the boy but they had failed. Jesus cured him immediately. When asked why he had succeeded and others had failed to cast out that kind of demon, Jesus was reputed to have said, "This kind can come out only through prayer."

XXVIII. In Capernaum, Jesus was approached by a tax collector demanding Temple Tax. Jesus told Peter to take his boat and go fishing, take the first fish in the net, remove the coin in its mouth, and give it to the tax collector. Peter successfully did as he asked.

XXIX. Before a crowd, Jesus healed a demoniac man who was both blind and mute. Free from the demon, he could see and talk. The crowds around him were amazed.

XXX. While teaching in the synagogue on the Sabbath, he saw a woman who had been crippled and bent for eighteen years. He called her over and cured her. Standing erect, she praised God.

XXXI. While dining on the Sabbath in the home of a leader of the Pharisees, a man ill with dropsy stood before Him. Jesus disputed with the lawyers and Pharisees present about curing the ill on the Sabbath. He told them they would all pull out a child or an ox that fell in a well on the Sabbath. They had no reply to his challenge. Then he cured the man with dropsy.

XXXII. In a small village on the way to Jerusalem, Jesus encountered ten lepers. As a test of their faith, he told them to show themselves to the Priests. When they did, they were cured. One, a Samaritan, returned to thank Jesus. The other nine were cured but did not return.

XXXIII. Jesus brought Lazarus back to life. Maryam Magdalene and Martha, sisters of Lazarus in Bethany, sent a message to Jesus that his close friend Lazarus was ill. Jesus was delayed, and arrived to find that Lazarus had been dead four days. He was buried in a cave with a large stone covering it. The stone did not prevent the stench of decay from escaping. The stone was moved, and Jesus called for Lazarus to 'come out.' Lazarus did, wrapped in his burial bindings, which were then removed.

XXXIV. Jesus healed a blind beggar, Bartimaeus, as he was leaving Jericho. Jesus was followed by a large crowd when Bartimaeus, sitting by the roadside, called for mercy. Jesus called Bartimaeus to his side, and cured his blindness.

XXXV. Jesus cursed a fig tree that was barren. It shriveled overnight. Jesus used this as a message that faith and prayers could move mountains. He further implored his followers to pray forgiveness.

XXXVI. When Jesus was arrested by the palace guard in the Garden of Gethsemane, Peter severed the ear of the servant of the High Priest. Jesus admonished Peter that those who live by the sword shall die by the sword, and then restored the severed ear. He was then led to the house of the High Priest for his trial by Caiaphas.

XXXVII. Jesus was instrumental in His disciples catching one hundred and fifty-three fish after His Resurrection. From a beach on the Sea of Galilee, He directed them to fish in a new location. When they did so, their nets almost tore with the catch. They struggled with it to shore where they counted one hundred and fifty-three large fish. The net was not torn even with so many.

There was an attempt to add three more miracles:

I. The purported virginity of the mother of Jesus. A messenger from the Jewish god had told her she was with child through that God, and that child would be God and man. Quintus didn't believe the tale. He suspected she had been raped by a Roman soldier and had invented the story to preserve her reputation.

II. The resurrection of Jesus from the dead, if indeed he did arise from the dead. This wasn't a miracle until it had been proven that Jesus rose from the dead. Quintus believed his body had been stolen by his followers to validate the prediction made by Jesus that he would rise from the dead on the third day.

III. His ascension into heaven some forty days after his resurrection, if indeed it was Jesus, and, if indeed, it was not a hallucination, and he did rise into heaven.

It was decided to consider these as possible miracles, but to exclude them from the list. It was determined that these needed substantially more investigation. Hence the number of miracles was set at thirty-seven.

* * *

Quintus found the list fascinating. He had not been aware of the extent of the trickery of the criminal Jesus. He decided to personally investigate the curing of a son of a Palace official, the three purported resurrections from the dead, and the miracle of the one hundred and fifty-three fishes ostensibly performed by a risen Jesus. In all these investigations, he would proceed in dress uniform, taking with him Sutonius and a group of five of his men. They set out the next morning.

Their first point of call was the royal palace of Herod Antipas, Tetrarch of Galilee and Perea. They asked to see Joseph, one of the ministers of the realm. When Joseph appeared, he was surprised to see a Tribune waiting to see him. This Tribune wore emblems of his position that indicated he was a man of great power. Joseph decided to be very wary of everything he said.

"I am Joseph, Minister to Herod Antipas, Tetrarch of Galilee and Perea" he said by way of introduction, "Is there anything I can do for you, Tribune?"

Joseph was an important looking official, richly dressed, with an air of command. His courteous introduction of himself could not hide the power behind his words. Quintus was certain this man would do everything possible to satisfy any request he made. The Tetrarch's position depended on the goodwill of Rome. He decided to stress that point by detailing his position, the charter from the Emperor, and his mission.

"Good morning, Minister," Quintus began, "I am Quintus Gaius Caesar, Tribune of the Praetorian, and Deputy Legate of the Guard. I have been sent here by the Emperor. I regret that I am taking you away from your important duties, but I have a mission from the Emperor that has been deemed very important." He handed Joseph the papyrus of authority, and waited while the royal minister read it.

Joseph's fears were confirmed. This man was very powerful, and he had to be sure he cooperated fully. Returning the papyrus, he asked, "How can I help you?"

Speaking directly and in an even tone, Quintus began, "We have heard rumors that your son was cured of serious illness by the executed criminal Jesus of Nazareth. Is that true?"

Joseph answered immediately, "Yes. When I approached him, he told me my son Jacob was cured. Later I learned that my son was cured at the instant Jesus told me it was so. From the point of death, Jacob was instantly fully alert and well. Without the intervention of Jesus, I am certain my son would have died."

Quintus was taken aback. This was something he had not expected. He just could not bring himself to believe it. He could sense that Joseph really believed it to be so. He decided to rattle him into the truth. In a stern voice and with a note of jeering he strongly asserted, "That is nonsense. Now tell me the truth, Minister, what illness did he have? Was he really even sick?"

Joseph sighed, and then quietly replied, "I know you find it hard to believe. When I asked Jesus to cure my son, I knew he was deathly ill. For me to approach Jesus was difficult and even a threat to my position. Jesus had already been identified by the High Priest as a threat to stability, and had recommended his execution to the Sanhedrin. Hence, I should not have spoken to Him." Joseph stopped, swallowed hard and continued, "As my son's condition worsened, I decided to find Jesus and ask him for help. I had complete faith that he could and would. I had seen him cure a blind man, a deaf man, a paralytic from birth, and a woman who bled." Joseph paused, and then added with great emotion, rare for someone of his rank, "Believe me, Tribune, it was my son, and he was dying. The mourners were gathering at the house and beginning to wail when I went in search of Jesus. I had absolute faith that he would cure him."

He paused, and looking eye to eye with Quintus, asked, "Shall I continue or are you absolutely convinced it is all a fraud?"

The details of this purported miracle by an official of the court of King Herod were significant. This man had no possible motive in lying. Joseph, Minister to the King, truly believed Jesus had cured his son of serious illness. But children were often very ill one minute and fine the next. Hence, this was either a miracle or a mistake. The Minister believed it was a miracle. Quintus wasn't sure yet, but he leaned to the possibility of a mistake.

"Thank you, Minister," said Quintus, "I am not sure what I think yet. I accept the facts as you have outlined them, and I accept your belief in their authenticity. For now, however, I must reserve my own judgment." With that, Quintus saluted the Minister and left.

* * *

Quintus and his escort rode to the synagogue, and sought Jairus, the leader. He strode into the synagogue and asked for Jairus. He was asked to wait in a small anteroom. While waiting, Quintus decided to become very thorough in his questioning of Jairus. He did not believe the story presented to him that Jesus had raised the daughter of Jairus from the dead. This was a magnificent claim. Yet, as he waited for Jairus to come to him, Quintus sensed a revelation coming that he was afraid would challenge his beliefs.

Jairus was a distinguished looking man. Tall and thin, with a short grayish beard, he had the look of significant intelligence. As he strode forward to meet Quintus, his bearing denoted leadership and command. Jairus was no fool, certainly a man of intelligence and decision. He looked quizzically at Quintus, and noting his badges of rank, smiled graciously and welcomed Quintus, "Welcomed Tribune, it is not often that we are honored by a visit from such a distinguished Roman. How can I be of assistance to you?"

"Thank you for your welcome, Jairus," Quintus stopped and directly gazed upon Jairus to determine the impact of his words, if any, "I am here to investigate the report that your daughter was cured of illness by the executed criminal Jesus of Nazareth." He then went on to explain his mission from the Emperor, "This is all part of my investigation into the questionable disappearance of the body of Jesus after his crucifixion."

Jairus seemed puzzled, but unperturbed, "Tribune, my daughter was seriously ill when I approached Jesus. I had delayed doing this because I knew the Temple authorities did not look upon him with favor. In fact, in my opinion, they probably wanted him removed in some way. For me to have him cure my daughter was a serious personal risk for me, but I was willing to take that risk for her sake." Jairus looked very sad and solemn as he said this, "Do you want all the facts, Tribune?"

"Yes, I do," said Quintus, "please, be as detailed as you can."

"When I found Jesus," continued Jairus, "he was busy with the blind man, Bartimaeus. He had been blind from birth. He was known all over Jerusalem. Jesus rubbed clay in his eyes and Bartimaeus suddenly began to cry for all to hear, 'I can see! I can see!'" The memory seemed to affect Jairus who paused and then continued. Quintus thought he detected a small tear in his left eye.

"I went up to him and asked, 'Master my daughter is ill. Will you come and cure her?' He told me that my daughter was not ill, and that he would come."

"Did he?" interjected Quintus.

"Yes, Tribune. When we arrived at my home, the wailers told me she had died. Jesus smiled, and told me she had not died. Then he said in a loud voice, 'Come out,' 'Come out,' and then she did, rubbing her eyes as if she had been asleep." Here Jairus stopped, swallowing hard to control his emotions. Then he continued.

"But she was alive, Tribune! Alive! Many people attested to her death, but now she lived." He stopped. His eyes gazed into Quintus' while he added, "When I thanked Jesus, he smiled and said to me 'Your faith has cured your daughter.' Tribune, that man was a god. He was full of goodness, full of good cheer, full of love for the people. When I heard that he was to be executed, I could not believe it. I was glad that Longinus was picked to command the cohort to carry out the execution. Longinus is a fair man who carries out his duties. He is not a man given to brutality or one who condones it. Even then it was extremely brutal."

Jairus hesitated a moment to control his emotions, "I was shocked when he was sentenced to be executed. The man had done no wrong. He preached goodness, not sedition. He broke no Roman laws. I tried to intercede with the High Priest, but Caiaphas would not tolerate any difference concerning Jesus. He insisted on proceeding to the Proconsul seeking the crucifixion of Jesus. Caiaphas had decided to defer completely to Pilate. He told me not to interfere. Yet I tried. When they mocked Jesus, I tried to stop them, tried to tell them what he had done, but they only laughed in disbelief." Jairus stopped, shaking his head, reliving a bad memory. Then he added, in a strong even voice, full of emotion, "I tell you truly, Tribune, on my honor as a leader in this synagogue, Jesus did bring my daughter back to life and that I believe he was from God. I believe he was the Messiah, but we did not understand his message. We killed him. Then he rose from the dead because a god cannot be killed." After a pause, he added, "Your mission is complete, Tribune. No one stole the body. He rose from the dead."

Jairus looked directly into Quintus' eyes, and stopped speaking.

Quintus stayed silent for a few moments. His mind was trying to grasp what he had just heard. A leader in the synagogue believed that Jesus was a god. How had his mind been twisted! How could he believe a carpenter had raised his daughter from the dead? Yet the girl lived! Had she really died? They thought so. Did he?

Jairus had no reason to lie. There were witnesses to what happened. If the girl was not dead, she had been in a deep coma. At the very least, she had been cured of a serious illness. He would have the Legionaries investigate further, seeking witnesses and corroborating every aspect possible of the story of Jairus.

Sighing inwardly, he wondered more than ever what was going on here. He decided not to ask to speak with the little girl. He would talk to the adult Lazarus. He decided to conclude the interview. He could always return if necessary. In the meantime, he would have the Centurions and Legionaries search for witnesses and other corroborating information.

He thanked Jairus, wished his daughter well, and left.

*  *  *

Next they travelled to Nain. The story concerning Jesus was that he was approaching the town with his disciples and a large crowd was following him. They encountered a procession to the burial grounds with a young boy dead on a litter, with his mother, a widow, following and weeping. Jesus went up to the mother and told her not to cry. Then he went to the litter, touched the boy and commanded him to rise. He did. Jesus restored him to his mother, told her to feed him, and then moved on.

They searched out the widow. She was with her young son. Quintus decided not to tell her of his mission, or to question her directly, but rather to engage in casual conversation concerning the rumor that her son had been raised from the dead by Jesus. She excitedly confirmed the story, full of good wishes for Jesus. The young boy became very interested in the discussion, adding that Jesus was a 'very kind man with love in His eyes.' Quintus was touched when the little boy then declared, 'I liked Him.'

Apparently she was not aware that Jesus had been crucified. Quintus did not tell her. He decided not to interview the little boy further since he could always return if necessary. Still he was full of wonderment. Once again Jesus had cured a serious illness or brought a young boy back to life from death; and this before a multitude of witnesses. He would have the matter fully investigated through witnesses whom he would have his Legionaries find. The more he dug, the more mysterious it became. His preconceived notions were being challenged repeatedly by the facts.

*  *  *

Quintus then led the Legionaries to Bethany. Once there, they asked directions for the home of Lazarus. There they found his sisters Maryam Magdalene and Martha. They were full of tears over the brutal execution of Jesus, but elated at his resurrection. In fact, Maryam Magdalene had been there the first morning. It was she, together with two other women, who had met the angel that told them Jesus had risen. It was she who had hurried to tell Peter, who then came to the tomb. Maryam, the sister of Lazarus, had been one of the closest disciples of Jesus. It was she who had washed his feet and dried them with her hair; it was she who anointed him with precious oil only a few days before his execution. This came as a pleasant surprise to Quintus. It would provide additional information for his investigation. Martha as well was aware of all that had occurred, learning from Maryam as well as from the disciples of Jesus, with whom they always kept a close association.

Quintus introduced himself and explained his mission from the Emperor. They were immediately drawn into the discussion, stressing the miracles and goodness of Jesus, how he had been the Messiah, and had risen from the dead. Quintus was tempted to question them thoroughly about what they knew, especially about the missing body, but he did not. He assumed if other information identified them as being truly knowledgeable, he could return and question them. He changed the subject and directed it toward the resurrection of Lazarus. He asked to see him to verify that he had truly been dead in the tomb, and that the resurrection from the dead was true.

His words evoked emotion and denial in the women. They answered that Lazarus was in the fields but would return shortly. Then they retorted that there was nothing supposed about his death. He had died and Jesus had brought him back to life. Then they told Quintus how Lazarus had died. He had been ill for some time, and they had sent word for Jesus to come in the hope and expectation that he would heal his friend. But Jesus did not arrive until he had been dead for four days, and buried in his tomb. All this was corroborated by what had previously been learned about the incident.

Quintus visited that tomb with the sisters. It was similar to that of Jesus. It was a cave, with no openings other than the hole in the front, with a large flat rock that rolled across the mouth to seal it from animals and to keep most of the decomposition odors inside.

He asked the sisters to continue with their story.

When Jesus arrived, they told him that Lazarus was already decomposing, and that odors were seeping from the tomb.

Accompanied by disciples and followers, Jesus went to the tomb, and in a loud voice commanded Lazarus to come forth. The stone rolled aside and Lazarus came out into the light with the burial cloths wrapped around him. The odor of decomposition was all about. The tomb smelled as did Lazarus. In haste, and in joy, the sisters removed the burial cloths, washed him, and dressed Lazarus in normal wear. Then they all went in for dinner.

Quintus said nothing. This was no magic. No trickery. Jesus had raised Lazarus from the dead, just as he had raised the daughter of Jairus and the son of the widow of Nain. What kind of man was he? Or was He more than a man? Quintus now had first hand information of miraculous resurrections from the dead, witnessed by many reputable people. He would have all of this thoroughly corroborated by the Centurion-led groups of Legionaries. Quintus was certain and resolute that this case would be exhaustively examined. He would continue his investigation until he had sufficient facts to arrive at an unassailable conclusion. His report to the Emperor must be correct, and complete. For now, he would await the return of Lazarus and question him.

Lazarus came in a few minutes later. After the mutual introductions, Quintus asked, "How did you survive in the tomb for four days with no food or water, and little air?"

"I was dead," replied Lazarus.

They went back and forth on this with Lazarus explaining his death, the feeling of everything going black, and then hearing a voice calling. He arose from the burial bench in the tomb and walked out. The stone had rolled back by itself. Here Quintus' eyebrows had lifted perceptibly, but he remained silent. He let Lazarus talk and talk, spurring him on with leading questions, expecting a contradiction somewhere in all the words. There was none.

After some minutes of this, Quintus interjected, "So you really believe you died and that Jesus raised you from the dead?"

"Yes," said Lazarus, "I was decomposing. The tomb smelled terrible when I rose," Lazarus shuddered.

"How did you feel lying in the tomb?" asked Quintus.

Lazarus was surprised, "I was dead. I felt nothing? When I heard the voice, I ignored it. I felt comfortable. I didn't want to get up. I knew I was dead and in a tomb, but I was not afraid. I even felt very happy. I did not want to come out. But the voice kept commanding. Then I realized it was Jesus, and that he was calling, so I got up and walked through the open entrance. That's when I knew I was alive, even though I smelled terrible."

"What happened then?" asked Quintus.

"My sisters cleaned off the burial clothes, washed me, and dressed me. Then I lay down to dinner with Jesus."

"Weren't you hungry after four days?" asked Quintus, still somewhat skeptical.

"No. As a matter of fact, I wasn't even hungry. But I wanted to socialize with Jesus. I knew he had raised me from the dead. I still wasn't sure if I wanted to be alive again, but I was." Then he continued with, "My sisters were ecstatic at my return. In time, I came to appreciate what Jesus had done. It is good to be alive, but I now have no fear whatsoever of death," with that, Lazarus stopped with a deep smile on his face.

Quintus stopped. He had his facts. He now believed that Lazarus had lain in the tomb unconscious or dead for four days. But witnesses claimed he had died before they buried him in the tomb. Hence, he could very well have been dead. In that case, Jesus had raised him from the dead. At the very least, Jesus had mysteriously moved the stone, and called him from a deep coma. The terrible smell could have been decomposition if dead, or body odor if alive. But body odor was not as bad as the smell of death. In either case, Jesus had performed a miraculous act. It was one of degree.

Quintus decided to just catalogue this as another set of facts. The Centurions would check these facts with witnesses. He thanked Lazarus and his sisters, and left. On the way back, he asked if Marcus had recorded notes of everything. Marcus said he had.

They rode on in silence, with Quintus deep in thought. Occasionally he glanced at Sutonius but both remained silent. Quintus knew that Sutonius believed Jesus had resurrected three dead persons. Quintus still was not sure what to believe. Finally Quintus did ask his opinion.

The Centurion told him he was not surprised. Jesus was certainly capable of doing all three miracles, just as he cured many who were lame, crippled, blind or deaf. No matter what the infirmity, alive or dead, he cured them. Sutonius pointed to a man walking along the road, “Jesus cured him. His legs had been crippled since his birth. Now you see him walking with no limp or problem whatsoever.”

He pointed further down the road where three people were walking along. They were shouting excitedly, “Those three were lepers, now they are clean. Jesus told them to go bathe in the Jordan, they did and they were cured. I can take you to the home of a man who had been deaf and a man who had been blind. Jesus cured them.” Here, the Centurion stopped for a moment.

“He was a good man. He helped the poor. He cured them. He told them their sins were forgiven. They would not have to make sacrifice in the Temple for their sins, a sacrifice which they could not afford. He was no threat to Rome, but I can see why he would be a threat to the High Priest of their religion.”

Sutonius stopped talking and seemed uncertain for a moment. Quintus sensed he was troubled by something. He asked, "Sutonius, you seem concerned about something. What is it?"

Sutonius answered Quintus with an expression that surprised him, "Tribune, pardon me if I appear impertinent, but I wonder why you didn't question Mary Magdalene more extensively. She was very close to Jesus. There are rumors she was his lover. Other rumors say he placed her above Peter in his esteem and confidence."

"But she is a woman," said Quintus, "You know as well as I do that women have little importance in affairs of state. They bear the children and act as servants of men. That is why I did not pursue that line of questioning." He lapsed into deep thought, “But you are right, Sutonius. You are not impertinent at all. I was wrong. I let my impressions of women from current common opinion cloud the great contributions women have made throughout our history." He paused again, "I will return another day to question her thoroughly." Then looking at Sutonius with new respect, he asked, "Anything else?"

"No, Tribune. I suspected you didn't realize that she was much more than just the sister of Lazarus."

They rode the rest of the way in silence. Quintus decided to keep his own counsel until he had every fact from all sides.

* * *

When they arrived back at the barracks, he waited for the return of the other two Centurions. Then he met with all three. He relayed the findings of the day, amplified to some extent by comments from Sutonius. Then Quintus commanded them to search vigorously for witnesses to these three specific miracles to corroborate and eliminate any lingering doubts of what really happened. Quintus summed it up with his comment, "We must verify that they occurred or did not; were they miracles or tricks? Or were they just illnesses that were cured?" The three confirmed that they would.

Then Quintus met with Aurelius and asked if he had found the close disciples of Jesus, Peter in particular. He asked him to arrest Peter and bring him in for questioning the next day, by mid morning at the latest. First thing in the morning, he was going to visit the site where Jesus was purported to have performed a miracle after his Resurrection.

That night, once more, Quintus was sleepless. He took one of the writing tablets from Marcus and began to make short notes on it. He kept staring at his notes, shook his head repeatedly, and finally fell asleep.

* * *

The next morning he set out alone with Marcus dressed in the clothing of the city. Once again he hoped to pass as a native or visitor. He found his way to the lake where the fishing miracle had occurred. They searched out fishermen who had seen the miracle. They found more than one. The stories were all the same.

The tale was that early one morning after the so-called Resurrection of Jesus, a man stood on the shore. He called to the disciples of Jesus, Peter among them, who were fishing, some one hundred yards from shore. When he called to them and asked if they had caught any fish, they said they had not. He told them to throw their nets over the right side of the boat where they would find fish. While they had done so before, they did it again. So many fish were caught that they found it difficult to pull in their nets. Then the disciple John shouted, 'It is the Lord!' as they recognized Jesus. Peter jumped into the water and hurried to the shore. The others followed in their boat, dragging the net with them. When they landed, they saw a fire of burning coals there with fish on it, and some bread. Jesus asked them to add their newly caught fish. Peter climbed back into the boat and dragged the net ashore. The net was full. They counted one hundred and fifty-three large fish. Even so, the net was not torn.

Quintus thanked the fisherman, and left with Marcus to return to the barracks. Quintus was looking forward to his interview of Peter.

That evening, he met with the three Centurions. Peter had been arrested and was ready to be interviewed in the morning. Quintus asked all three Centurions in turn if there was evidence of any kind that the body of Jesus had been stolen by anyone, especially the disciples and associates of Jesus. Were there any rumors, possible hiding places, averted faces, suspicious glances, anything? Each Centurion reported that all their Legionaries had uncovered nothing further towards clarifying the mystery of the missing body. With regard to the companions and followers of Jesus, at the time of the crucifixion they were all fearful and in hiding. It was doubtful they had the courage or capability to steal the body. Yet they were the only ones who would benefit from an empty tomb. It would give credence to their preaching. But why the sudden reversal in their demeanor? From being fearful, they were now courageous, and apparently willing to die for their beliefs. One of their number, Stephen, has been stoned; still proclaiming that Jesus was the Messiah and God. That factor gave a new dimension to this investigation.

More and more it was beginning to appear to Quintus that Jesus had been innocent, and might have been a god. The interview of Peter the next day would be very important. Doubts began to creep into his mind. If Jesus was a god, then Maryam could very well have been a Virgin, and her story could be true. So could the claim of resurrection from the dead. The key to the whole mystery continued to be what happened to the body. Was it stolen or did Jesus truly rise from the dead?

**The Resurrection: A Criminal Investigation of the Mysterious Disappearance of the Body of the Crucified Criminal Jesus of Nazareth**

# Chapter Five
# Jerusalem - Peter

Quintus had Peter brought into the small meeting room. As in previous interviews, he sat behind a small table and had Peter stand before him. He had Longinus on one side of Peter, and Sutonius on the other. He was chained to both men. As planned, they stood before a stern Quintus. In that fashion he hoped to intimidate Peter.

Peter was a large man, well-muscled and apparently very strong. His beard joined his hair to form a circle in which a calm face with a humorous look upon it almost beamed at Quintus. Contrary to what Quintus expected, Peter was not cowardly but rather calm and dignified. His attitude and posture portrayed a man of conviction, ready to suffer whatever came his way, and to do so cheerfully. His body language spoke of leadership.

Quintus had expected that Peter would appear defeated and fearful. He was surprised at the actual demeanor of Peter. This was no fearful man. No coward!

Quintus looked at Marcus seated behind Peter and the Centurions. He detected a slight nod from Marcus. So Marcus too had noticed the difference between rumor and fact. So the stories of the change in the disciples of Jesus that occurred on the Hebrew feast of Pentecost must be true. Quintus looked at Peter with some respect that he was careful to hide.

He tried Greek and Latin but Peter shook his head. He obviously did not speak either language. When Quintus tried Hebrew, Peter responded quietly asking that they speak in Aramaic.

This would be more comfortable for Peter. Quintus agreed to do so. This confirmed to him that Peter was not well educated, a fisherman, he understood. Quintus also knew, from what he had learned about the execution itself, that Peter had been a cowardly man who was easily intimidated, but was also given to bursts of anger, rage, and even to violence. It was reported that he had cut off the ear of one of the arresting soldiers when Jesus himself was arrested. Quintus had been told that Jesus had put the ear back in place as if nothing had happened. Peter's reputation then was not that of a leader. But today he gave every appearance of being one - and a strong one. Quintus was hopeful that his interrogation of Peter would further his investigation. He decided on a strong questioning process.

"Simon, bar Jonah," Quintus began, "or Peter, as you seem to be called now, you have broken the laws of Rome. You are known to have consorted with a known criminal, the executed carpenter, Jesus of Nazareth. You were with him when he was preaching sedition against Rome, and seeking followers for his kingdom - a kingdom that would vanquish the Motherland. Since his execution, you have been spreading stories that this Jesus was a god, and that he committed no crimes against Rome," Quintus glowered at Peter. He was surprised to see Peter completely unperturbed.

Quintus slammed his hand on the table and almost shouted at Peter, "What can you say in your defense before I order you flogged and executed?"

Peter remained silent, with a smile tugging at the corners of his lips. Then he began to speak in a calm, yet forceful voice. His manner was direct, a tone of equal to equal, and perhaps, speaking as a parent to a child. He did not thunder, but his voice carried a note of authority. Again the thought flashed through Quintus' mind that here was a fearless and dedicated man.

"Tribune," Peter began, "welcome to Judea. I heard that you were sent by the Emperor to find the truth about Jesus of Nazareth. I can tell you that truth."

Quintus was not surprised that Peter knew of his mission. It was no secret. But he was surprised at the tone Peter was taking. Quintus once again slammed his hand in the table, and stood, pointing his finger in Peter's face. Raising his voice, he said, "Stick to the point. Answer my question."

Peter's smile now became apparent. His voice took on a small note of impatience as he continued, "You know that I am not a criminal and that I have committed no crime. You must also know that Jesus was not a criminal but rather divine. He was God, you must know, in the guise of a man. He was a man but He was God. You killed the man, but after three days God came out of the tomb, once again in the body of a man, although now His body showed more of the nature of God. I will explain this as I proceed," As Quintus was about to object, Peter raised his shackled right hand, much to the surprise of the Centurion Longinus, who sat to his right, and continued to speak.

"Tribune, I am trying to answer your question." Lowering his hand, and now with a deep smile that lit his face, Peter continued, "I will tell you the story that proves what I have just said is true."

"Please do. And also tell me how you stole the body and where it is hidden," said Quintus, as he sat back in his chair with an air of expectation, still with a stern look on his face.

Peter showed no emotion. Quintus had expected Peter to rise at the bait and become sidetracked. It was almost as if Peter had shaken his head mentally, and stifled an irritated outburst. Peter expelled his breath slowly, and then, taking a deep breath, began.

"I was a fisherman in partnership with my brother Andrew and my kin James and John. We had a few boats and a few workmen. One day when I was mending my nets, Jesus walked by with a crowd behind Him and asked if He could use one of our boats as a platform on which to speak. He gave an eloquent talk about the need for repentance and forgiveness by us and of us. The people were enthralled by this message of hope. As they drifted away He came ashore and asked me to follow Him and become a fisher of men. I did. I followed Him away from my boats, my partners, and my livelihood. I could not at that time explain why, but I can now. This will become clear to you as I tell my story."

He paused for breath. "I had heard of Jesus before. My brother Andrew had heard Him speak to multitudes. He came back and told me he had seen the Messiah. I told him he was ridiculous, especially when he told me Jesus preached repentance and forgiveness, that He was the Messiah. This was not in accordance with what I knew of the prophecies. The Messiah would lead the promised people back to freedom and greatness. Jesus preached goodness, and went around curing people, praying for them, telling them their sins were forgiven, expelling demons, and even bringing the dead back to life. But He did not preach power and supremacy. He cared for the people. He loved them. He had great compassion for their problems and illnesses. He took their grief upon himself," Peter paused again. His voice took on an even stronger tone, "He even died for their sins, as a sacrificial lamb, just as was prophesied in our holy scriptures. He was the Messiah!", he exclaimed forcefully. "But we misunderstood the promise of the Messiah. We wanted to think the Messiah would be a worldly leader with great power who would bring that power to the chosen people of God. Jesus was the real Messiah, the leader sent to guide us to the new promised land of the kingdom of God, a kingdom not of this world, but a kingdom in the next world of goodness, redemption, and eternal happiness."

Peter paused again and put great emphasis into his next words, still spoken in a forceful voice that carried conviction without belligerence.

"Tribune, Jesus rose from the dead as He predicted." Peter stopped as if seeing the scene play out again before his eyes.

Quintus could no longer keep his stern pose. He leaned forward, enthralled by this matter-of-fact recitation of what Jesus had done. It all confirmed what he had heard from many witnesses and beneficiaries of the goodness and acts of kindness and compassion of Jesus of Nazareth. Now he had a glimmer of hope, if not belief, that Peter's words would dispel his lingering doubts about the missing body.

Quietly Quintus questioned, "Well, what of the missing body?"

Peter continued, "There are only three possibilities. First, that Jesus did not die; that He awoke, removed His burial clothes, folded them, put them on the bench, and then walked out of the tomb. Secondly, that His body was stolen. Or thirdly, that He rose from the dead since He was God."

Peter paused for emphasis, "I am sure you have come to the same conclusions," glancing directly at Quintus, and then sideways at Longinus and Sutonius, asked each, "is that not so?"

All, with difficulty, remained impassive. Peter was right. They had all come to the same conclusion.

"Go on," said Quintus. With a full smile, now, Peter continued.

"The first case just does not work. If Jesus had been alive, and then became conscious, He had to roll back the stone. You know that is impossible. No single person could do that, and certainly not someone who had been as abused as Jesus had. Besides that, He was dead when placed in the tomb. Your own Centurion, the man shackled to me on my right can testify to that."

Here Peter looked at Longinus calmly, with no rancor or anger towards him for killing Jesus. He went on, "This Centurion put a lance through His body. He can verify He was dead. I am sure he has already told you that."

Longinus nodded.

Quintus interrupted, "Yes he did. I will accept that Jesus was dead. Go on."

Peter remained silent. Quintus repeated, "Yes that is all true. We will accept all that. Even if we were fooled, and he was alive, he needed help to roll back that stone." Firmly and quietly he asked, "So, it comes down to accomplices. They either helped him if he was not dead, which we doubt, or they stole the body. Were you and your associates those accomplices? And if not, why not? Who else would benefit from stealing the body?"

Peter grinned, "Of course we did not, we were not, and are not. Jesus rose from the dead as he foretold," Quietly and pointedly, he added, "You know that is true. You also know neither we nor anyone else stole the body."

Quintus started to interrupt, but once again Peter raised his hand, shackled as it was to Longinus who almost seemed to anticipate and cooperate with Peter. Once more, Quintus just sat back and listened, while also glancing at Marcus to make sure he was taking all this down on his tablets.

This was not going as Quintus had hoped. Everything Peter said confirmed what he had heard from others. All the testimony pointed in the same direction. The carpenter was dead when placed in the tomb. It would take a number of persons to roll back the stone. Guards were on duty. Under torture and even when they were being put to death they repeated the same story: that Jesus had walked out of the tomb. It was either a case of mass hysteria, or in reality a true resurrection of Jesus, the Carpenter from Nazareth. Quintus did not believe that it was mass hysteria. He still refused to accept the resurrection. It must have been theft of the body. But how could that have been done with the guards present? He decided to pursue that point.

"Why should I believe you that no one stole the body?"

Peter replied, "Because it could not be done, and because we were too afraid to do it. Even if we had swallowed our fear, we would have to drug the guards, steal the body, and tell the stories that have circulated about His appearances after His resurrection. Hundreds of people say they saw Him. They are willing to die for that belief. Stephen did. I am willing at any time. So are my companions. A conspiracy of such a magnitude is impossible. The risk of discovery alone is too great to justify it. No, Tribune, we did not steal the body. No one had any reason or desire to do so. You are left with only one possibility; and that is that Jesus rose from the dead."

Quintus had followed the argument closely. It paralleled what he had been thinking, and what others, especially Longinus, had said. It now came down to examining the witnesses and testimony of those who claimed to have seen and talked to Jesus after he had been crucified. If that was verified, then the possibility that Jesus was a god had to be seriously considered. He continued his questioning, now more inquisitive than stern.

"Tell me, Peter, which witnesses saw Jesus after he supposedly rose from the dead?"

Peter smiled. His face telegraphed his conviction that he was now on safe ground, "Hundreds of people saw Him. I saw Him on that first day and spoke with Him."

Quintus interrupted him asking, "How did you come to do that?"

"Why, Maryam Magdalene came running to me at the start of day to tell me she and her friends had visited the grave and found it open, and that an angel dressed in white had told them that Jesus had resurrected. I ran with her to the grave and saw Jesus and talked to him," related Peter.

Peter said all this in a matter-of-fact voice. The importance of Maryam, Lazarus' sister in his investigation was now becoming apparent. He would pursue this later. For now he wanted to hear what Peter had to say. He prompted him, "Go on."

Peter did, "Jesus appeared to all of us shortly after His resurrection, in our meeting room where we were assembled in hiding. He came back a week later when Thomas was with us. Thomas, not having been present at our first meeting, said that he did not believe, and would not believe, until he had put his hand into the wounds in Jesus' side, hands, and feet. When Jesus came that second time, He insisted that Thomas do just that. Thomas did, found the wounds, and then said apologetically, 'My Lord and my God!'"

Peter paused, wrapped in thought, before he continued, "I can tell you as much as you wish to know, but I am sure that you are hearing the same stories from others. Do you want me to go on or will you accept what they say?"

Quintus was pondering deeply both the words and the intent. After a moment, he replied, "Yes I have heard some of these stories, and for now, I will defer hearing more from you. I may or may not come back to you for additional information concerning sightings of Jesus after he is claimed to have resurrected from the dead." He saw disbelief on Peter's face. Peter was so convinced of the fact of the resurrection that he found it hard to believe others would deny the evidence. Quintus pressed on, "But perhaps more evidence will convince me. For now, however, please tell me why you and your companions followed Jesus?"

Peter refused to abandon the topic of the resurrection, "Tribune, you must have heard that Jesus raised others from the dead! Surely if he could raise others, He could raise himself! To have the power of life over death is to be God. If you are God, you can do anything. If you can raise others from the dead, you can raise yourself from the dead. If you are God you created the universe. Raising someone from the dead is nothing." Peter emphatically added, "Jesus was God!"

Quintus sighed inaudibly. It would be difficult to dispute this point with Peter. All the evidence pointed in the direction of the resurrection of Jesus from the dead. Quintus was not yet ready to accept that fact. Peter added, "Tribune, check on these other cases. There are at least three: his friend Lazarus, the daughter of Jairus, an official in Tetrarch Herod's court, and the son of the widow of Nain, whose name I can't recall at this time."

"I already have," said Quintus, who had nodded as each name was mentioned. They were on his list of interviews he had already completed. Once again before Peter could interrupt, he attempted to change the subject to the selection process used by Jesus in picking his close followers, a dozen as Quintus had come to understand. "Peter," he said, "how did Jesus pick you and your companions, and why did you follow him?"

"That is an easy question to answer, Tribune. Why He picked us, and not others, we do not know. We are gratified that He selected us. We followed Him because He asked us, challenged us, and promised to make us 'fishers of men.' Initially we were intrigued. As we came to know Him, we came to love him. He was pure goodness. He loved us and he loved all people, even when they turned against Him."

"How many close associates did he have?" asked Quintus.

"He picked twelve of us," Peter replied. "Initially they were Andrew my brother, then my kin, James the son of Zebedee, and his younger brother John. Levi whom he called Matthew, who was a tax collector, was the fifth chosen," then he went on to add the other seven, "Philip, Bartholomew, Thomas, James, son of Alphaeus, Jude, Simon the Zealot and Mathias, the last of whom replaced Judas Iscariot, who betrayed Jesus to the Temple guards."

Here Peter paused and became very sad, as he added, "It was difficult to accept that Judas betrayed Jesus..." another pause, "difficult!"

Longinus decided to change the subject, "Were there any women in your group?"

Peter replied in a matter-of-fact manner, "Why of course, His mother Maryam, and her close friend, Maryam Magdalene, the sister of Lazarus. Maryam's sister Martha also came with us at times," He bit his lip in deep concentration, and continued, "and of course we had many families follow us to hear Jesus. There were many women in the crowds He attracted."

Quintus decided that he had to question Maryam Magdalene as quickly as possible. Apparently she had been quite close to Jesus. The thought crossed his mind whether they had been lovers. If that were so, then Jesus was not the all perfect person everyone said he was. That had to be pursued. He nodded to himself that this had to be investigated. Looking directly at Peter, he abruptly he changed the subject. Turning to Longinus, he said to him, "Didn't Jesus pray for you and your men as you killed him?" he asked.

Longinus winced, but nodded, "Yes, he did."

Peter interrupted, and Quintus directed his gaze to him, "Tribune, do not blame your men. They carried out their duty as they knew it. That is why Jesus forgave them. Jesus tried to teach them, and us, that the kingdom of God, the kingdom of the next world was one of love, repentance, and forgiveness; the next world was ready and waiting for all of us. Entry would depend upon whether or not we repented and performed good works. He told us that our only commandment was to love God above all else, and to love our neighbors as ourselves. It was a simple path, and a simple message. He did not quote our rules. As Jews, we understood the old law. It was a law of fear as well as love, of sacrifice for sins, and continual remorse. Jesus preached a new law of repentance, forgiveness, and moving forward. It was a message of the heart and not of a mechanical following of rigid rules. The difficult part for us was to understand how simple it was, how possible it was to follow, and how worthwhile it was to do so. There can be no joy in evil. There is great joy in doing good, especially in helping others. We saw the Master's joy as He cured people of their illnesses, and how He always found the path to goodness and righteousness no matter how many obstacles were placed in His way. This is especially true of the many traps placed in his way by the Pharisees. I am sure you have heard those stories as well."

Quintus nodded as he interrupted, "What did he preach?"

Peter went into a long discussion of how Jesus preached goodness, the need for repentance, and the pardon they would receive from God simply by asking, so long as they were truly sorry.

Peter also went into a discussion about the use of parables by Jesus. In particular, Peter stressed the parable of the Bridegroom who found that his invited guests were too busy to attend the ceremony; he scoured the neighborhood and brought to the wedding feast all those that he could find. Peter went on further to describe how the bridegroom also insisted that the guests wear the wedding garments that he provided. When someone appeared without a gown, the bridegroom had him thrown out into the cold. The moral of the story was that those who did not heed the invitation, or did not follow it, were doomed to weeping and gnashing of teeth.

Peter then added the story of the Master who called in his stewards and reduced, the amounts owed to him by half or more if they were unable to pay. One of the stewards then called in his debtors and demanded that they pay or be put into prison. When they could not, he had them locked up. When the master heard of this action, he recalled the Steward, berated him, stopped the reduction of his debt, and had him in turn imprisoned for his debts because he had refused to follow the lead of the master.

Peter relayed a third story about the parables of Jesus. This was the story of the Prodigal Son. The son had requested his inheritance from his father, had left his father's home, and squandered the entire fortune in a foreign country. Then he turned to his father full of repentance, begging only to be made a servant. The father feted him, and restored him as an heir and son. Another son wondered why he was treated so well when he had deserted the father. The father's answer to the faithful son that he was a good man who would always be with him but that his brother had been dead and was now alive. Peter went on to amplify this parable with the one that Jesus told of the lost sheep and how the Shepherd would leave ninety-nine sheep to search for the one that was lost, praising God when that one was found. Both stories emphasized the love of the father for one who was lost and was then found. By implication, Jesus was showing how God would rejoice over a repentant sinner with true remorse.

Peter continued for the better part of the day, retelling the parables of Jesus one after another. During all of this, Quintus listened with deep attention and great patience. He well understood the constant repetition was driving the point home. Simply said, Jesus preached good. He did good things. He performed miracles to help the people. He cured their ill, expelled their demons, and even raised their dead. He helped people. He did not preach sedition. He did not preach revolt against Rome. Peter even quoted what Quintus had heard before, that Jesus had repeatedly called upon the separation between religion and the state; that of Caesar was to go to Caesar, and that of God was to go to God.

Suddenly Peter look directly at Quintus, and a look mimicking that of fury crossed his features, "Why did you Romans kill Jesus? You murdered an innocent man! You murdered God!"

Quintus was surprised at the attack. He was tempted to sidestep the question, since it had no bearing of the reason for this interrogation of Peter. The immediate issue was the missing body, yet he decided to represent Rome on the issue. His words were dry and somewhat official. He wasn't sure he believed them all, and would not think of that issue until he met with Pontius Pilate. But for now, he would summarize the official position. In a dry, authoritative voice, he answered Peter's outburst.

"Peter, Jesus was tried before Pontius Pilate and sentenced to death. The High Priest, Caiaphas, and the Sanhedrin accused Him of blasphemy, in their law punishable by death. That is not a crime in Roman law, fomenting unrest in the people *is*. As an occupying military and governing force, we are charged with keeping the peace, and with protecting both the people of Judea and the interests of Rome. Pilate acted on that premise. Even then, he tried to free Jesus. He gave the people their choice of releasing Jesus or Barabbas, a known murderer scheduled for execution. They chose Barabbas and went into a frenzy to have Jesus crucified. They even called for his blood on themselves and their children. So Pontius Pilate had him executed. It was not murder."

Before he could add anything else, Peter blurted out, "You know that mob consisted of two parts only: the followers of Barabbas who knew of the Passover amnesty and wanted Barabbas freed, and those bribed by the Sanhedrin and the High Priest. The followers of Jesus were not there. They were frightened and in hiding. I was one of them." The last was said with deep remorse. Peter continued, "We did not come out of hiding, or support Jesus, until the Holy Spirit came on Pentecost. Then we truly told every one of the teachings of Jesus."

Quintus decided to change the subject. Before Peter could say anything more, he abruptly asked, "How did Jesus teach you?"

Peter looked directly at Quintus, shook his head, raised his hand, and pointed at Quintus. He paused. Then he lowered his hand, expelled his breath, and looking calmly at Quintus said, "Tribune you seem to be a fair man. I know you are investigating the disappearance of the body of the Master. You will find that this execution, or murder as I believe, was a mistake. Your real issue is the resurrection of the body of Jesus," And Peter nodded to give emphasis to his words. A look of prophecy came into his appearance and words, "You will find, Tribune, that Jesus was God."

Then Peter went into a long discussion of how and what Jesus taught, "Jesus taught in parables, stories that were understood by all. His words were amplified by His miracles. Everything was meant to be a lesson. We moved about Judea going from town to town, staying with friends in their houses, and teaching our followers or those who came to hear. Jesus preached in homes, in fields, from boats, or in the town and village square. Often we had meetings with hundreds if not thousands of people in the countryside."

Then Peter gave a great smile, "You know Jesus fed two crowds of four or five thousand each with only a few loaves and fishes. On one occasion the crumbs from a few loaves and fishes had filled twelve baskets after everyone had their fill." Grinning broadly, he added, "And the crumbs exceeded what he started with by far. Jesus certainly had a sense of humor." Looking directly at Quintus, he asked, "He did it twice with two groups in two different locations. Did you know that, Tribune?"

"Yes, I did," answered Quintus, "It was reported to me from two of the purported miracles of Jesus."

Peter laughed outright, "Fancy words, Tribune, but they cannot hide the facts." Almost jutting his chin out, Peter added, "Jesus performed real miracles. Let me tell you more."

Peter went on for hours. Everything he said was confirmatory of what the Legionaries and Centurions had discovered and reported. Quintus was pleased at the corroboration, but still wanted more proof. He decided to change his tactics. Without warning, Quintus asked Peter, "Why did Jesus pick you?"

Peter suddenly lost his aplomb. His face took on a very sad look, "I don't know. Maybe it was because I am such a fool. Maybe by picking me He proved to everyone that anyone could be saved if they just followed His path," Peter paused, "He loved me, and I loved Him. It wasn't a love of familiarity, or a physical love. I loved Him differently than I loved my wife and my family. It was more than physical. It was all consuming. I knew He loved me totally. I just returned it, reflected it in a way back to Him." Here Peter paused and looked enigmatically at Quintus, "I even loved Him more when He berated me for my clumsy mistakes and words. Sometimes I even thought He was just picking on me. But then I realized that in reality He was preparing me to be a leader, honing me for criticism and rejection," Peter shook his head slowly as if clearing it, and went on. "Just before He died He placed Hiss arms on my shoulders and, calling me Peter, said that I was His rock and He was building His church on me, that rock." Looking directly at Quintus he said softly, his words as a cry of anguish, and certainly with no exaltation or pride, "He picked me to head His church. As unworthy as I was, He picked me! I, who had denied Him three times in his moment of trial."

Peter stopped, and fought hard to gain control of his emotions. Tears began to form in his eyes. He looked down, obviously in shame. In a tightly controlled, and tear-filled voice he added, "At His hour of need I failed him repeatedly. I slept as He prayed in the garden; when He was before Pilate, I denied Him three times, just as he had prophesized. Just after the third time, He passed by and looked at me. I could not face Him. I ran away and cried. Tears have formed ridges in my face since then whenever I remember my denial of Him," He seemed to shudder inwardly. Raising his head and standing up straighter than ever, Peter looked at Quintus, and said in a strong voice, "I will never deny Him ever again!"

Quintus looked at Peter. He saw before him conviction, firmness, and no note of worry or fear. He was convinced of Peter's determination never to let Jesus down again. For Peter, Jesus was certainly still alive. What a noble person. A fisherman. He would have made a brilliant general. A true leader. Jesus was right to call him a rock. He was beginning to admire Peter. Peter was a rock. What a Legionary he would have made, or a Centurion, perhaps even a Tribune or Legate. Peter in turn was impressed by the Tribune. Here was a man who should have been the Proconsul. He would never have sentenced Jesus to be flogged and executed. The thought crossed Peter's mind, he might even have removed Caiaphas from office for trying to use Rome to do his dirty work. He wondered where Quintus would end this interview. He had the power to have Peter executed, flogged, or released. Peter was ready for whatever fate was in store. He was, however, determined to bear witness to the truth. Both men remained silent for a short time for the emotions of the moment to pass.

Finally Quintus asked, "Did Jesus ever promise rewards for you and your associates? Did He promise you great power when he succeeded and came into his kingdom?"

Somewhat ashamedly, Peter answered, "There was a time I thought I would achieve great rewards in His kingdom, especially when James, John and I saw Him transformed into a godly figure on top Mount Tabor, talking to Moses and Elisha. From the sky we heard thunder that sounded like a voice saying, 'This is my Son in whom I am pleased.' We were afraid. We knew He was divine. In our awe, we did not seek position, but only to follow Him. We needed no further proof. Up until then, we had jostled in terms of who would sit on His right hand in the kingdom. Since then, I seek only to serve Him and others, to tell them the good news, to tell them about the resurrection, to tell them of His promise to return and to send the Holy Spirit as He ascended into the sky. He kept his promise on Pentecost. We were afraid, and now we are not."

Peter became silent, and a glow came over his face. He proceeded, "But most of all I want to tell everyone of his resurrection," Looking intently at Quintus, he said, "He was God, you know!"

The room became deathly silent.

Peter gave Quintus a quizzical look. "Well, are you going to free me or kill me?" he asked, with some humor in his voice. With no fear at all, he said, "I would prefer you free me because I have much to do to spread the word of God among my people." Then looking directly at Quintus, and after glancing at the two Centurions on either side, he added, "You can all join us too."

Quintus smiled. The bravery and brashness perhaps had won the day. There was no reason to hold Peter any longer. He was certain Peter and his associates had not stolen the body. Nor had anyone else. Quintus still refused to admit it, but it did appear as if Jesus had risen from the dead.

But he needed more information for his report. He would have Peter return with the others, "Peter, I would ask you to return in a few days with your eleven associates. Also, please ask Maryam Magdalene to expect me to visit her the same day. Can you do that?"

Peter laughed. Quintus appreciated the humor and strength of this man more and more. He might be an ignorant fisherman, but he could be a Tribune, or even of higher rank. What a leader he made. He too laughed as he heard Peter's words.

"Tribune, here I am chained to two of your Centurions and you are asking me a favor? Of course I can come here with the other apostles, and of course I will ask Maryam Magdalene to expect you. Do you want anyone else?"

"No," answered Quintus, "I will speak to Maryam his mother separately."

Once more Peter grinned, lifted the chains, and looking at Quintus repeated his earlier question, "Well, are you going to free me or kill me?"

Quintus grinned and gave the order, "Free him!"

**The Resurrection: A Criminal Investigation of the Mysterious Disappearance of the Body of the Crucified Criminal Jesus of Nazareth**

# Chapter Six
# Jerusalem – Pontius Pilate

Pontius Pilate arrived from Damascus on the Sabbath as scheduled. On the first day of the week, Quintus was summoned to the palace. Quintus strode rapidly to the meeting, escorted by a soldier of the palace guard, followed by his scribe, Marcus. The meeting site was the room where he had met Legate Lucius on his arrival. During that meeting, he and Lucius had sat in chairs beside the elevated platform which reminded him so much of a throne room. As he entered, he saw that Pontius Pilate was sitting in the ornate chair on the elevated platform with a seat beside him at a lower level. Quintus hid his surprise. Pilate gestured to Quintus to sit at the chair to his right, and motioned at Marcus to find a place. Quintus saluted Pilate with his right hand over his heart, "Hail Pontius Pilate, Procurator of Judea."

Without rising from his chair, Pilate in turn saluted him, "Hail Quintus Gaius Caesar, Tribune of the Praetorian Guard and Legate of the Emperor Tiberius." Then he clapped his hands. When his steward appeared, he directed him to bring wine for the Tribune. He sat, lifted a cup of wine, and gestured to Quintus, who had remained standing, once again to sit in the chair at the lower level on his right. Again he waved at Marcus to sit wherever he chose. Quintus hid his displeasure at what he considered to be treatment more befitting a subordinate than a Legate of the Emperor. He also detected a sense of uncertainty on the part of the Procurator. This was going to be an interesting meeting!

"How can I help you?" began Pontius Pilate. "I understand why you are here. Since my return from Damascus I have received a full report from the Legate Lucius of your activities and the arrangements the two of you made to work together. I have instructed him to continue his close cooperation with you. I am aware of your orders from the Emperor contained on the papyrus which I see you have with you."

Quintus took the papyrus and handed it to Pontius Pilate. The Procurator unrolled it, read it, and then returned it to Quintus. He then continued:

"I had received a separate dispatch from the Emperor commanding me to tell you everything that has happened concerning this man Jesus and to do as you request as if commanded by the Emperor himself." He paused as if searching for his words, "Please tell me what you have discovered, and how I can provide any information to you that would be of assistance in your mission from the Emperor."

At that point, the steward returned with a goblet of wine for Quintus. He also placed a carafe of wine on a small table to the left of Pontius Pilate. This gave Quintus an opportunity to think for a moment.

Quintus had prepared a plan for this meeting. His objective was to secure as much information as possible from Pilate, and divulge the least amount of information, until he had formed his conclusions. His decision was to use this meeting strictly as an introduction and to follow it up with other meetings as he progressed with his investigation. Looking at the Procurator, he began, "Proconsul, in your absence, I worked with Tribune Lucius and must thank you for having commanded him to be of maximum assistance to me during your absence in Damascus."

Pontius Pilate nodded, sipped his wine, and waved his left hand to continue. Quintus hid his irritation at such cavalier treatment.

He then related in summary fashion his activity; Quintus began with his meeting with Saul the tent maker in Tarsus, his investigation of the tomb of Jesus, his inquiries in various areas of Jerusalem, his trip to Nain and Bethany, his meeting with Lazarus, and his interview the day before with Peter. As he relayed the facts, he could see the impact it was having on Pontius Pilate. The Procurator seemed not only impressed, but Quintus detected a sense of unease, uncertainty, and perhaps even fear. Was Pontius Pilate hiding something? Was there some fact he feared that Quintus would discover?

Quintus decided to get directly to the point, "Why did you have Jesus executed?"

"He was becoming a problem," said Pilate, "the High Priest wanted Him executed, and so did Herod Antipas, but neither had the courage to do it. They could have had him stoned. They were afraid they would lose the support of their people. Only a few days previously Jesus had entered Jerusalem in triumph. While they could bribe some of the people to perjure themselves at the trial, and to scream 'Crucify Him!' at my meeting with Jesus, they did not have wide support. In addition, they were afraid that word of their prejudicial activities would create an even greater problem for them if they actually executed Jesus. So they decided to use me, to have me order and carry out the execution of Jesus."

"So, why did you?"

"It was difficult."

"Why?"

"I could not find any guilt in Jesus."

Quintus grunted in disbelief to hear such a statement from a Procurator of a Roman Province. Then he remembered the Emperor's words, "All in good time." With a total straight face, he continued, "So?"

Pontius Pilate sighed, "If I had freed Jesus, I would have injured my relationship with Caiaphas and Tetrarch Herod. I use them to keep the peace. I had Jesus executed to keep that peace. I decided and wagered that Jesus had less power, and less support than they did. Executing Jesus would cause less mischief for Rome, than losing the support of Caiaphas and Herod."

"So you washed your hands of the blood of that just man?"

"Yes. My act of washing my hands was to show everyone that I understood the situation but that I was willing to execute an innocent man to protect the power of Rome."

Quintus was not surprised since he had formed his own opinion. Pontius Pilate was a man lacking courage and nobility. No wonder he was Procurator of a post no one else wanted. He stared at Pontius Pilate trying to keep the distain from his face. "Why didn't you just have him executed without the charade of washing your hands?" He pressed on, "Would not that have been nobler? In fact, would not it have been much nobler to have freed him?"

"My wife, Procula, virtually told me to do just that." Seeing Quintus' quizzical look and raised eyebrows, he continued, "While I was sitting in the judgment hall, she sent me a message: 'Have nothing to do with that innocent man, because in a dream last night, I suffered much on account of him.' That just added to my unease in handling this man. I knew he was innocent, but I also knew I was expected to execute him in return for having continuing peaceful relations with the Jews. It became a case of personal belief against political expediency."

Pontius Pilate meekly added, "Now I know that releasing him would have been a better course of action."

"Why?" interjected an exasperated Quintus, "Why were you hiding behind a woman's skirts, or were you too frightened to exercise your power as a Roman Proconsul?" In a stern voice, he repeated, "Why?"

Quintus had finally been able to penetrate the shell of the Procurator's composure. Pontius Pilate slammed the wine cup against the table. He leaned forward and almost screamed at Quintus, "No! I did the right thing acting in the interests of Rome. I should have freed him because now I know I killed a god. He even rose from the dead!" Calming down, Pilate continued, still with a note of exculpation in his voice, "The guards placed in front of the tomb swore the stone rolled away on its own, and that Jesus walked out of the tomb as a bright light, and walked right through their midst." He stopped, sipped his wine and sitting back in his chair, stated matter-of-factly, "You know, these were Roman guards. In their fear, they went to Caiaphas for support before I, as Proconsul, found out. They were bribed by Caiaphas to tell everyone that they were sleeping but were awakened by the noise of the stone being rolled away from the opening. They claimed they saw disciples of Jesus go into the tomb and come out with the body, then run off with it."

Quintus controlled his anger, "I assume you questioned all the guards and found the truth!"

"Yes," said Pilate, "we sought them out. We interrogated them vigorously," said Pilate with a slight smile.

"You mean you tortured them?" said Quintus.

"Yes," admitted Pilate, "we tortured the guards extensively. They all told the same story. They went to their deaths claiming he had risen from the dead. They were all crucified upside down, which is a punishment for guards who fall asleep on duty." Here, Pontius Pilate stopped, and took a sip of wine.

Quintus took the opportunity to interject an important question, "On what basis did you arrest, torture, and execute these guards?" he asked.

Pilate sputtered, almost choking on the sip of wine he had just taken, "Why? Because I am the Procurator."

"But that doesn't mean you are above the law," said Quintus. "You have the authority, but you do not have the right. Even if it was the right thing to do, it was a mistake. You should have forced Caiaphas to tell the truth about the incident."

"It was all unfortunate," Pilate gave a long sigh, "I think the guards were telling the truth. It just added to the mysterious events that occurred the day we crucified Jesus."

Quintus looked up - something new! "What happened?"

"In about the third hour, I was told that Jesus had died. But I already knew. At the third hour, there was a great thunder storm. Caiaphas later told me the veil in the temple tore apart on its own at that instant. There were stories of graves opening and that the dead walked. All matters of strange reports came. That was the first time I heard the phrase, 'You killed God.' That came from the High Priest. Now I think he was right." Pontius Pilate sipped his wine again, "The next day, Caiaphas came to me asking that a guard be posted at the tomb. He said that Jesus had foretold his death and prophesized he would rise again on the third day. Caiaphas made strong arguments that if his body disappeared, then his followers could claim he had risen from the dead, and this could lead to civil disorder." Pontius Pilate stopped once more. Gazing at his wine goblet for a moment, and taking another sip, he went on, "So I posted a guard, but they claimed the body had walked out of the tomb after angels came down and rolled the tomb stone away." Pontius Pilate stopped. Looking once more into his wine cup, and persevered, swirling it as he spoke, "I had them all arrested, tortured, and executed. They claimed it was a risen Jesus that had left the tomb." After a moment, almost as an afterthought, softly, in a voice full of anguish and emotion, he noted, "Apparently he did."

His story was becoming more and more unbelievable. Quintus had received a charter from the Emperor to investigate the disappearance of the dead body of Jesus of Nazareth. Now he was hearing that Jesus was not a criminal, that he was a god and that he had risen from the dead. If he had risen from the dead, then he was God. But was he dead in the first place…if he had been placed in the tomb unconscious, could he have opened the tomb himself and walked away? But that was impossible! That tomb could not be opened from the inside. In fact, no single person can roll the stone back. Accomplices would be needed. And it would be noisy. If the guards were on duty and the stone had rolled back, even if they were asleep, it would have awakened them. Sixteen guards would be more than a match for a small group of untrained followers of Jesus. So the soldiers could not have been asleep, or could not have been overcome. A group of followers could not have rolled back the stone and taken the body. They would have been stopped. Even if Jesus was alive inside the tomb, he would have been unable to move the stone. As Quintus went through the possibilities, only one seemed to make sense. Even that seemed to make less sense though. If Jesus were God, then it could all happen, but how could a god be killed? How could a god allow himself to be brutalized as Jesus had?

Quintus looked at Pontius Pilate, "What do you truly believe?"

"I believe that Jesus was a god and that he allowed his human nature to be killed when he could have stopped it with one twitch of his eyebrow."

Quintus was shocked, "How can you be sure he died?"

"Because the Centurion passed a lance into His side and blood and water rushed out, which is usually a sign that someone we have crucified has died. There is no doubt in the mind of the soldiers who executed him and those that buried him, that Jesus died on the cross and was buried in the tomb. There is no doubt that he has risen from the dead." With that, Pontius Pilate got up and began pacing back and forth in the front of the room, occasionally sipping wine. After a few moments, he returned to his chair, sat down and remarked, "What other explanation do you have?"

"I am not sure," said Quintus, "I have a great deal of information but I have more people I wish to interview. I delayed talking to the High Priests, Caiaphas and Annas, and with Tetrarch Herod, until I had met with you. Now I will proceed with those meetings."

Quintus stared doubtfully at Pontius Pilate for a moment and then proceeded, "I have to interview the close disciple of Jesus of Nazareth, one named John, who did not run away during the execution. I also wish to interview the mother of the carpenter, Maryam. Then I will report back to you with my findings and with some of my opinions. Then I will discuss with you some of the details of my report to the Emperor." He then questioned, "If this Jesus was a god, why did he let the crucifixion happen?"

Then he looked directly at Pontius Pilate, and in a very stern voice, befitting his position, he asked, "Why didn't you do this kind of investigation before I arrived? Why did you leave it up to the Emperor to initiate this investigation, and to send me to do what you should have done?"

Pilate was startled. He almost dropped his wine goblet, seized almost by panic as he realized what a terrible mistake he had made in not investigating further. He put his wine goblet on the table, rose, and began to pace back and forth, muttering to himself, until he suddenly stopped and stood before Quintus, who had also risen from his chair. The two men stood facing each other, inches apart. Attempting to control his emotions, and speaking through clenched teeth, Pilate spoke, each word almost exploding from his mouth, yet subdued in volume, "Because it was over! Jesus of Nazareth *was* the Messiah! We executed him but he rose from the dead! What more was there to uncover?"

Pilate turned away, began pacing again, at first quickly and then slowing as he regained control of his emotions. At that point he walked over to Quintus and said, "As you know I reported all this to the Emperor. Why are you here?"

Quintus looked directly at Pontius Pilate, "Because the report you sent was not believable. You cannot tell anyone, and certainly not the Emperor, that you executed a carpenter who turned out to be the Messiah and who later rose from the dead, and have people believe that statement at face value. You need facts and proof. I am here to get those facts and to find the truth. I am here to do the job you should have done and did not do!"

Quintus looked steadily at Pontius Pilate. Visibly shaken, Pilate regained control of his emotions and his composure. He had made a terrible blunder in how he had handled his meeting with Quintus. He should have treated Quintus as a superior instead of a subordinate. He decided to redirect the attention away from himself to others.

"Quintus," he began, "my job as Procurator, reporting to the Governor of Syria, is to maintain Pax Romana, the peace of Rome. This is done not through the exercise of power, but through the threat of exercising the use of that power. We used that power to conquer these people. Now we keep that power in the background as we occupy. We work with the people. We let them have their religion and customs, but they know and we know, that *we* have all the power. Do you not agree, Tribune?"

Quintus nodded. In a quiet, matter of fact voice, he approached, "We all know that, Pontius. What are you getting at?"

Pilate let out a long breath and continued, "These people have their own quarrels and power struggles. Some are not so petty. In this case, Jesus of Nazareth started touring the countryside of Judea, preaching about the kingdom of God, and performing miracles. Reports were continually coming back to me of how his following was becoming larger and larger. The reports also indicated that he was no threat to Rome, and was in fact advising his followers to obey the Roman law. I believe the statement was something like 'Render unto Caesar that which is Caesar's, and render unto God that which is God's.'" He paused for dramatic effect, not knowing that Quintus had already learned most of this. He went on.

"The same reports were being received by the High Priest, Caiaphas, and his father-in-law, the High Priest, Annas. Herod Antipas was also aware of what was happening. In fact, most of the activity was in his territory of Galilee. The three of them were concerned about their power base."

Quintus resisted the temptation to interject with the question, 'And what about you and <u>your</u> power base', but he did not. He let Pontius Pilate continue.

"Caiaphas went to the governing Council of their religion, the Sanhedrin. A continuing discussion had occurred over some weeks concerning the growing power of Jesus and its threat to the established order. Caiaphas began a campaign which upheld that it would be better for one man to die than for a nation to come asunder. He rapidly convinced the majority of the Sanhedrin that Jesus had to die. But that was even before Jesus entered Jerusalem. When he did, on the first day of the week in which he was executed, it was a triumph. The people greeted him as if he were a King. This caused even more alarm in the Sanhedrin, with Caiaphas, and with Herod. They all came to me. They lied and claimed he was preaching sedition when he claimed that he wanted to create a new kingdom. In their eyes, religion and government are connected. For them, an attack on religious belief or practice is an attack against the common order. If we were not the conquerors, then their government would have had him executed. They claimed that Jesus was a threat to their orderly conduct of controlling their people, and as such was a threat to us," Pilate paused in thought, "I laughed at them. I told them we, or Rome, had no problem with the activities of Jesus and his followers since we saw they were no threat to the sovereignty of Rome. I reminded them that we separated religion and government. All the demonstrations were peaceful, a manifestation of religious belief and acceptance, even if exuberant."

Here, Pilate paused. He became consumed in thought for a moment, and then pressed on, "There was one act of Jesus that solidified the decision by Caiaphas and Herod to have him executed; the act of Jesus upsetting, berating, and beating the money counters in the Temple. He had gone too far. It was then that they sought a traitor amongst his followers who would lead them to Jesus at a moment that they could arrest him. They found such a man, a despicable man, Judas Iscariot. He led the palace guards to Jesus where he was praying in the Garden of Gethsemane."

"I think you know the rest. Essentially he was tried by Caiaphas, and then Herod, and then finally me. They wanted him executed. They manipulated everything to have this done. They scared the people demanding an execution. I thought they probably bribed instigators because I could not believe that in three days the people who had welcomed Jesus into Jerusalem now wanted to condemn him to death. I knew it was an arranged demonstration." He paused before a brutal admission, "They prejudiced my questioning of Jesus. When I asked him if he were 'King of the Jews,' He told me of his kingdom not of this world. I began to see the potential for rebellion. Caiaphas and the Sanhedrin had set the seeds of doubt in my mind. The result was my decision to chastise Jesus, and to have him mocked. Later it led to my order to have him executed. I am now convinced they poisoned my mind to act as they wished against my will."

Quintus decided that Pontius Pilate had let himself become a pawn in the hands of Caiaphas. There seemed little point in disputing the fact. He remained silent and let Pontius Pilate break the silence. It lasted for a moment or two. Finally, Pontius Pilate emitted a long sigh and walked back to his elevated chair. He sat down, took a sip of wine and said in a somewhat normal voice, "How else can I be of help to you?"

Quintus decided to change the subject dramatically in order to close the meeting on some kind of positive note, leaving the door open for further meetings.

"Procurator, when I met with Saul, the tent maker in Tarsus, a man dedicated to stamp out any following of Jesus, he told me he was proceeding to Damascus on behalf of the High Priest Caiaphas and the Sanhedrin to arrest any followers of Jesus he could find. Did you learn anything of his activities before you left Damascus?"

Pontius Pilate looked up in surprise, "Yes I did. But what I heard was somewhat surprising. Apparently Saul has gone through a conversion and is now an ardent follower of Jesus."

Quintus could not hide his surprise, "How could that have happened? He was very zealous against Jesus and his followers when we met in Tarsus. What changed the mind of this tent maker, Saul?"

As Quintus asked the question, in his mind he remembered the hesitancy in Saul. The Procurator's next words added to his surprise, "You say Saul. I heard him referred to as Paul. In any event, he was apparently struck from his horse on the way to Damascus and heard a voice identifying itself as Jesus asking why he persecuted his followers. Paul was blinded and arrived in Damascus without being able to see, with scales over his eyes. A few days later, his sight was restored by a follower of Jesus, someone called Ananias I heard, and since then he has become a vocal and vibrant supporter of the teachings of Jesus of Nazareth."

Quintus quietly catalogued this new fact. He would try to learn more. Apparently the teachings of Jesus could convert even extremely zealous opponents. The Emperor was right. The movement started by Jesus could have a major impact on Rome. A startling thought briefly crossed his mind. It could change Rome forever! The Emperor's gut feeling certainly had merit.

He immediately suppressed the thought and turned his attention back to Pontius Pilate. Quintus had remained standing. Pilate once more sat on his elevated chair, which Quintus refused to think of as a 'throne.' The meeting had provided significant information for him, but his disdain for the Procurator had significantly increased. He was tempted to banish and remove him on the spot but he remembered the words of Tiberius, 'All in good time.' He hid his feelings and in an agreeable tone of voice, with a smile on his face, he said, "Thank you very much for your time, Procurator. The information you have provided has been very helpful. You must overlook some of my pointed questions but I felt it was necessary because of the complexity and seriousness of the situation. What is done is done! Our job now is to preserve and enhance the power of Rome. This whole episode concerning Jesus must be examined in that light."

Quintus paused for a moment, then began his concluding remarks, "I have much more information I seek, and certainly more interviews including, as I have told you, a meeting with Caiaphas and Herod. I would appreciate the opportunity to meet with you again when I have completed these inquiries and visitations. Thank you, Procurator!"

Quintus saluted, and was saluted in turn by a somewhat cowed Pontius Pilate. Quintus left the room, with Marcus following him.

They returned to the barracks. Marcus began to transcribe his notes into the report being prepared for the Emperor. Quintus used the time to collect his thoughts. When Marcus had completed his work, Quintus dictated the dispatch for the Emperor. This would be sent via chariot to Caesarea for the next galley leaving for Rome.

Quintus read the dispatch before he signed it. He had omitted all his editorial feelings and had reported only the facts. It carried the location, Jerusalem, and the date. It read:

*This morning I met with Pontius Pilate. He has been manipulated by the High Priest Caiaphas and by King Herod. He sentenced the carpenter Jesus of Nazareth to death because of their bribery of perjuring witnesses and crowd demonstrators. Jesus was a threat to their power. They plotted to have him executed, and connived to have this done by the Romans. Jesus was innocent of breaking any Roman law.*

*The execution was successful. Jesus was definitely dead on the cross. The dead body was placed in a tomb with only one access point, the entrance. This was covered by a large stone which requires two or three strong men to move. Doing so is very noisy. Because Jesus had predicted that he would rise on the third day after his death, Roman guards were placed on duty at the tomb. When the tomb was found empty, the guards had disappeared. They told differing stories; first that of a brightly illuminated resurrected Jesus walking through the opening; and secondly, that they had fallen asleep and his disciples had come, rolled back the stone, and run away with the body. Under torture the guards insisted Jesus had resurrected. They were executed by order of Pontius Pilate, guilty of conspiring to hide the facts concerning the disappearance of the body of Jesus. .*

*Pontius Pilate had instituted no investigation concerning the missing body. Since my arrival, under my direction, three Centurions and one hundred Legionaries have combed Jerusalem for the missing body. They have uncovered no rumors or possible locations for the missing body. The closest associates of Jesus were fearful of the Sanhedrin and us at that time of the execution. It is doubtful they had the courage or capability to steal the body.*

*There is much conjecture that Jesus was a god, and that he did indeed rise from the dead. In my investigations, we have catalogued some thirty-seven miracles attributed by witnesses to the carpenter Jesus of Nazareth. Three of these miracles involved raising dead persons back to life. I investigated these and found them authentic, and spoke to each of the three persons who were raised from the dead.*

*Jesus has been seen since his execution by over five hundred people in various locations. I investigated one such sighting and believe it to be true.*

*On the death of Jesus on the cross, strange events occurred simultaneously. Many said at that time that we had executed a god.*

*Sire, if you will recall a prior dispatch concerning a zealous antagonist of Jesus, one Saul, a tentmaker from Tarsus. Apparently he is now converted to belief in Jesus as a resurrected deity. This conversion is indicative of the power of the message of Jesus, and could be an indicator of the future growth of the sect of followers of this man. I will investigate further.*

*My summary findings to date are as follows:*

- *I. Pontius Pilate is incompetent and should be replaced.*
- *II. Jesus truly died on the cross.*
- *III. Jesus performed miracles in his lifetime.*
- *IV. Jesus was seen alive after his death.*
- *V. No one stole his body from the tomb.*
- *VI. The conversion of Saul is a straw in the wind compared to the wave of potential change which might become a threat to Rome. This will be investigated further.*

*From this analysis, I conclude that Jesus most likely was a god and that you were right to be concerned. There is much more to this entire affair than merely a missing body. My investigation will continue.*

Quintus signed the papyrus, rolled it, placed his seal along the edge, and handed it to Marcus for dispatch to the Emperor. Then he went in search of the three Centurions to discuss and plan their activities for the next day.

**The Resurrection: A Criminal Investigation of the Mysterious Disappearance of the Body of the Crucified Criminal Jesus of Nazareth**

# Chapter Seven
# The Apostles and Maryam Magdalene

By mid morning, the conference room had filled with the close disciples of Jesus, the Apostles as they were known. There were twelve of them. Aurelius greeted them as they arrived and had them escorted in. When they were all assembled, he sent word to Quintus. A few minutes later Quintus entered the room in dress uniform accompanied by Sutonius, Longinus, and Marcus. The three Centurions took up positions at the back of the room behind the Apostles, and Marcus moved to a table off to the side, in the rear as well. Quintus walked to a small platform at the front of the room. The voices stilled in expectation of his remarks.

Quintus looked at the men before him. Peter was in the very front, in a position of leadership, just as he expected. Looking at the others, he was agreeably surprised. They were mainly fishermen, dressed somewhat poorly except for one whose robe denoted considerable wealth. Their bearing, however, was surprisingly alert for such a group. Fishermen they might be, but at first sight they were impressive. It seemed to Quintus that they exuded an air of strength and confidence. These men would be formidable in any undertaking. Two thoughts circulated in his mind as be prepared to address them. First, that Jesus had chosen wisely in selecting each of these men. The second thought was a puzzle. These men were confident, probably fearless. Yet he had been told they had been frightened away at the execution of Jesus. Was that true, or had something happened to give them that air of confidence and strength?

Perhaps what he had been told about Pentecost was the answer. He was going to find out.

"My good men," he began, "thank you for coming." His words were greeted with silence. He went on, "I am Quintus Gaius Caesar, Tribune of the Praetorian in Rome, special emissary of the Emperor." The silence continued, "I was sent to Judea by the Emperor to investigate the mysterious disappearance of the body of the criminal Jesus of Nazareth."

Hardly had he finished when he heard Peter say in a very strong voice, "Jesus was no criminal. He was an innocent man condemned to death because He spoke the truth," Peter looked hard at Quintus, "Tribune, I thought we covered that in our meeting."

"Yes, Peter," said Quintus, somewhat resignedly, "but I am stating my mission as indicated in the mind of the Emperor. In his eyes, Jesus was a criminal, the body has disappeared, and there are potential disturbances in Judea. And so, I am here to investigate and report back. What I think will not necessarily be what the Emperor decides. For that reason I must be thorough in considering every aspect of the situation. Now do you understand?" Quintus thought he heard, "Oh." He continued:

"Since my arrival here, I have engaged in a very extensive investigation of all the circumstances surrounding the death, burial, and empty tomb of Jesus. Three Centurions and one hundred Legionaries have scoured the country for witnesses, information, and documents that would help establish the truth. I personally visited the tomb, and met with Roman and Jewish officials, and a number of the followers of Jesus. I also met with Peter," Quintus raised his arm to point to Peter as he mentioned his name. Peter smiled broadly at this point.

Quintus went on, "And I interviewed Lazarus," A buzz of appreciation filled the room. The Apostles realized they were dealing with someone determined to find the truth. Quintus punctuated his next words by looking at each Apostle in turn as he spoke, "And so I wanted to speak to each of you and to all of you in a group." He made his way into his closing remarks, "My objective is to find the truth and report it to Tiberius." Then he added to punctuate his remarks, "He is the Emperor, I am the investigator." The group became very sober and quiet. Quintus decided to get to the heart of the underlying problem concerning the Emperor, "The Emperor has charged me with the responsibility to report back to him whether or not you are a threat to Pax Romana." Raising his right hand, Quintus closed his fist tightly as he added, "If so, you will be quashed!"

There was a deathly silence in the room. Quintus decided to go directly to the point of meeting with them. Looking carefully at each in turn, he asked, "Which of you stole the body?"

There was a startled gasp and a torrent of voices immediately started. Peter was the first. With some anger in his voice, somewhat under control, yet with a certain amount of exasperation, he challenged Quintus, "Tribune, I thought we settled that when I met you!" Controlling the strain and anger building as he spoke, Peter continued, "Jesus would never have condoned such an act by any of us. All of His teachings were based on and directed towards honesty. We are honest men. I can give you solid reasons why your question is totally out of order. Jesus rose from the dead. No one stole his body, Tribune."

Peter stopped for emphasis, and then stepped forward a pace and continued, "Tribune, we are here at your bidding, but as willing witnesses to the truth of the Resurrection of our Lord, Jesus." Peter then became very strong in his statements, "We know the truth and wish to tell you what it is." He paused, and looking even more forceful than ever, went on, "Jesus said, 'I am the way, the truth and the life. Those that follow me shall have eternal life.' He commanded us to go forth and teach all nations. We are pleased at this opportunity to begin obeying Him by teaching Rome through you and the Emperor." Then taking one more pace forward, Peter raised his right arm, and pointing let it sweep the entire room, "Our message is one of peace and love. We are no threat to Rome."

The assembled group erupted with, "Yes. Jesus was Truth."

Quintus was surprised, but not entirely. His meeting with Peter had prepared him. Otherwise, from the information relayed to him, he might have expected a cowed and frightened group of men concerned about their fate. These men seemed to have no concern for what might happen to them. Their only concern seemed to be the dissemination of the knowledge they had of Jesus. They said they were no threat to Rome, but a group of such cohesion and zeal could very well grow and become a threat. But first he had to finalize his investigation of the disappearance of the body. If anyone had stolen the body, it was probably members of this group since they had the most to gain.

Quintus decided to sidestep Peter and go directly to the men before him, "Peter, you and I have had an opportunity to discuss Jesus at length. Now I wish to speak to each of your companions." He searched his mind for names from his meeting with Peter. He remembered that his brother Andrew had first called Peter's attention to Jesus, "Andrew," Quintus said, looking around the men before him, "are you here?"

A tall man stepped forward. He had some of Peter's facial characteristics. He had a distinctive bearing, confident, and eyes that sparkled with a keen intelligence, "I am Andrew."

"Tell me, Andrew, how you came to follow Jesus, and why?" Andrew began the tale, "I had heard of John the Baptist who was preaching repentance and was baptizing people in the Jordan. I went to see for myself and became interested in what the Baptist had to say. One day, Jesus came and was baptized. Then I started listening to what He had to say. I told Peter. We discussed it, but did nothing more since we were busy with our fishing business. Then Jesus came by when we were fishing, and called Peter to join him. And also me. We both followed Him, staying with Him longer and longer as we gradually wound down our involvement with our fishing business. Jesus then called James and John, sons of Zebedee, our kinsmen, who also worked with us. They too followed Jesus," Andrew stopped, obviously turning over in his mind why they all followed Jesus. Then he began to explain:

"Tribune, as you know, life is a continual series of episodes of hard work, intermingled with moments of relaxation with family and friends. Each day passes with little change as you strive to pay your bills, support your family, and build a cushion for hard times. Suddenly there is a change, an opportunity to do more than scratch and grub for daily bread; something that enables you and helps those around you. Some ignore the opportunity. For us, Jesus became that shining beacon that we followed. He offered involvement in being of service to our fellow humans who were suffering, and who also looked for a beacon to truly brighten the hum-drum of their lives. We followed Jesus because He offered an opportunity for us to be complete, to fulfill the purpose of being alive, and to pave the way with our work in this world for eternal life in Paradise,"

Andrew became silent, staring directly at Quintus, "You are a soldier, Tribune. You believe in the nobility of your cause, you believe in the ascendency of Rome. You are willing to give your life for that belief." Again he stopped, and directed a piercing look at Quintus, "We are willing to give our lives for our beliefs as well."

Quintus listened with increasing respect. His mind worked quickly on the aspects of what he had heard from Andrew, and previously from Peter. If Andrew and Peter truly represented all of these men, then here was a force that could constantly grow. Would it be a threat to Rome? He didn't know yet. He would have to keep pursuing that aspect. For now, he had to concentrate on the missing body. The motivation of his closest followers became important in determining any possibility that they had stolen the body. First he had to reply to Andrew.

"Andrew, thank you." Looking around the room at the assembled men, he asked, "Do you all share this view? Did you all receive a calling from Jesus to join Him?" He then went around the room to each man to confirm that all had received a call from Jesus, which they had followed. When he asked if they all agreed with Andrew that they would die for their belief in Jesus, they were resounding in their confirmation that they would. Peter even added, if crucified, he would ask to be executed with the cross upside down since he was not worthy to be crucified in the same manner as Jesus. Quintus was impressed. If only he could believe these men.

For three more hours he badgered, shouted, threatened, coaxed, and demanded answers and opinions from them. He questioned them as a group and individually, examining the teachings of Jesus, the miracles, and the lessons with parables. There was agreement among all of them, not only with information garnered in today's meeting, but also with the information separately obtained by the Centurions and Legionaries. Jesus had certainly been a remarkable man.

Then Quintus suddenly went into the Crucifixion. He confirmed that the followers had been frightened and ran away. They confirmed that Peter had cut off the ear of a guard, but that Jesus had miraculously reattached it and chastised Peter that those who lived by the sword would perish by the sword. Quintus winced when this was said. How true!

To Quintus, they agreed that Caiaphas had engineered the execution, and that Pontius Pilate had ordered the death of Jesus because he feared a civil disturbance. The farce of offering the Passover amnesty was easily explained; the supporters of Barabbas, and those bribed outshouted the few supporters of Jesus brave enough to be present. They were vehement in their denial that the followers of Jesus had turned against Him. The crowds that witnessed and praised His entrance into Jerusalem still believed in Him, but out of fear had either hidden, remained silent, or been outnumbered by the followers of Caiaphas and Barabbas.

All of this confirmed what Quintus already knew. It was significant that everything any of the twelve had said was independently corroborated.

Quintus abruptly returned to the main point of his investigation, "Which of you stole the body and hid it to increase the belief in Jesus?" Quintus asked.

There was an immediate cascade of voices. All of them vehemently protested the accusation. Jesus would never tolerate such a conspiracy. None of them would be guilty of such a collusion of falsehood. On and on the arguments went, all at full voice. Quintus let them all talk. Finally Peter waved his arms and restored order. Turning to Quintus, masking his anger with cold logic, he began, "Tribune, you know that is not what happened." Peter held up his hand, extending a finger with each point.

"First, there were guards. They attested to a brilliant body that came out of the tomb and walked through them. They were Roman soldiers knowing that failure on duty meant death," He extended one finger to maintain his counting.

"Second, I saw Jesus the day He arose from the dead. Others saw Him as well. In all, hundreds saw Him," He extended a second finger.

"Third, Thomas, before all of us here, put his hands into the wounds of Jesus. Ask him," Peter extended a third finger.

"Fourth, Tribune. There is no other explanation other than the fact that Jesus rose from the dead. If he did not, then hundreds of people are guilty of a terrible conspiracy, a conspiracy contrary to all their beliefs, a conspiracy that has no whisper of proof," He extended the palm of his hand with four fingers open and the thumb not.

"And finally, Tribune," he said as he opened his entire palm and waved it before Quintus, "we are willing to die for our belief. We are neither fools nor idiots."

Quintus remained silent before quietly asking, "Thomas, are you here?"

A nondescript man in clothing that had seen better days stepped forward, "I am Thomas," he said, and remained silent.

"Did you actually put your hands into the wounds of Jesus?" Quintus asked.

"Yes," answered Thomas with no elaboration.

Obviously facing a taciturn and self-possessed man, Quintus asked further, "How could a body pass through walls and still be solid enough for you to put your hands and fingers into his side and into the wound on his hands and feet?"

"I don't know," answered Thomas, "all I know is that the body I felt was solid, warm, and alive." He paused, and almost against the better judgment of his laconic nature, he added, "Everyone in the room saw it."

Quintus persisted, "Do you believe Jesus rose from the dead?"

"Yes," said Thomas, "and I believe He was and is my Lord and my God."

"Will you die for your beliefs?" asked Quintus.

"Willingly," replied Thomas instantly.

Quintus decided to try a naked threat, "Longinus, please have fifty Legionaries come here immediately. On my command they are to arrest these men and scourge them until they tell the truth. Then they are to be executed."

When Longinus left the room, Quintus turned again to Peter, "Well, this is your last chance. Tell the truth or you know the consequences."

Peter turned to look directly at Quintus, and said in a voice full of determination, "Tribune, we have. There is nothing you can do to make us tell you what is not true," Peter then folded his arms and looked sternly at Quintus.

Quintus then asked each of the other eleven the same thing. They affirmed what Peter had said. By this time, the Legionaries had entered the room and circled the twelve. Longinus approached Quintus, "Tribune, what is your command?"

Quintus looked around the room. He saw no sign of fear in the twelve. There was not a single flicker of uncertainty in their eyes. They were willing to die for their faith. They truly believed what they said was true. Quintus was not really sure, so he quickly devised a stratagem. He looked at the twelve and spotted one who seemed the youngest. He appeared to be barely more than a boy. He pointed him out to Longinus, and ordered five Legionaries to surround him and upon his command, to escort him to the torture chamber and await his arrival.

There was a stunned silence. The men looked at each another in wonderment. The fist was coming down. Quintus turned and looking directly at Peter, in a stern voice asked, "Who is this lad?"

In a calm voice, Peter answered, "John, the son of Zebedee, of whom I spoke earlier." Then in a resolute voice he asked, "Would you replace him with me, Tribune?"

"No," said Quintus, “I will make an example of him first and then come back for the next one. I will execute one at a time until I get the truth." Quintus ordered the Legionaries to escort John to the torture chamber, but to await his appearance before beginning. Next he ordered the Legionaries in the room to guard the eleven until he returned. They were not to receive food or water in his absence. Then he beckoned to Marcus and Longinus to join him as he left the room.

He proceeded into a small chamber well away from the meeting room. Quintus took Longinus aside and ordered him to beckon the two most vicious torturers in the barracks to come to the chamber but to do nothing until he arrived. They were asked to explain their implements of torture to John, and to crack their whips on the ground to frighten John without touching him in any way. Food and water was denied John, but the guards were to eat and drink lustily before him. Quintus ordered Marcus to stay with John and record everything he said at all times. He too was permitted to eat and drink as much as he wanted, and perhaps more.

Then Quintus went for a long walk, taking with him an escort of Legionaries. As he walked, he replayed in his mind everything he had heard. All the evidence seemed to act like a circle, always coming back to Jesus rising from the dead. But that was impossible!

He must have been alive when placed in the tomb. But that was impossible! The body must have been stolen. That was impossible! The only remaining possibility was that Jesus, absolutely dead, had walked out of the tomb alive. There were witnesses that he was seen alive after he died. On and on it circled in his brain as he walked. These men knew the answer. He had to break them. He was prepared to carry out his threat. He would find out the truth today.

After walking for an hour, Quintus returned to the barracks and summoned Longinus and Marcus, "Longinus," he asked, "do you have anything to report?"

"No, Tribune," replied Longinus, "nothing has been said by any of them. They are prepared to die for their beliefs."

Turning to Marcus, he asked about John.

"He has said nothing Tribune. He seems to be praying to his God, talking softly. I heard him say almost inaudibly, 'Forgive them Lord; just as you said on the cross, they know not what they do.'"

Quintus then had Longinus and Marcus accompany him to the torture chamber. As he entered, he heard the growls and shouts of the torturers baiting John. As Quintus entered, he ordered them to stand back so he could interrogate the prisoner before allowing the torture to proceed. Both the torturers seemed to lick their lips, but moved over to the end of the chamber. Quintus approached the stretching bed on which John lay. He was spread tightly on his stomach with arms and legs stretched to their fullest. He looked at Quintus with no fear in his eyes.

"John," Quintus began, "I demand the truth. This is your last chance before I turn you over to the torturers. Do you understand me?"

"Yes, Tribune," John gasped out as best he could, "but we have told the truth; Jesus lives."

"But did you not see Jesus die?" asked Quintus.

"Yes," said John. "I was there with His mother, Maryam Magdalene, and Lazarus." He gasped for breath, difficult as it was in his stretched condition, "We anointed Him, wrapped His body, and put it into the tomb." Again he gasped to breathe and talk. After a moment, he struggled to continue, "We rolled the stone in front of the grave and left." One final gasp, and looking directly at Quintus, he declared, "He was dead, Tribune. The Centurion with you put a spear through His heart." John's speech ceased for a moment as he lay there panting, fighting for breath. Then he added, "Killing me will not change the truth. Jesus rose from the dead," More gasps, followed by, "I saw Him and I talked to Him."

Without a word, he walked to the front of the stretching block, leaned down, and looked directly into John's eyes. "Listen to me, John," he said, "with the snap of my fingers you can be ripped apart by these brutes. Do you want that?"

Looking directly at Quintus, John spoke quietly and firmly, "Tribune, you have the power of life and death over me. That is true. But you cannot force me to tell a lie. I have told you the truth."

"Are you ready to die for your faith?" asked Quintus, still looking directly into John's eyes.

"Yes." The word came out full of pain, but steadfast, without fear or pleading. Quintus straightened up. This man was not lying.

Were they delusional? Was the whole episode of the appearance of Jesus mass hysteria, mass delusion on the part of many people? It was possible, but unlikely because so many witnesses were corroborating details of each appearance - hundreds over many occasions over a protracted period of time. It did not seem likely.

"Free him, give him food and drink, but await my instructions to return him to the meeting chamber with the others." Ordering Longinus and Marcus to accompany him, he exited the tortured chamber and went to the meeting room where the eleven waited, guarded by the legionaries.

He strode into the room, walked to the front, looked around at the eleven, and asked, "Who is next?"

There was an immediate outcry. Peter's face contorted with rage, "Will you not be satisfied with logic, Tribune? Must it be blood that convinces you?" Now Peter raised his hand and shouted, "If you must have blood, take mine next!"

From the others, Quintus heard "No!" and "Take me!" and "I am prepared to die for our Savior!"

His stratagem had worked. Quintus was now absolutely convinced that all of them would choose to die; to a man, faithful to their belief that Jesus had risen from the dead. The evidence presented by Peter in his five points, together with the strong evidence by Thomas, was very convincing.

Quintus decided to continue the charade for a moment. He issued the command: "Legionaries, keep these men in this room. Restrain them if necessary. Centurions, please come with me." Quintus exited the room with the Centurions and led them into another chamber where they could not be heard, "Longinus, do you think they are telling the truth?"

"Yes, Tribune. I was there at the crucifixion. My lance pierced the body of Jesus. I know he was dead. I know we buried a dead man. I know the tomb had no other exit. I know the Roman guards were placed on duty before the tomb and that they fled at the apparition of Jesus walking out of the tomb. These guards were executed, still claiming the truth of what happened. I also know, Tribune, that Jesus appeared on many occasions to hundreds of people after the incident at the tomb. The evidence is irrefutable. Longinus paused and confirmed, 'Yes, I believe.'"

Quintus remained silent, digesting what Longinus had said. He had come to respect Longinus as a dedicated, professional soldier. Without showing any emotion whatsoever, inwardly he was pleased that Longinus' opinion and thoughts matched his own. It was important, however, to consider all of the alternatives since it would be necessary for him to report to the emperor. He could just imagine telling the emperor this and hearing his reaction: "What nonsense!" He had to be absolutely certain of everything he told the emperor.

Turning to Sutonius, he asked the same question, and received virtually the same answer, of course with different words. In his turn, Aurelius confirmed that he, too, saw no other logical explanation.

"Can I assume, Centurions that you all agree that Jesus was not drugged to feign death, but rather to appear dead when he was only unconscious for a short period of time?" The three centurions were in agreement that that would be impossible. Longinus in particular related how weak Jesus had been after the scourging. He went so far as to say Jesus was almost dead as he was forced to carry the beam of the cross, which he could not do. One bystander, a man called Simon from Cyrene, was impressed into carrying the cross. That explained why Jesus had died so quickly after being crucified. As Longinus related this, Sutonius nodded his head in agreement since he too had been on duty that day. Aurelius, who had been in Rome, listened attentively. Quintus turned to him and asked, "Aurelius since you are hearing this and were not present, does it make sense to you? Would you accept that explanation?"

"Yes, Tribune, it would appear that no other explanation is possible. In my opinion, from all the evidence presented, not just today, but from all investigations to date, Jesus was dead when placed in the tomb."

Longinus continued the discussion concerning the appearances of Jesus after his supposed resurrection from the dead, "Centurions, can any of you offer any explanation for the reported appearances of Jesus after his death? Was it mass hysteria, hallucination, or conspiracy?" The three of them remained silent, obviously wrestling with their thoughts. Longinus was the first to break the silence.

"Tribune, the appearances were in too many places with too many people. We have to rule out mass hysteria. We also have to rule out hallucinations. As far as a conspiracy of collusion in falsehood, while that is possible, is it highly unlikely. Such a conspiracy could never be as widespread as this one without someone, somewhere, telling the truth, or hinting at it. I would discount the conspiracy theory, although there's no doubt in my mind that some people will believe in it, seeing as there are some that are always looking for a conspiracy theory when none exists." Longinus paused in deep contemplation and concluded, "Hundreds of years from now, there are some who will claim that Jesus never existed. Such claims will never change the historical fact that Jesus lived, died, and was seen to be alive after his death."

Quintus was pleased. He continued the discussion seeking confirmation from the three centurions in the group. Sutonius, almost immediately after Longinus had spoken, added, "I must agree with Longinus, Tribune. I might see it much differently, but there really is no other explanation. When we take into account the testimony of the Roman guards concerning the apparition of a risen Jesus as an intense light emerging from the tomb, we have to accept a resurrection from the dead."

Aurelius submitted another factor, "Tribune, we must also remember that Jesus raised at least three people from the dead, all of whom you've met or been introduced, most especially Lazarus. If Jesus had the power to cure the sick and the disabled, and raise the dead, then surely he was not a normal mortal as we know mortals."

Aurelius seemed to gather all his thoughts and with deep emotion went further, "From all the evidence it appears that he was a god. I think the men in that room are telling the truth."

Quintus looked at the three, searching their faces and eyes for any flicker of doubt. He saw none, just as he had none. He would have to review all of this again in putting together his report for Tiberius. He knew his session with the emperor would be turbulent. He had a message to deliver that was probably not what Tiberius was expecting, hence he was being overly cautious in considering and assessing every alternative.

"Thank you, Centurions," said Quintus wrapping up the conversation, "we will speak again of these matters when we prepare the final report for the emperor. For today, are you satisfied that these men are telling the truth?"

It was Longinus who answered for all three, "Yes, Tribune; I not only believe they are telling the truth, but I also believe that in days and years to come, each of them will face execution for their belief, and suffer it gladly as a witness to the truth of what they say. I hope that is not the case, but I suspect it will be so."

Quintus nodded and asked if the other two centurions had anything more to say. Neither did, except to confirm the same opinion.

"It appears we are all of the same opinion," said Quintus, "my threat, as you may have suspected, was a stratagem. I think it is time to go back and see if there's anything further we can glean from this group." Quintus and his centurions went back into the meeting room where the apostles were being guarded by the Legionaries. As they walked in, they were met by silence. Quintus walked to the back of the room, turned, and looking back at the group said, "Do any of you have anything further to say before I issue my commands?

Peter strode forward, and the legionaries moved to restrain him, until Quintus moved his hand, giving Peter permission. Peter kept moving and stopped with his face within inches of Longinus'. "I repeat," Peter replied sternly, "we are telling the truth. If blood is needed, take mine."

Quintus gave a small smile, causing great surprise to Peter. He stepped to the side, and gave the command, "Legionaries, you are dismissed, please leave the room." Then turning to Longinus, he ordered, "Bring John back into this room. Centurion Sutonius, have food and drink brought here for these men."

The silence of the room was broken by the excited sound of many voices speaking in surprise and relief. Looking about the room, and letting his eyes scan Peter and his associates, Quintus said, "You have passed the test, under duress." Then becoming very subdued with a look of sadness, he added, "A day may come when you may have to become martyrs," and he paused for emphasis, "but not at my hands. It was necessary to put your faith to the test. I must report to the Emperor concerning all these matters. The Emperor hears many stories in his position. He must have an open mind in trying to discern what is true from what is not."

John entered the room and joined the others. Quintus stopped and said nothing as he looked at each man, seeking to pierce their outer shell, and through their facial expressions and eyes, to look into their hearts for the truth. He was satisfied. He saw no doubts, only zeal and belief. So be it. In their eyes, they were telling the truth. They would die for their beliefs.

Turning to Peter Quintus said, "What is your mandate from Jesus? If I free all of you, what will you do?"

Somewhat puzzled but relieved at the use of the word 'free,' Peter reflected momentarily, and then answered directly, "Jesus told us to go and teach all nations. We have already decided the destinations for some of us. My brother Andrew will go to Greece; Bartholomew to India; James, the son of Alphaeus, will stay here in Jerusalem; James, the son of Zebedee, and brother of John, will go to Spain; John, as the youngest of us, will be asked to prepare documents of these events, as will Matthew. Philip will go to Turkey; Jude will go to Greece and Turkey, Thomas will go to Persia and India, and Simon and Mathias will stay here in Jerusalem with me as well."

Peter paused, flipping through his thoughts and added, "We must also consider the role of the Gentiles in the church. The lead in that will come from our brother Paul, whom you know as Saul of Tarsus, a tentmaker." Quintus nodded. "I am sure you have heard of his change of heart because of the vision of Jesus that he experienced as he travelled to Damascus." Here Peter looked directly into Quintus' eyes, "Tribune, Paul is a Pharisee, once dedicated to uprooting and extinguishing the followers of Jesus; now he is one of us promulgating the teachings of Jesus," Peter paused for emphasis, "That is important, Tribune. A Pharisee is one of us by conversion."

Peter became quiet, staring intently at Quintus. Slowly he nodded, and added, "I repeat, the Pharisee Saul is now our brother Paul. So it will be with many who initially oppose the teachings of Jesus." He stopped. And then with a twinkle in his eye, Peter once again looked directly at Quintus, and stared eye to eye, "It all depends on whether you execute us or free us. Well?"

Quintus truly appreciated Peter. Life would not be comfortable with him since it would always include the potential for differences in opinion, but it would certainly be interesting. What a Tribune he would have made.

Once again, he scanned the faces of all those in the room. "Tribunes are never disposed to say 'thank you.' In this case, I must express my gratitude for your help in seeking the truth which is very important to you, to me, to the Emperor, and as we both foresee, to the multitudes that follow us," he stopped, looked down at the ground lost in his thoughts for a moment, and looked up and said "I wish you all well. You are free to go."

* * *

Later that day he rode out to Bethany with Longinus and Marcus, to the home of Lazarus. There they asked to speak alone with Maryam Magdalene. Sitting on a bench outside their home, Quintus skipped directly to the point.

"Maryam, were you and Jesus lovers?"

Maryam gasped. Her face reddened in anger, not in shame, "How dare you insult the memory of our Lord and God!" she almost shrieked. Her voice shook with anger she continued, "I love Him because He was God. I loved Him because he taught truth and preached forgiveness. You would have loved Him, Tribune." Then her anger eased somewhat, and staring deep into his eyes, she added quietly, "And maybe you have learned enough to do so," then she looked away, shook her head, and looked back with a completely open face.

"Tribune, I am a woman. The role of women in our time is to serve men, and await their orders. But Jesus treated us as though we were equal. He made no distinction between man and woman. He gave His love to everyone; the good, the tax collector, and the sinner were all the same to him. They were souls that could be saved. He told us repeatedly that there was more joy over one repentant sinner than over one hundred who did not sin."

She choked a small sob, and tears began to trickle down her cheeks, "And in return for His goodness, He was crucified, murdered horribly, before our eyes."

Seeking corroboration, Quintus asked, "Were you there?"

"Yes, together with Maryam his Mother, John the son of Zebedee, and Lazarus. We took his dead body down from the cross, cleansed it, wrapped it in burial clothes, and laid it in the tomb." She said this with deep sadness, and then seemed to stiffen, but then she looked up, radiant, "And on the third day I spoke to him at the tomb. I was there with his mother who is a great friend of mine."

"Tell me what he said," implored Quintus.

"He told me to find Peter and tell him to come."

"Did he?"

"Yes," said Maryam, "Peter came and spoke at great length with Jesus."

They talked for over an hour, with Maryam corroborating in every detail what she had learned or heard from others. Finally, as the conversation started to repeat itself, Quintus gave a long sigh, and said, "And so, Maryam, I come back to my fundamental question, 'Were you and Jesus lovers in a carnal sense?'"

This time she did not erupt in anger but resignedly stated, rather intensely, "You are a fool to think of a normal man-woman relationship between us. Yes, Jesus was a man, and I am a woman. But He was more than a man. He was God. He was unattainable. He loved all, but did not seek sexual gratification with me. Nor I with Him." She added in exasperation and asperity, "You are a fool to hear of His miracles, parables, and teachings to think He would stoop to have a sexual encounter with me." She began to sob, "You fool! To think I would try and seduce such a noble man! But, Tribune, He was also God, and I knew it." Looking at him with defiance she added, "Yes, I loved Him, I loved him as a person, not as a woman in the sense you imply. And I know He loved me, as He loved all of us." Then she stopped and abruptly stated, "Can't you realize that love need not be carnal?"

Quintus sat silently. This woman was angry, but not ashamed to admit her love. He believed that there was mutual love. He began to believe it was not carnal. He pondered more fully the basic issue here. If Jesus was divine, then the love of Jesus was as Creator to Creation, full of love, but not desire; the same as love of parent for a child. Only aberrant individuals would seek sexual encounters with their child. Such action was evil. Was Jesus evil? Nothing pointed that way. Was Jesus more than human? Much pointed that way. Was he divine? Probably. Then the possibility of sexual relationships with Maryam was not possible.

But if Jesus were not divine, then it could be possible despite Maryam's denials. If Jesus was not divine, the so-called resurrection was nothing more than the theft of his body. But if that is impossible then Jesus was divine. That would explain the miracles as well. That was the nub of the entire dilemma.

He decided not to trouble Maryam with more questions. He would have to meet Maryam, the mother of Jesus as a final witness before using all the testimony and the findings from all the other sources.

He thanked Maryam for her assistance, asked her to remember him to her brother Lazarus, and left.

# Chapter Eight
# Caiaphas, Annas, Herod and the Sanhedrin

The next morning, Quintus left the barracks in his dress uniform, on horseback, to meet the High Priest. He was accompanied by the Centurion Longinus, Marcus, and five Legionaries, all mounted, and with all the banners of his rank. They proceeded to the Temple, creating a significant stirring of interest. Once they arrived at the main entrance, Longinus dismounted, walked to the guard on duty, and informed him that the Tribune Quintus Gaius Caesar, emissary from the Emperor Tiberius, had arrived for his meeting with the High Priest.

Shortly, a Priest accompanied by six Temple Guards in dress uniform came and stood at attention in front of the mounted Quintus. The priest extended his arm in greeting, and asked Quintus to follow him to the quarters of Caiaphas. Quintus dismounted, as did Marcus. They, together with Longinus, they followed the priest into the Temple living quarters.

They were escorted into a sumptuous meeting room, hung with tapestries and with a thick rug on the floor. Caiaphas alone stood at the head of a table surrounded by six chairs. He was dressed in all the splendor of his office as High Priest. Caiaphas stood tall, erect in his splendor. His pose was almost one of disdain, seeming to look down on the world of inferiors. Caiaphas gave every indication of a proud man who relished his power.

"Good morning, Tribune," he said in a smooth and polished voice, almost oily in its unctuous tones, "welcome to Jerusalem, and to the Temple." He bowed slightly, formally deferring to Quintus' rank. "Please seat yourselves," he added as he used his hands to sweep around the table area, gesturing for the Tribune to sit on his right. "Can I offer you any refreshments, some wine perhaps?"

"Thank you for agreeing to see me, Caiaphas," Quintus said, in a matter-of-fact tone that totally ignored his title of High Priest. He noted a quick look of pique cross Caiaphas' face, but then the diplomatic smile returned. Quintus inwardly girded himself for battle. This was a wily opponent. He continued as he sat, "And thank you for your courtesy about refreshments, but I would rather proceed since I know your time must be limited with all your duties."

The hidden barb was not lost on Caiaphas. He smiled, and as he sat, said, "How can I be of help to you, Tribune?"

Quintus nodded to Marcus. Marcus rose, walked over to Caiaphas, and handed him the papyrus from Tiberius. He stood waiting at his side until Caiaphas returned it to him after reading it. As Marcus went back to his chair, Caiaphas took both hands and formed a figure with all his fingers touching. He sat there, looking directly at Quintus for a moment, obviously lost in thought, before he spoke. Quintus was amused at the pretense. The gist of the letter from Tiberius had been imparted to Caiaphas asking for the meeting. Furthermore, Quintus was certain Caiaphas had been fully informed of all his activity, one way or another. Quintus waited patiently for Caiaphas to speak.

In his most disarming tone of voice, Caiaphas began, "Tribune, I was aware of your mission before today." Quintus was pleased that he was not going to hide his knowledge. "I trust you have found evidence to justify our contention that Jesus was a fraud, and was justly executed as a criminal for his crimes against Rome?" Caiaphas added with a crooked smile twisting his lips almost into a grimace, "Have you made any progress in uncovering who stole the body, and indeed, where the body is?"

Quintus kept a straight face during what he knew to be a charade. In a calm, but blunt voice, he replied, "Caiaphas, you know that is nonsense. Jesus violated no Roman law except the one you fabricated in the mind of the Procurator." Caiaphas sat up straight in his chair, a look of surprise on his face.

Quintus continued, "You also know that no one stole the body; you know that it walked out of the tomb, accompanied by angels." He paused, and looked head-on at Caiaphas, "As a Pharisee I know you believe in angels and in an afterlife". With a note of great sternness, he continued, "I also know you look upon us Romans as a necessary evil to be used to perpetuate your power." Caiaphas looked as if he was going to interrupt, but Quintus waved his hand to be silent, and continued, "I represent the Emperor, Caiaphas, and in that role I demand that you be forthright with me." Then looking directly at Caiaphas, with no emotion on his face to be interpreted in any way by the High Priest, Quintus said, "Well, what can you tell me now concerning the circumstances of the arrest, execution, and resurrection of Jesus of Nazareth?"

Caiaphas looked down, his right hand stroked his beard, and he lapsed into intense but rapid thought. He was surprised at the strength of the man before him. This was an exceptional Roman. While young, Quintus had all the trappings of command. Tiberius had been very wise in selecting him to resolve this open issue of who and what had been Jesus of Nazareth. He had certainly been much more than a carpenter. In Caiaphas' mind, he had been a threat. He had been gradually increasing his circle of supporters in the countryside. His triumphant entry into Jerusalem during the week before Passover had been an alarm signal to him that Jesus was now a major threat to the status quo, and possibly to his survival as High Priest. When Jesus had attacked the money changers, Caiaphas knew it was close to a declaration of war for control. For Caiaphas control was more than religious. It was everything that affected the daily lives of the people. The Mosaic Law, the Mitzvot, gave him that authority over them. Jesus, on the other hand, was ignoring the Mitzvot, obeying the commandments, yes, but seeking a separation of religious belief from governance on a daily basis. The role of High Priest, without the Romans, was akin almost to being King. With a King, he would be the Prime Minister, exercising daily power. With the Romans, he had to exercise his power through them if necessary. That is why it had been necessary to use Pontius Pilate to do the actual execution of Jesus.

Caiaphas pondered. His control of the Sanhedrin had resulted in the agreement, as proposed by him, that it would be better to sacrifice one life, that of Jesus, to save the nation, the Jewish people. There had been voices raised in protest in the Sanhedrin, but he had swayed the majority. The Jewish people were starting to favor Jesus more and more. Soon they might very well revolt against Caiaphas' authority. But the will of the people did not matter. It was his will that counted. He knew better than they what was best for them. But he must be careful not to show his hand. He had to get rid of Jesus without antagonizing the people who looked upon him as their Messiah, their Savior. That was a problem for him, but also an opportunity to use as a lever with Rome. Rome had to carry out the execution. With that decision made, he had convinced Pontius Pilate that executing Jesus was the best course of action for Rome. Now to convince Quintus. Caiaphas looked up, gazed at Quintus for a moment, and then he looked down again, stroking his beard a few more times. Quintus would be difficult.

Then he looked up at Quintus without deviation, and began, "Tribune, I am sure you know the facts, and the sequence of events. You must be pleased that we were helpful in working with the Roman authorities to preserve the peace of Judea. What specifically do you wish me to comment upon?"

Quintus in a very direct way, still dispassionate, asked, "Why did you not have Jesus stoned? If he blasphemed, as you say, then you had the authority to issue the command to stone him to death. If you felt confirmation was needed from Rome, I am certain it would have been granted." Quintus now raised his voice somewhat, into a commanding tone, "Well, why did you not do that?" The last word came close to being a shout.

Caiaphas almost began to sputter. His aplomb was shattered. Groping for words, he tried to answer in a calm, reassuring way, but failed. He began to sound like a schoolboy caught doing something wrong, "Because...because...because the carpenter had preached sedition, and was turning the people against Caesar."

Quintus' fist slammed the top of the table. Glaring at Caiaphas, he thundered, "That's a lie! He committed no act of sedition against Rome. He has been quoted as saying words to the effect of 'Give to Caesar what is Caesar's, and to God, what is God's.' Here he was speaking of a single God, the God of the Jewish people. The Romans believe in the separation of government from religion. You don't!

You have your rules which give you control over the lives of your people. He was a threat to you, not to Rome!"

Here again Quintus slammed his fist on the table, and once more thundered, "How dare you connive to distort the truth to use the Roman Procurator as your pawn!"

Exercising supreme control over his emotions, Caiaphas assumed a calm exterior to hide the tumult inside his brain and stomach. In an even voice, he answered, "I regret that you feel that way, Tribune. I only did what I felt was right. The information I had led me to a different conclusion." Then he paused and brightened as he recalled the crowd at the trial, "Tribune, you must know that the people called for his crucifixion. They chose a known murderer at the Passover amnesty and not Jesus. These are the same people who welcomed him only three days before."

"Not so, Caiaphas," countered Quintus, "you and I both know the crowd at the trial did not represent the Jewish people." At this Caiaphas looked up abruptly, his jaw hanging down. Quintus continued, "The Passover amnesty is a well known event. The followers of Barabbas undoubtedly gathered there and loudly chose their own man. Their shouts were augmented by those you bribed." Here Caiaphas began shaking his head. Quintus raised his hand to stop any comment and continued, "And as for the followers of Jesus, they were too frightened to do anything but hide." Quintus suddenly had a thought, "And by the way, did you spread the word that he might not be freed if his followers came and demonstrated?"

Quintus stopped speaking and sat there, waiting for the High Priest to speak. Caiaphas remained silent. Then he quietly asked, "And what other accusations will you make against me?"

"Well, then, tell me about the problem with the guards at the tomb," answered Quintus. "There is considerable evidence that you bribed the guards to claim his followers stole his body."

Caiaphas remained silent.

"Well?" asked Quintus once more.

They were interrupted with the entrance of a much older man, also garbed in the robes of a High Priest. Caiaphas rose and walked rapidly over to the older man, who was shuffling slowly, lending his arm for support. Slowly they made their way to the table, where they both came to a stop before the seated Quintus. In a very deferential voice, Caiaphas said, "Tribune, it is my honor to present the High Priest Annas, senior to me, my predecessor, and my wife's father." Turning to Annas, he said, "Father, this is Tribune Quintus Gaius Caesar, emissary of the Emperor Tiberius. He was sent here by the Emperor to investigate all the matters concerning the death and the disappearance of the body of Jesus of Nazareth."

Quintus stood to greet the older man. As he did so, he noticed with an inner sense of caution, that Caiaphas had not added adjectives such as criminal before the name of Jesus. After a few moments of quiet introductory conversation with the older priest, they all sat, Annas across from Quintus, with Caiaphas between them.

"Thank you for dropping in, High Priest Annas," said Quintus, "we had just about concluded our conversation, but perhaps you can add any details you wish." Quintus omitted the strong disagreements and in a few moments he came to the crux of the situation. "High Priests Annas and Caiaphas, as I understand the situation, you, Annas, and the Sanhedrin, led by Caiaphas, questioned Jesus. During this, in your opinion, he blasphemed. That merited death. But you did not stone him. You took him to the Procurator, and refusing to enter his residence, forced him to conduct a trial in his front yard. You then convinced the Procurator that Jesus was a threat to the stability of Judea, and that only his execution could perpetuate Pax Romana here."

Annas remained silent for a moment before quietly answering in a wavering voice weakened by either age or emotion. Quintus believed it was the latter. "The end result is as you say, Tribune, but the rationale is not so," he paused, took a deep breath as if to fortify himself, and went on, "we merely presented the facts. Pontius Pilate came to his own conclusions."

They went on for another quarter of an hour, with Annas calmly deflecting each point made by Quintus. Still, Annas seemed rattled by the confusing set of facts presented by Quintus that contradicted his version of the facts. Quintus had obviously completed a very thorough investigation of the entire matter. But then again he had significant resources to use. The Emperor's mandate in writing, plus the three Centurions and one hundred Legionaries scattered on investigative missions all over Judea was sure to produce results. In addition, Quintus gave every indication of being a thorough, brilliant, and commanding presence. Annas envied the Emperor in having such a man for this mission. He tried to catch the eye of Caiaphas to make sure he followed his lead in calm assertion of their position. He failed to do so.

As Annas stirred as if to stand and leave, Quintus turned to him and asked, "Can you both call a meeting of the Sanhedrin so I might speak to them?" While Quintus had addressed this request to Annas, it was Caiaphas who answered.

"Of course, Tribune. It may take a day or two to arrange. I will send word to your quarters when that meeting can take place." In a most obsequious voice, Caiaphas then added, "Would that be convenient for you?"

"The day after tomorrow would be fine," replied Quintus without elaboration. He had reserved the next day to visit Herod. Arrangements to confirm this visit were being made even as he met here with the High Priests.

With a sigh, Annas rose. They all followed suit. Turning to Caiaphas, he said, "My son, thank you for your continuing representation of our position in this matter." Then turning back to Quintus, he spoke to reassure, "I must bid you good morning, Tribune. I am sure that Caiaphas will be able to provide you with all the assistance you need from us, and with all the true facts we have at our disposal." Then the old High Priest shuffled out of the room, aided by Caiaphas. A few minutes later, Caiaphas returned and sat once more in his chair.

In an even voice, Quintus summed up the meeting, "High Priest Caiaphas, I believe I have all the facts I need to complete my report to the Emperor concerning your activities associated with Jesus of Nazareth. Is there anything further you can add, or that we can discuss?"

The High Priest remained silent. After a few more minutes of silence, Quintus rose from his chair, as did Longinus. Marcus remained seated, taking his notes. Quintus walked over to Caiaphas, and assumed a neutral pose as he concluded his remarks, "Thank you, High priest, for your time this morning. I repeat what I just said. I am close to completing my investigation of the circumstances surrounding the execution and disappearance of the body of Jesus of

Nazareth. I came to Judea believing he was a criminal justly executed for his crimes, and that his body had been stolen. After my extensive and exhaustive investigation, I now believe he was the innocent victim of a conspiracy by you, assisted by Tetrarch Herod, to have him executed. As for the disappearance of his body, it is beginning to look more and more to me that he was a god, and did rise from the dead."

Caiaphas averted Quintus' gaze. Then he rose, and taking a deep breath, said, "Tribune, I disagree with you. That is your opinion. You have yours, and I have mine. I did no wrong." Then, in a voice clearly controlling his exasperation and anger, almost through clenched teeth, he raised his right hand, and waving his index finger at Quintus, started speaking, "Tribune, you are a man of action. You kill your enemies and think nothing of it. Battle, blood, and execution are your normal way of eliminating enemies. Now you lecture to me about the sanctity of life. I tell, you, Tribune, the life of one man is nothing compared to the fate of a nation. He blasphemed. He was leading our people away from us, into the unknown with no control. No one knew how far that heresy would spread. The triumphant entry into Jerusalem, followed by his attack on the moneychangers in the temple sealed his fate." Looking at Tiberius he ended with his chin thrust out, and in a belligerent tone added, "He had to go! In my place, you would have used your sword. I used diplomacy."

Quintus remained silent throughout the outburst. His eyes hardened as Caiaphas spoke. When the High Priest finished, Quintus, in a voice loaded with patience and suppressed anger, replied, "High Priest. You are wrong! I am a soldier. I kill in battle on the orders of my superiors, and to avoid being killed by the men I am fighting. You were not ordered to kill Jesus. He was not trying to kill you. Yet you had him killed. High Priest, that was an act of murder." Then his anger burst forth, "In fact, it was a cowardly act of assassination!" He stopped, and looked directly at the High Priest, gradually letting his anger subside.

Caiaphas stood there, somewhat stunned. He had no reply for the accusation Quintus had made. He wrung his hands, seemed to stiffen up, and looking into the distance instead of gazing on Quintus, said, "If there is anything I can do or say to dissuade you from your opinions..." He stopped. Quintus made no reply. Caiaphas gave a deep sigh, and then said, "Let us then conclude this meeting." In his most diplomatic voice, he then looked at Quintus and closed with, "Please tell the Emperor he has my deepest loyalty and adherence to his commands."

With that, Caiaphas bowed, and clapped his hands for the Palace Guard. Quintus began leaving the room even before the guard appeared, followed by Longinus, and by Marcus who rose quickly from his chair after having put his easel back into his case.

* * *

Once distant from the Temple grounds, Quintus beckoned Longinus to ride beside him. He had come to appreciate the sterling qualities of Longinus. He would recommend his promotion to Tribune on his return. He now sought his counsel.

"Longinus, tell me truthfully, was I too strong in my accusation?" Then he added with a grin, "As one soldier to another, I was tempted to use my sword to make my point."

Longinus was quick to answer, a knowing smile crossing his face, "No, Tribune. The High Priest violated his office because of his fear for his position and influence. That is completely understandable. The measures he took to protect his position are not. You were correct to point out to him his violation of not only his post, but of Roman law. While we keep Pax Romana by force of arms, we also keep it by working with the conquered people. When the battle is over, we cooperate. That is the Roman way."

As they rode along, Quintus voiced a question that piqued his curiosity, "One further point, Longinus, if you know the answer. Tell me, how is the High Priest selected for his post?"

Longinus was silent for a moment, and then answered, "So far as I know, Tribune, they are picked by the Sanhedrin. Every High Priest has a group of close followers from whom the Sanhedrin, or the High Priest himself, picks a successor."

"Then there is a continuity of temperament and thought," said Quintus. After some reflection, he concluded a realization, "That thought came to mind when Annas appeared. I understand he had two of his sons succeed him prior to appointing Caiaphas. Is that so?"

"Yes," said Longinus, "that is what I have heard."

Quintus nodded as they trotted along, "Thank you, Longinus." Then he added with a broad grin, remarking, "It seems, then, that the Sanhedrin is political rather than religious. That reminds me of the Roman Senate," then he burst into laughter, and nudged his horse to pick up the pace.

Back at the barracks, Sutonius and Aurelius joined Quintus and Longinus. Aurelius told Quintus that word had been received confirming a meeting the next morning with Herod Antipas at his palace to the south of Jerusalem, a ride of close to two hours. Quintus designated Longinus to accompany him. Then they entered into an extensive discussion of the investigative findings of the day. Everything uncovered was pointing more and more to the miracles of Jesus being real, not associated with magic tricks, and that no one had any evidence at all that justified the rumor that Jesus' body had been stolen by his disciples or apostles. The more he heard, the deeper Quintus lapsed into his inner rationalization. Mentally he nodded to himself, *yes, yes, yes. Jesus was murdered; He died on the cross; His body was not stolen, it left the tomb on its own. Yes. Neither the Romans nor the Jews were responsible for his death. Caiaphas bore that responsibility, with Annas and Pontius Pilate as his accomplices. Yes. Yes.*

Their meeting soon concluded. As they went their separate ways upon the conclusion of the meeting, Quintus reminded Longinus that he wanted him to accompany him to visit Herod.

* * *

The next morning, Quintus set out for Herod's palace with Longinus and twenty Legionaries. Before they left, a message had been received by Longinus from the Temple that the Sanhedrin could meet with Quintus the next morning as he had requested. When informed, Quintus immediately sent a message back accepting the invitation, and indicating that he would bring the three Centurions, Longinus, Sutonius, and Aquarius with him.

The ride gave Quintus adequate time to be briefed by the two Centurions stationed in Jerusalem, Longinus and Sutonius. Herod, or Herod Antipas, had been appointed a client Tetrarch of Rome by the

Emperor Augustine. He had succeeded his brother Herod Archelaus who had been judged incompetent. They were both the sons of Herod the Great who had also been a client king before them. He was reputed to be a madman who murdered his own family and a great many others. It was he who had ordered the slaughter of all male children born in Bethlehem around the time of the birth of Jesus. The prophecy had been that a King would be born when the super star lit the skies. In fear for his power, Herod had ordered the killing of all male children under the age of two.

As he heard the story unfold, Quintus was impressed by the similarity of the thirst for power and the murderous use of power to preserve it. It seemed so typical of the politics of Rome. He mentally thanked the gods for the longevity of Augustine and now Tiberius at least to have brought stability to the throne of the Emperor. It was so much more stable than the chaotic rule under the Consuls in Rome prior to the ascent of Augustine. In his mind, Quintus equated Roman politics now with Judean politics.

The visit itself was of little consequence. Nothing new was learned, except that Quintus was able to form the first hand opinion that Herod was totally untrustworthy, and would sacrifice anything to retain power. His role in the murder of the carpenter Jesus of Nazareth was clearly one of compliance in a hidden conspiracy with Caiaphas. Nothing was evident or could be proven; but just as a leopard had spots, Quintus knew that Herod would be vicious with anyone who might in any way challenge his power. The thought went rapidly through his head - 'like father, like son.' The father had killed innumerable babies in the attempt to kill the newly born Messiah. Jesus was purported to have been the Messiah that fulfilled the prophecy. The son had ensured the death of Jesus by crucifixion.

Quintus was most diplomatic in his meeting with Herod. He hid his true feelings, as he felt that Herod did. It was as if they both jockeyed around the truth. As he rode away from the Palace, Quintus laughed out loud, to the surprise of the Centurions riding with him. He chose not to tell them why. As they rode, he elicited from them their reaction. It mirrored his. The three Centurions felt that Herod had played a diplomatic game, providing statesmanlike answers with no way of verifying whether true or not.

They spent the rest of the ride back discussing the meeting the next day with the Sanhedrin. Quintus actually felt lighter of heart than he had since coming to Judea with his investigative assignment. The meeting with Herod had been 'refreshing, if of little value to his quest. That night he slept soundly.

* * *

The next morning, accompanied by the three Centurions and an honor guard of ten Legionaries, all in dress uniforms, Quintus set out for the Temple area. Once there, they were greeted by a contingent of Palace Guards. After being saluted, Quintus, the Centurions, and Marcus dismounted, while the mounted Legionaries took up position in front of the entrance, forming a square to control access and egress from the Temple. Quintus and his group then followed the leader of the guard unit into a sumptuous meeting hall filled with the voices of the assembled members of the Sanhedrin. As they entered, the noise subsided, and Caiaphas rose to greet them. The members of the Sanhedrin were sitting around the room, leaving an area in the center for Caiaphas and Annas, with chairs in place for Quintus and the Centurions. Marcus found a place against the wall opposite the entrance.

"Welcome to the Sanhedrin, Tribune. You and your associates are most welcome," said Caiaphas, using Greek as the common language. He then raised his arms in a sweeping motion embracing the Sanhedrin members, and added, "My colleagues too welcome you." At this point, all of the Sanhedrin rose in a body with a buzz of welcomes filling the air.

In a gracious tone of voice, Quintus thanked them for their greetings, and explained his mission from the Emperor Tiberius. He asked their cooperation in searching for all the facts concerning the disappearance of the body of Jesus, and for any information concerning the possibility that Jesus' miracles and preaching would create any kind of problem for the civil order. He then asked them to voice their opinions and to provide any information they had.

The Sanhedrin erupted in a cacophony of voices, some in favor of Jesus and others opposed. The majority seemed to side with Caiaphas in terms of blasphemy, whereas the minority favored acceptance of Jesus as the Messiah. Caiaphas alternately beamed and frowned as the members voiced their opinions. Although they all talked at once trying to be heard, when one did manage to quiet the others, he was listened to attentively by the Sanhedrin members until he completed his presentation. Joseph of Arimathea seemed the calmest and most supportive of Jesus. It was then that Longinus whispered into Quintus' ear that this was the man who donated his newly created personal tomb for the use of Jesus following his death. Quintus nodded in understanding.

The discussion went on for the better part of two hours without cease. Both Caiaphas and Quintus let it proceed without comment. Finally the voices of the members decreased in volume and intensity. They had just about said everything they wanted to say. Silence reigned.

Caiaphas then addressed them, "Members of the Sanhedrin, thank you for your comments." Bowing towards Quintus, he asked, "Tribune, has this discussion been of help to you?"

Quintus rose and strode to the center of the open space in the center of the group. He addressed them directly, turning so as to meet the eye of various members of the Sanhedrin. As he spoke, he made every effort to address each individually, moving his eyes from face to face, trying to make eye contact, if only for a fleeting moment. At the same time, he mentally assessed their reactions to his words.

"Members of the Sanhedrin," he began, "in the name of the Emperor I thank you for coming to this meeting and giving me your opinions, thoughts, and information." Here he paused as he let his gaze circle the room. With a smile that broadened as he spoke, he added, "I must compliment you. For a few moments I thought I was in a meeting of the Roman Senate. The atmosphere was the same. The differences were the same, but the language was Greek instead of Latin, although some Greek is usually present during the discussions." The room erupted in laughter. Members of the Sanhedrin looked at each other, shrugged, laughed, and looked pleased. Quintus had made an immediate hit with these men. They recognized a true professional and leader. The mood seemed to shift to one of expectation rather than apprehension, to one of potential cooperation as opposed to one of foot dragging.

Quintus paused dramatically for a moment or two, and then proceeded calmly, "My men and I have conducted extensive investigations of all aspects of the circumstances surrounding the execution, death, and disappearance of the body of Jesus of Nazareth. I believe this investigation will help me to finalize my report for the Emperor. This discussion today now leads me to ask all of you to carefully consider three questions that I will now prompt. In each case, please answer as I direct, with a yes or a no." He then swept the group with his eyes as he circled with his body, "I wish to exclude the High Priests Caiaphas and Annas from these questions, and please answer as you feel rather than how you think I, Caiaphas or Annas might wish you to reply." As he said this he looked sternly at the two High Priests staring them into remaining silent. Turning back to the members of the Sanhedrin, once more circling and scanning their eyes, he began.

"My first question is this," Quintus said. "Can any of you provide direct witnesses of any activity associated with the disappearance of the body of Jesus. If you say yes, then I want the names of the witnesses, and how I can speak with them. If you have no such information or witnesses, please answer 'no.'" After a short pause, he said, "Who can say 'yes?'" There was absolute silence. Quintus circled three times with his body, sweeping the group with his eyes as he did so. They remained silent. "Then there is no point in asking 'no.'" he said.

"I will move on to my second question," once again he circled the room three times with his eyes as he rotated his body. "Can you verify that the preachings of Jesus constituted a threat to Pax Romana? The answer must exclude any opinion you may have that it affected the relationship of the followers of Jesus to the teachings and rules of this body. A 'yes' reply must be directed concerning only Rome and Pax Romana, and if answered in that way, I will meet with you to examine your reasons and any witnesses or documents you may have to prove your conclusion or opinion." After a lengthy pause, he snapped out, "Who is prepared to say 'yes?'" The silence was deep. Some of the members shuffled their feet, or moved in their chairs, a quiet hum seemed to fill the room, but no one said 'yes.' Once again Quintus closed out the 'no' vote with his remark, "I believe there is no point in calling for a vote of 'no.'" As his eyes circled the room, he sensed consensus.

"I will now ask my third and final question," Quintus stated. As before he circled and stared before asking, "How many of you truly believe that Jesus was a god-man?" There was a gasp in the room. Quintus continued, "Once again, if 'yes', I may wish to discuss with you individually why you believe this to be true. If you vote 'no', that will not be necessary." Quintus knew his question would dispose members to say 'no.'

After a period of silence that stirred great tension in the room, Quintus carefully and slowly said, "Who votes 'yes?'" He was astounded that many of the members of the Sanhedrin voted 'yes.' When he asked for the 'no' vote, almost as many responded.

Quintus remained silent. Staring in turn at each member of the Sanhedrin as he turned his body, he continued his silence. In his mind, he considered asking further questions now as a follow-up but decided against a change of that nature. He had what he wanted for now.

"Members of the Sanhedrin," he stated, "I will keep my word concerning only three questions. My Centurions will now speak with each of you who said 'yes.' Those who said 'no' may leave now, and as you complete your discussion with the Centurions, you may also leave." He then bowed towards the two High priests in turn as he spoke, "In the name of the Emperor I thank the High Priests for convening this meeting, and I thank you all for attending."

With a grim look and in a tightly controlled voice, Caiaphas added, "This meeting of the Sanhedrin is adjourned."

Quintus called the three Centurions to him and held a short, low voiced discussion with them. During this he asked them to broaden the interview to include some discussion concerning the Sanhedrin member's evaluation of Jesus as being the Messiah.

The individual discussion went on for over an hour. Throughout, Quintus remained standing in the center of the group, calmly walking back and forth, in deep meditation.

When the individual discussions were completed, Quintus, the three Centurions, and Marcus left the room and the Temple, mounted their horses and returned to the barracks.

Once there, Quintus met with the three Centurions to discuss their findings. Marcus took careful and complete notes of that meeting. The gist of what the three had discovered was nothing specific. The individual members of the Sanhedrin spoke of the miracles, the missing body which they believed had been resurrected, and the public appearances after the empty tomb was discovered. The two strongest voices in support of Jesus had come from two men, Nicodemus and Joseph of Arimathea

Many commented on the strange circumstances that attended the death of Jesus. The earthquake, the tearing of the veil of the temple, and the strange appearances in the city of people considered long dead. There was comment over the controversy of the guards at the tomb. At first they had claimed they were asleep, and the body was stolen. Then they claimed the body had floated out of the tomb. Some believed the High Priest had bribed the guards to tell false stories. Apparently the guards had been executed for dereliction of duty. The final point of great importance to the members of the Sanhedrin was the change in demeanor of the followers of Jesus at Pentecost.

After a short discussion of the three Centurions with Quintus, they began to summarize the information derived from the members of the Sanhedrin who answered 'yes' to the third question. Caiaphas and Annas were not among them. The reasons stated were summarized as:

I. The miracles before and after the crucifixion.
II. The universal acceptance that Jesus had truly died on the cross.
III. The empty tomb pointing to resurrection rather than theft of the body.
IV. The events during the death of Jesus on the cross.
V. The contentious testimony of the guards at the tomb.
VI. The changes in the disciples at Pentecost and afterwards
VII. There seemed to be no consensus about Jesus being the Messiah. Opinions ranged from yes, to maybe, to definitely not.

Quintus was pleased with the results of his meeting, especially the last. It seemed that even in the group that accused Jesus of blasphemy, the same group that approved the death sentence, there were some with an open mind as to his innocence and to his being the Messiah. This seemed very significant to him, and would weigh heavily in his deliberations for his final report and conclusions to present to Tiberius.

Quintus thanked the Centurions for their assistance, and asked each for his opinion of the meeting with the Sanhedrin. All three were in agreement that more and more evidence was pointing to a god-man situation with Jesus.

Quintus thanked them and retired for the night. He decided that the next day he would make an extensive search to find the mother of Jesus and interview her. Once again he slept soundly.

**The Resurrection: A Criminal Investigation of the Mysterious Disappearance of the Body of the Crucified Criminal Jesus of Nazareth**

# Chapter Nine
# Maryam - Mother of Jesus

Quintus decided to search for Maryam accompanied only by Longinus and Marcus. He further decided not to dress in uniform, but to wear clothes as if a native. He asked both the Centurion Longinus and his scribe Marcus to do the same. Peter had told them that Maryam spent most her time with John. She had moved out of her home and had gone to live with him and his family. When Quintus and Longinus went there, they were told she had gone for a walk, probably to the Temple. They started walking there when they saw a single woman sitting on a bench under a fig tree in the Temple square. They thought it strange that a woman would sit alone. What really surprised them was that they had no memory of the fig tree or the bench even though they had been to the square many times.

Longinus quietly told Quintus, "That is Maryam." Quintus decided to talk to Maryam alone. He bade Longinus and Marcus not to come with him but to walk on. He approached the bench alone.

Before he could say anything, she said, "Good morning, Tribune Quintus." She beckoned to the bench beside her, "Please sit beside me so we can talk a little." Her voice was like a flowing brook, soft and gentle. A smile gave radiance to a face that shone with peace and love. And yet, there was latent power in the background. This was a woman of great authority, yet with a demeanor of comfort. As surprised as he was, Quintus still became again the little boy who always went to his mother for comfort and love whenever he had a bruise or bloodied his nose. Quintus had an urge to kneel before Maryam and put his head in her lap. He could almost feel her arms circling him with protective love as her soothing words would say, "There, there, my son. Do not be afraid. All will be well." For a fleeting moment he let this vision warm his spirit. He began to smile, but abruptly returned to the present. The moment had passed.

He sat, and as he did so, blurted out, despite himself, "How did you know my name?" But even as he said this, he assumed word of his mission and travels about Jerusalem were sure to have reached her ears. There was nothing mysterious about that.

Her smile remained calm, serene, and enigmatic. "I knew you were coming even before Tiberius summoned you to Capri," she said in a matter of fact way.

Quintus was startled. He now knew he was dealing with more than the mother of a simple carpenter from Nazareth unjustly crucified when he posed a threat to the power of the High Priest. He felt a glow of anticipation that in Maryam he might find the key to assembling the pieces of information he had unearthed since his arrival. Yet he was unnerved. He pulled himself together, and began in a halting voice, backed with a spirit that was full of awe and curiosity.

"Good morning, Maryam. Yes, I am Quintus Gaius Caesar, Tribune of the Praetorian in Rome. I am pleased that you know who I am and what my mission is." Here he paused for a moment. In a contrite tone he went on, "I am sorry that we, the Roman occupier government of Judea, crucified your son, but we did our duty as we were commanded."

Before he could go on she smiled and said, "I know. Tiberius sent you to find the truth." Her voice once again reminded him of a gently flowing brook, "You were wrong to crucify Jesus, but you are forgiven." She smiled and added, "His death fulfilled the prophecies, and His sacrifice purified the world." The sounds seemed to follow a melodic lilt to him. They were accompanied by an unbelievable smile. Quintus felt completely comfortable with Maryam. Once again he was suffused with that same feeling he had as a little boy when his mother would cuddle him in her arms and sing to him. Maryam could have been his mother. He almost felt like addressing her as mother. His soldierly discipline took hold and once more he recovered his poise, asking her softly, "You were pointed out to me as the mother of Jesus. Are you?"

Once more the serene smile and gentle words, "Yes," she replied, "I am the mother of God. Jesus was God, you know." She paused, looked directly at Quintus, and once again her enigmatic smile lit her face with a glow. "How else could He have come back from the dead?" After a pause, she went on, "He did, you know. Many people were witnesses, and many more have come to accept it as true." Once more she paused as if to give emphasis to her next words, "Oh yes, I saw and spoke to Him. Over five hundred did as well. You have interviewed many of these." Quintus nodded. "You have found nothing to disprove His resurrection." With a twinkle in her eye, she added, "You even verified the story of the one hundred and fifty-three fish!"

Then she gave a little laugh. "Have you ever wondered why one hundred and fifty-three fish and not one hundred and fifty-four or one hundred and forty four?" When she saw a slight shake of his head, she went on, "It was to call attention to the fact and not to the number of fish. It was a sizeable number. That's all that mattered. They were fishermen, you will recall." Again the smile.

Quintus nodded at each point. She continued, "You spoke with Thomas who did not believe until he put his hands into the wound in Jesus' side, and in the wounds in His arms and feet." With a knowing nod, she proceeded softly yet firmly, "Now he believes. My son blessed him for his belief and blesses all those who would not see, but would believe."

Quintus made no reply. She smiled at him, "Does it not dawn on you that this is very important? Jesus walked through the doors to enter the room, yet Thomas put his hands in the side of a solid body." She added for emphasis, looking directly at Quintus. "A solid body!" Looking into Quintus' eyes, she asked, "Do you believe?"

"I don't know," said Quintus, "It would be easy for me to believe with all the evidence that I have, and all the evidence associated with the fact that nothing contradicts that belief with certainty." He stared into space for a moment before adding, "But he looked different! His associates and followers often did not immediately recognize Him. How could that be?" he asked as he looked expectantly at her.

Once more the gentle breeze of her voice seemed to whisper into his ears, "Of course He did. It wasn't His physical body. It was the glow. Thomas put his fingers into His side and in His hands and feet. The wounds were there. The body was the same. What changed was His face - no longer bloody from the thorns which were gone. Of course He looked different, because He was glorified more as God than as man. Before the crucifixion, He hid the divine nature, letting the human dominate. After His resurrection, it was no longer necessary to hide the divine. Only the divine could raise itself from the dead. Only the divine could raise others from the dead. The divine raised His human body, a body with the wounds of His crucifixion, a body into the wounds of which Thomas placed his hands, but a glorified body that glowed, glided over the ground, and went through walls."

She paused to let this thought circulate in the mind of Quintus. Then she continued, "Before the crucifixion the divine sometimes appeared as Jesus let His love dominate his caution and patience. He cured the lame, the blind, the deaf, the lepers; He raised from the dead the young man in Nain, Jairus' daughter, and his friend Lazarus. Even as a young boy, He lectured in the Temple, disputing with the learned their interpretations of the scriptures." Again she paused so Quintus had time to reflect, "After His resurrection, it became important to let the divine dominate. That is why He walked through walls, but had a solid body for Thomas to check. That is why at first His friends going to Emmaus didn't recognize Him. Then He broke bread and they knew. They ate with Him." She nodded as if remembering, and delved deeper, "I knew Him. Peter knew Him." She stopped and once more her smile engulfed him in tenderness, "You would have known Him!" Then she added, the words confusing Quintus completely, "But you can see Him, my son. He beckons, Quintus. Follow Him."

Quintus was not sure what she meant. Was it a call to be a disciple of Jesus, to join Peter and his associates in proclaiming the gospel of Jesus, or did he misunderstand? Was Maryam merely asking him to confirm in his report that Jesus had been a god? Quintus won the battle within his mind by abruptly changing the subject. He almost addressed her as 'Mother.' He could not address her as 'Maryam.' He remained neutral by just asking the question without any specific correlation.

"Why did he have to die, then, in such a brutal way?"

"Because then the people would understand that He was a sacrifice for their sins which were forgiven," she responded. "He had foretold His death, and He had foretold His resurrection. His Apostles could not understand the full meaning of what He said. It was not until afterward that they fully comprehended His words that the Temple would be destroyed and then He would rebuild it in three days." She paused, "He was the Temple. He was crucified, then in three days He arose and that is what He meant, saying that the Temple would be rebuilt." With a quizzical addition to her continual smile, she asked Quintus, "Do you now understand as well what His prophetic words meant? He preached the new commandments - to love God above all else, and to love our neighbors as ourselves. He did not preach a set of rules that controlled every aspect of life. Rather he preached love, joy, repentance, and forgiveness. Recall that He forgave the executioners on the day of His crucifixion."

Quintus was humbled by her logic, grace, and a quality he couldn't quite put his finger on. He kept probing.

"Where is he now?" he asked.

Once again the matter of fact reply was delivered gently, but this time with a touch of rebuke. "Where He belongs," she said, "in Heaven, overseeing His kingdom." She still smiled, but with that new note of rebuke, "Where do you think He is? Peter told you He had ascended."

This gave Quintus no difficulty. If Jesus was God, then he could of course rise to the heavens. He could be the son of Jupiter. That, too, was no problem for Quintus. What was one more son of a god, or another god? In his religion he had a god for just about everything. One more or less mattered naught. But Maryam was claiming a single god, almost as if only Jupiter existed and no other gods existed. The Jews believed in a single God. Maryam was claiming to be the mother of that single God, and that Jesus was part of the nature of that single God. It made no difference to him if there was one or many. He firmly believed there was a power beyond what was natural or that he could comprehend. In his belief up to now, he was satisfied with the explanation of multiple gods and multiple evil spirits that controlled what happened on earth. To him, the only thing that really mattered was Rome and Pax Romana. So now it came down to a single God with many attributes, almost as if there were three Gods, Jesus the son, the father, and the Holy Spirit that had suffused the disciples of Jesus with strength for their faith to counter the threats against them. If that was correct, this was a new idea that could have great repercussions in Rome. An alliance of this religion with the strength of Rome could sweep the world. The thought almost took his breath away. He had to learn more.

He sensed a new factor in his reasoning. Maryam seemed to be playing with him, as if she could read his mind and words even before he spoke. This was a remarkable woman. He had to inquire further.

"When did you first realize he was a god?" he asked.

"You mean - don't you Quintus? - when did I first know He was God, the one and only God?"' After a break for effect between her last words, she went on, "I always knew. The messenger told me. I knew not man. My conception was from God."

Quintus smiled in disbelief. She stopped him. "You think I was raped by a Roman soldier and fabricated this story to keep shame from my family." She was not angry. Her voice remained firm. She continued, "Think, Quintus! If God could make the universe He could easily make any woman with child. In fact," and she smiled broadly, "He could make every woman in the world with child in one blink of an eye." Then she added with words that had a scatter of humor, even a gentle laugh, in them, "He could have made men unnecessary for the propagation of people. Wouldn't that have been a blow to the male belief that women are subservient!"

"Why didn't he?" asked Quintus, now completely unnerved by her logic and wit. She did not answer, just sat looking into his eyes. Hers did not blink. His did. The smile was fixed on her lips. She was playing with him, teasing him like a little boy. It was not malicious. She was not that kind of person. She exuded goodness and love. He felt only awe and even a strong attraction to her. He struggled to concentrate on her words and their meaning. She was giving him an important message.

Quintus remembered the commandments from Peter. He began to understand and accept, and almost to believe this woman, really a lady. His tone changed to one of great respect as he asked her something that had bothered him for some time now, "My lady Maryam, was Maryam Magdalene his lover here on earth?"

She laughed outright, "But you already asked her that, Tribune." Her laugh came like bells tinkling in the breeze, "You now want my corroboration. You are a very good investigator, Tribune. That is good. Like Thomas, you must see to believe, and prepare the way for those who cannot see, so they can believe."

With a small sigh she continued, "Maryam Magdalene is my close friend. She was a close friend and follower of Jesus. You might even think of her as His greatest Apostle. While He made Peter the head of His Church, it was not to slight Maryam. It was to make it coincide with the culture of these times where women are considered lesser than men." Then she stared into space for a moment, and added softly, "The day will come when women will be considered equal, and in some cases superior. But not in these times," she added.

After a few seconds, she persisted, "Of course Jesus loved Maryam, and she loved Him. She washed his feet with perfume and dried them with her hair. A few days before His death, she anointed Him with oil. She worshipped Him." Then she added with a strong voice, "But she was not His sexual partner. It was not an erotic love, but a filial and paternal love."

"Why and how?" asked Quintus.

"Because God loves all his creatures. He made man, and then He made woman to be a companion for man. They were equal in his eyes. All of this was done for love of us. In His Kingdom, there is no distinction between the human man and woman. All are spirits. There is no sex in heaven."

Quintus bowed his head. The nobility of the lady, the love that shone in her heart, the love that bound Jesus to His followers and the people began to penetrate his belief barriers. He began to understand, and almost to believe this lady. She noticed the change but gave no indication of surprise when he asked, "How can you reassure me that his disciples did not steal his body?"

With no exasperation or sign of impatience, but as if she were explaining to a little boy, she replied, “If you think about it, it would have been impossible for them to do it. First the guards, and second their fear. They had seen their leader brutally murdered - or executed as you prefer - and they feared they were next. Peter denied him three times even though he loved him. They were not then ready to die for Him." She stopped. Her warm eyes directly staring into Quintus', "Now they are. After the Holy Spirit came on Pentecost, they were readied." A sad look came over her face, "And they will die for Him, in horrible ways."

Then, the sadness dissipated, "Before the Holy Spirit came, they were afraid. They lacked the courage to undertake something as dangerous as stealing the body of Jesus with the guards before the tomb. Even if they tried, it would defeat the purpose of Jesus' life. No. They didn't steal His body. He rose from the dead. He was God."

They were both quiet. Delving into his thoughts, Quintus remembered to ask about Jesus as a young man, "What kind of son was Jesus?"

Maryam gave a gentle laugh, "Like all other boys. He played, hurt himself, came crying to me for comfort when He did, but He was always obedient, never did anything bad, and always tried to please Joseph and me." Her eyes twinkled. "He always did anything I asked. He even changed water into wine at the wedding feast in Cana," the laugh became stronger, "and it was the best wine anyone had ever tasted." The flicker of light in her eyes reappeared, "That was one of the miracles you listed, isn't it Tribune?"

Quintus decided to ignore the comment. They both knew it was true. As her laugh subsided, he asked, "What kind of learning did He have? Where did He become so proficient in his knowledge of the Scriptures?"

She sighed and replied patiently, "He read voraciously. He seemed to know before He even read the Scriptures. His Bar Mitzvah was superb. The priests deemed Him exceptional. When we went to Jerusalem for Passover, He disputed in the Temple with men much older than Himself. We had actually left for Nazareth when we found Him missing. He disputed for three days until we found Him. He came back with us, gently explaining He was on 'His Father's business."' She looked at Quintus, with a look of tenderness as she pulled the scenes of his younger days out of her memory, "He was exceptional. A good boy; but then again, He was God."

Quintus was affected but still persisted with his questions. He had to be complete in his report to the Emperor. "How did he come to be a carpenter?"

"Why, Joseph taught Him," Maryam said. "They worked well together until Joseph died. They both knew that Joseph was only a surrogate father, but they acted as true father and son." With a broad smile bordering on a grin, she proceeded, "He was a good carpenter. He made all of our furniture." Before Quintus could ask "Why" almost anticipating the question, she continued, "He wanted to show His nature as that of any man. Only then could His brutal death be accepted as the sacrifice of a man for the sins of all. By His death, He purified the world."

"When and why did Jesus begin to preach about the country?"

Without any delay she answered immediately, "In His third decade, when He knew it was time. He started with a trip to the Jordan River to be baptized by His cousin, John, whom they called the Baptist. Then He spent forty days and nights in the desert alone, before coming back and beginning His mission here on earth. He challenged men to follow Him, and they did. He performed miracles, travelled the countryside, staying with friends or out of doors, and He taught his Apostles and His followers about his kingdom." Then her smile faded, "He entered Jerusalem in triumph, but that sealed his fate." The smile vanished, "He was crucified for all of us, as you know." The smile returned, "Then He rose from the dead to prove He was divine." Now she beamed.

Quintus was moved by this image of Jesus. It raised in his mind the image of Maryam as Mother, proud of a son. There was another image as well. One of sadness and anguish. In his mind, he pictured her as she stood at the foot of the cross as he died, quietly grieving. She must have felt terrible anguish. "I have a final question, my lady Maryam," said Quintus. As gently as he could, he posed his inquiry, "My Lady, you impress me as a loving and caring person and mother." Maryam's features took on a sad hue as if she knew what he was going to ask her, "How did you have the courage and stamina to witness the brutality of his execution, and to stand there at the foot of the cross as he died?" he asked.

She gave a long sigh, as her features softened and her eyes glistened as tears welled in their corners. "I was His mother. It tore at my heart to see Him suffer such pain. When they nailed Him to the cross, they were nailing me too. When He bled, I bled. I would willingly have traded places with Him if I could. I knew He was divine, but He was also human, and ultimately, my son." She stopped as the memory of that terrible time filled her mind. Then she continued, the words soft and full of sorrow.

"I always knew He would suffer someday. Simeon the aged priest had foretold that 'a sword of sorrow would pierce my heart' when we first took Him to the Temple to be Presented some time after His Circumcised. I lived with that apprehension all His life."

A slow tear trickled down her cheek. She wiped it away with the edge of her scarf, and continued, softly and full of anguish, "It tore at my heart to see them nail him to the cross. Each blow hit me." She stopped, seemed to swallow a few times, and went on, "I prayed to God to let me take His place, but the horror continued." Now she stopped entirely. Her breath came in short gasps for a few moments until her will took over, she sighed, and pushed through, "As He hung on the cross, dying, in terrible pain, struggling to breathe, He pardoned the repentant robber on His right and prayed for the one on His left." She stopped and looked directly at Quintus, "He pardoned His executioners. He pardoned the Centurion who came with you." Quintus' head jerked up as she said this. How did she know? Her eyes glistened as she added, "He gave John and me to each other."

Then she seemed to brace up, and continued, "He died for all of us. He died for our sins. He died to redeem us all. He died so He could rise from the dead to prove He was God." Looking directly at Quintus, she quietly said, "He rose from the dead, Quintus, my son. No one stole His body!"

She folded her hands. She looked at him. From nowhere she seemed to change her tone and the subject. "Quintus you have a glowing future before you. You will affect the minds and hearts of multitudes with your words and deeds. But your great contribution will not come from your sword or from the throne, but rather from the word of God. Be a fisher of men like Peter, Quintus. Follow the Lord. Follow my son." She stopped and looked at him. Quintus was shaken. She smiled enigmatically, arose and walked away. He followed her with his eyes until she turned the corner and was gone.

Quintus felt his emotions tumble within his mind and heart. He was stunned. The conversation had taken a turn he had not environed. He was a soldier, a Tribune, perhaps the son of the Emperor. He had a glowing future before him. Yet she had asked him to give it all up - to follow her son, to follow the carpenter. Or was it to follow God? Quintus believed in multiple gods. Now she spoke of a single God, a God only of love and forgiveness, even if all powerful. His head up in a whirl, he walked back to where he saw Longinus and Marcus standing. He stood there for a moment, stuck deep in thought. His reverie was broken by Longinus asking if he wanted to return to the barracks. He turned to Longinus and said, "She pardoned you. She knew you commanded the Legionaries who executed her son. She knew you were with me." Then looking directly at Longinus, he repeated, "She pardoned you."

Longinus was silent for a long moment. "Yes I imagined she would. Her son did, from the cross." After a short silence, he added, "It affected me. It will affect me all my life." His emotion-filled eyes pierced Quintus'.

"How did your conversation affect you?" Longinus asked. "Will it help in your mission to discover the truth about the disappearance of the body of Jesus?"

Quintus stood for a moment, and then quietly said, "Yes, but not in the way I thought when I sought this meeting." He casually looked back at where he had met Maryam. The bench was gone. So was the fig tree. He turned to Longinus. "Centurion, did you notice the fig tree and bench are no longer there?" The Centurion looked at the Temple square where the bench had been. A surprised look came over his face.

"But it was there!" Longinus gasped. He was about to speak again, but then he stopped. He looked at Quintus. Then at Marcus who shrugged. Then back to Quintus, "Tribune, was it not there?"

Still somewhat startled, Quintus stared back at the wall. After a few seconds he turned to Longinus and said, "Yes it was!" After a moment, he quietly said to Longinus "I am not surprised. Are you?" Longinus gave him a long look of understanding.

Beckoning to Marcus, Quintus said, "Let's get back to the barracks. I want to start on my report."

They walked back to the barracks in silence, with Quintus' mind spinning a mile a minute. Could he have imagined it all? No. It was real. But even Longinus saw the bench that wasn't there. Like the 153 fish, the fig tree was the 'extra' that drove the point home. Inwardly Quintus smiled. He knew.

**The Resurrection: A Criminal Investigation of the Mysterious Disappearance of the Body of the Crucified Criminal Jesus of Nazareth**

# Chapter Ten
# The Evidence

In the morning, Quintus met with the Captain of the flotilla of galleys who had come from Caesarea for the meeting.

"Captain," he asked, "When can you be ready to leave? Is it possible to leave the day after tomorrow?"

"Yes, Tribune," answered the Captain, "I have made all the arrangements to provision the galleys on short notice. That can be done to meet your departure date."

"Then proceed," ordered Quintus, "The Legionaries we brought with us will march to Caesarea tomorrow and will be ready to board the galleys by nightfall. We sail in the morning upon my arrival." Then he added, well-knowing the answer, but exercising the cardinal rule of command of having those commanded willingly follow, "Thank you, Captain. It is always a pleasure to be supported as you have supported me. I wish to leave then. If that is impossible, we can make accommodations." Then Quintus added, as the true essence of command, "However, I think it imperative we return as quickly as possible to report to the Emperor."

"There is no difficulty meeting your target date, Tribune. That is all possible. I am sure everyone will be happy to return to Rome." The Captain grinned, but said nothing more. Quintus was pleased that the lessons Tiberius had taught him concerning leadership could be very effective.

"Then see to it, Captain," he said in a light voice, "and thank you for your efforts."

"It has been my pleasure, Tribune." With that, the Captain left. Quintus was certain the next two days would be spent in frenzied preparations, but that all would be ready to leave upon his arrival in Caesarea on the morning of the third day.

Then Quintus met with the three Centurions. Marcus took detailed notes of the discussions. Each Centurion reported in turn what had been discovered from the extensive and exhaustive investigation. They sat in a square, with the documenting Centurion standing to make his report. Marcus sat taking his notes to the rear of the group.

Longinus and his Legionaries had been assigned to study all aspects of the disappearance of the body of Jesus from the tomb. No real evidence had been uncovered about anyone stealing the body. There were no witnesses to such an act, and no direct rumors about where the body might be if stolen. There were rumblings that the guards placed to guard the tomb had initially spread the story that they had been asleep, and that the body had been stolen. But all their stories differed and little credence was given to them. On the whole, then, Longinus could report that no evidence existed to prove that the body had been stolen.

On the other hand, there was significant evidence that Jesus was seen alive, walking and talking with many persons. Hundreds had seen him, and all attested to the fact that he was alive after being entombed. He was even reported to have performed a miracle. This miracle, being his direction of his fishermen disciples to a specific location where they caught one hundred and fifty-three fish, was verified by a number of persons, including Quintus.

The actual death of Jesus was verified by numerous witnesses. Longinus himself had thrust a spear into the side of Jesus. Blood and water had flowed immediately from the wound indicating that he was dead at the time.

Longinus then proceeded to catalogue the witnesses, the circumstances surrounding each event, and the dates. Then he summarized all his evidence into nine conclusions. These were, as Longinus stated:

I. There was significant evidence that Jesus was dead when placed in the tomb.
II. There was no evidence that his body had been stolen.

III. There was no evidence of any other exit from the tomb other than the opening in the front sealed with a massive boulder.
IV. There were no persons identified who might have stolen the body.
V. There was no evidence of a conspiracy to hide the body or bury it elsewhere.
VI. There were hundreds of witnesses who claimed to have seen Jesus fully alive after the disappearance of the body from the tomb.
VII. There was corroborated evidence that Jesus performed a miracle after the disappearance of his body from the tomb.
VIII. One of his disciples, before witnesses, had placed his hands into the five wounds from the crucifixion in the body of Jesus - his side, his two hands, and his two feet. Also in front of witnesses, he had pronounced his conviction that Jesus now lived, whereas he had doubted before this test.
IX. There were many statements to the effect that Jesus had risen from the dead as he had predicted; on the third day after his death, as he had also predicted. Such a conclusion would be consistent with the findings.
X. The majority of the very group that had sought the death of Jesus in representations made to the Proconsul, the Sanhedrin, accepted that he had been dead in the tomb, and that no evidence existed that his body had been stolen.
XI. Guards had been posted at the tomb. They would not have been easily overcome. They related a mixed story of being bribed by the High Priest to say the body had been stolen, or they claimed the body had risen from the dead and walked from the tomb. Their story of being overcome or having fallen asleep was not seriously accepted.

After Longinus had summarized his findings and report, Quintus decided to ask Longinus' personal opinion. He began with thanks for the well-conducted and thorough study and analysis, and then asked, "Longinus, do you think Jesus was dead when placed in the tomb?"

Longinus looked at Quintus, "Yes, Tribune. I was certain of it while Jesus was still on the cross. That was my assignment in command of the crucifixion Legionaries." As he said this, Longinus looked down, a sense of shame overcoming him. Quintus was quick to notice that Longinus was deeply moved by the image of Jesus on the cross, and the fact that he, Longinus, had been instrumental in his execution.

Quintus went on, "Longinus, based on your own findings and those of all the Legionaries assigned, do you personally believe any one person or group stole the body?"

Longinus looked up, and in a strong voice stated, "No, Tribune. I firmly believe that the body was not stolen from the tomb."

Quintus then asked his most intriguing question, "Do you personally believe, Longinus, that Jesus rose from the dead?"

Longinus was silent for a moment. The looking directly at Quintus, said "The evidence points that way, Tribune."

Quintus thundered in reply, "Centurion Longinus, I asked for your personal opinion! I am well aware of what the findings are."

After a long pause, Longinus, after a long drawn out release of breath, said, "Yes, Tribune. There is no other possible explanation."

"Thank you, Longinus," said Quintus, "your report is thorough. I am sure the Emperor will be pleased that this evidence will lead to some closure on the question of what happened to the body of Jesus." Then abruptly changing the tone, he moved from investigative comrade to commander, "Longinus is there anything else you wish to do or are you satisfied your investigation is as complete as possible."

"It is complete, Tribune," replied Longinus.

Quintus nodded, “Very well done, Longinus. Compliment your men for me." Turning to Sutonius, Quintus asked what he and his Legionaries had discovered.

Sutonius began. "I was given the assignment to trace the supposed miracles of the carpenter Jesus of Nazareth. The Legionaries assigned to this function, and I, questioned witnesses of these miracles. Every miracle that we listed, all thirty-seven of them, had numerous witnesses. We questioned a number of them and in all cases there was corroboration of the cure or the raising from the dead of three specific persons." Looking directly at Quintus, he added, "These verification witnesses included you, Tribune Quintus. You visited each of the three, and even spoke to them about their experiences."

Sutonius went on to relate at length the corroborative evidence he and the Legionaries had uncovered and found. All the miracles had been verified. The possibility of trickery and collusion had also been examined thoroughly. There was no collusion when a woman touched the hem of Jesus' robe and was cured, or when Jesus responded to a cry for 'mercy,' or 'cure me, Lord.' With regard to trickery, it would be difficult to cure a man blind from birth, or deaf, or a leper, or to raise three persons from the dead. In the latter case, they were all different."

"Jairus is a high ranking person in the court of Herod," continued Sutonius. "He placed his position in jeopardy when he asked Jesus to cure his daughter, who subsequently died. Her death was witnessed. Conspiracy is unthinkable in this case because of Jairus' position. Such a plan would be detrimental to his position and his future. As a father, he grieved for his daughter, and sought Jesus to do something for her." Sutonius stopped. He looked at Quintus, and then over at Longinus and Aurelius in turn, "Jesus brought her back to life." He paused again, and then continued in a strong voice, almost biting out each word, "Jesus asked Jairus not to tell anyone about the miracle, but it soon became evident when the little girl whom everyone thought had died, and for whom they were mourning, was now alive and well." Even strongly voiced, he proceeded, "There could be no collusion or trickery here. It was a real major miracle," he placed great emphasis on the next point, "with witnesses whose testimony is unassailable, and who would have no motivation whatsoever to lie."

Sutonius then mentioned the story of the widow of Nain, "In this case, Jesus was passing by, and brought the young boy back to life." He looked eye-to-eye with Quintus. "Tribune, you too can verify the facts of this case." Quintus nodded. Sutonius went on, "There was no collusion or trickery here. There were credible witnesses, the boy is alive, and the meeting was one of chance. Jesus was saddened at the plight of a grieving widow, and taking pity, raised her son from the dead."

"Could the boy have been merely ill?" asked Aurelius.

"Unlikely," said Quintus, "I questioned all about that, as I am sure Sutonius did." and here Sutonius nodded, as Quintus went on. "The boy was dead. Jesus brought him back."

There was silence for a few moments before Sutonius continued.

"Some of the most powerful evidence of the power of Jesus came when he raised Lazarus from the dead after he had lain in his tomb for four days." Sutonius paused, "Think about that." He looked about, at Quintus and the other two Centurions, "Authoritative witnesses saw him die. They buried him. He was in his tomb four days. Putrefaction had commenced." He paused for dramatic effect, "Jesus came, called him from his tomb, and Lazarus emerged in his burial clothes. After being cleaned, he dined with Jesus and his sisters." In a strong voice bordering on thunder, he reaffirmed, "Jesus raised His friend Lazarus from the dead four days after he was buried..."

"Are you sure he was dead?" Quintus interrupted before he could go on. "Yes," said Sutonius, "if he wasn't dead when he was put into the tomb, he probably would have died while in it. He was wrapped. That alone is enough to suffocate. He must have been at least very ill, and weakened from the illness. Without food and water, he would have died. My opinion is that he was dead. Whether he died before being placed in the tomb, as I believe, or after being placed in the tomb, he was certainly dead when Jesus appeared." Looking inquisitively at Quintus, he challenged, "Tribune, you talked with him. What is your opinion?"

"My opinion is unimportant," said Quintus. "My findings are! He was certainly dead in the tomb, and he was certainly alive after Jesus commanded him to come out. He remembers that and we spoke about it." He advanced, "And yes, my opinion is that this is a valid miracle, a great one in fact." The others nodded. Then he added, "Sutonius please summarize your findings and those of your Legionaries."

Sutonius did. He documented interviews, names, places, and dates. Finally, he came to his summary conclusions, which were as follows:

I. All the thirty-seven miracles were authentic. Trickery and collusion were not possible.

II. In three cases, the miracles were resurrecting lives of dead persons.

III. The probability is high that the greatest miracle of all was Jesus' own resurrection from the dead.

Quintus remained silent for a rather lengthy period of time, obviously immersed in thought. The addition of this report only reinforced his own findings and thoughts. Together with Longinus' report, this pointed more and more to a divine nature for Jesus. His meeting with Jesus' mother, Maryam, would have to be added to this analysis. He decided to do this last, after the report from Aurelius. He looked at Sutonius, and expressed his gratitude. "Thank you Sutonius. Your report is well done. The Emperor will be pleased." Then, almost as an afterthought, he quietly added, "Sutonius is there anything else you and your men wish to do in this investigation?"

"No, Tribune. The investigation is complete."

.Quintus nodded, and complimented Sutonius and his men, "Good. Well done, Sutonius. Please give my thanks to your men for all their hard work."

He then turned to Aurelius. He inquired of the third Centurion, the one who had accompanied him from Rome. "Aurelius, you were assigned to investigate the teachings of Jesus. What did you and the Legionaries find?"

"Tribune," he began, "our investigation was in two parts. In the first part, we scoured the nation, going into towns throughout the country where we were told Jesus had visited and preached. We sought witnesses to verify what he said and what he did. While we discovered information concerning the miracles, we informed Sutonius of this for his thorough investigation, as he has related. We concentrated on the message of Jesus to the people of Judea. The second part of our investigation concerned what Jesus had said to his disciples; how he recruited them, what he told them, what he promised, what he trained them to do, and what he commanded them to do. Some of this we garnered from our visits and investigations around the country. However, the meeting here with Peter and his disciples added significantly to our findings." Quintus nodded.

Aurelius proceeded, "During that meeting, we spoke to the twelve closest disciples of Jesus, known as 'the Apostles.' The leader is, as you all know, Simon bar Jonah, whom Jesus called Peter, the rock upon which to build His church. These twelve men are a mixed lot, mostly uneducated fisherman. Yes, despite their minimal learning, they displayed unusual bearing, confidence, and ability. They appear to have been well trained by Jesus during their time together. Apparently he taught them using stories or parables to make his points. We have encountered a number of these in our interviews, and have found them remarkably instructive and illuminating of the point at issue. Jesus was a great teacher."

Aurelius paused in thought for a moment, "As a teacher, Jesus leaned to pacifism. One quotation related to us was his comment to present the other cheek if someone strikes your cheek. This is certainly not the statement of a zealous revolutionary seeking to overthrow Roman rule. In all of our inquiries, we could uncover nothing that would indicate Jesus in any way was planning such a revolt. We could find no evidence that he sought anything other than to have his followers 'love God above all else, and their neighbors as themselves.'"

Again Aurelius paused, looked at Quintus and the other two centurions, and continued, "These people are not a threat to the civil or military rule of Rome. They are a threat to the rigid and arbitrary rule of the Sanhedrin and the High Priest. The threat they pose is one of having their followers question the purpose and value of rigid observance to rules. Jesus, on the other hand, demanded that his followers add good deeds to their code of belief. His actions in curing the sick and disabled, his offer to forgive sins, and his willing death as a sacrificial lamb to cleanse the world of their sins are the mark of a divine nature rather than a human nature."

Aurelius stopped for a rather lengthy time. Just when the silence was becoming unbearable, he concluded with a summary, "Jesus was a man of and for his god." Slowly he added, "his teachings were a harbinger of his resurrection from death. Based on our findings, Tribune, no evidence has been found to justify his execution. We can find no evidence that he did not rise from the dead. We could find no evidence that he was not divine."

Aurelius stood silent for a moment, and sat down. The others too remained silent for a few moments, all wrapped in thought over what Aurelius had verified.

Quintus broke the silence by walking over to Aurelius, clapping him on both shoulders with his hands, and saying, "Well done, Centurion." Then turning towards Sutonius, he repeated the same action and commendation; and then repeated again the entire process with Longinus. Then he walked to his chair but did not sit. He motioned the other three to sit.

"Centurions," he began, "thank you for the diligence of your work, and the excellence of your reports." He paused. "In two days I shall depart for Rome. Aurelius will accompany me, together with all the Legionaries we brought with us. I have discussed this with the flotilla Captain and all is ready. Aurelius will leave with the Legionaries in the morning and will embark tomorrow night. I will arrive the next morning and leave for Rome then."

Turning to look at Marcus, he began with announcement of a difficult decision he had made. He wished it could be otherwise, but he found it necessary. "Marcus, I believe it necessary to leave you in Judea to continue the task of recording events here. I believe that is necessary." He noticed the quick intake of breath by Marcus. Then it was over. Marcus gave no further reaction to this sudden change in his life. Quintus continued. "I wish to thank you profusely, Marcus, for your excellent work in recording the minutes of our meetings and the conclusions of our studies. I will sign these and take one copy with me to present to the Emperor with my verbal report. The second copy is to be sent to Rome via courier galley in case the first set is lost with me in a shipwreck. Marcus, I leave you here with your notes in safekeeping in the event we are all shipwrecked and all the documents are lost. You can always re-create them from your notes and memory if necessary."

Then turning to Longinus, he continued, "Longinus, I will discuss with Lucius your assignment here to be my liaison in the event additional investigation is needed. Marcus will report to you. I would ask you to keep in contact with Peter and send me dispatches periodically about his activities."

Turning once more to Marcus, he assured, "Marcus, I believe you and Peter will spend time together. Perhaps you can document additional material to add to these reports." He paused and was about to begin another thought when he stopped, and looking at Marcus again, asked, "Will all be ready for my signature tomorrow?"

"Yes, Tribune," answered Marcus, showing no sign of emotion whatsoever at this sudden change in his life. Inwardly, however, he was pleased. His own observations were that Peter was a good man, easy to work with, and very interesting. He looked forward to documenting the progress of this sect.

Quintus walked over to his chair, but remained standing, in a position which allowed him to look periodically at each of the three Centurions as he began.

"Centurions, I have a few remarks to make as a report of my personal activities and observations." He then proceeded to discuss his meetings with Peter, Mary the Mother of Jesus, Lazarus, Mary Magdalene, and Caiaphas. He did not present his comments concerning Pontius Pilate.

He concluded his remarks, "Centurions, it has been a pleasure working with you. I am sure the Emperor will be pleased with the results of your hard work which will be incorporated into my verbal report to him, and which is evident in the written reports prepared by Marcus which I will present to him." After a short pause, he went on, "Please thank all the Legionaries for their assistance in this investigative effort." Quintus adjourned the meeting at the lunch hour. He told the three Centurions and Marcus that they would reconvene early the next morning for each to sign their reports. He then informed them of his scheduled final luncheon with the Proconsul. He asked Marcus not to come with him to his luncheon meeting with Pontius Pilate, but rather to freshen his notes from their morning session.

Again after a short pause he added, quietly, in a voice almost bordering on some regret, "This meeting is adjourned." As the Centurions left, Quintus beckoned Marcus to stay. When they were alone, Quintus decided he had to impress upon Marcus the importance of the document he had been preparing, and how many elements required secrecy until release of their contents was approved by the Emperor. This was especially true of any revelations concerning officials of the Empire. Like the Emperor, Quintus felt that history was to a large extent governed by a few individuals. Looking directly at Marcus, Quintus issued a stern warning concerning secrecy. "Marcus what I am about to have you write is to be kept secret. If you reveal any of this in any way to anyone, you will be executed, as will all those who learned any of this because of your crime. Do you understand me Marcus?"

Somewhat shaken, Marcus looked up and said, "Yes, Tribune, I understand. I promise that nothing that you say to me or that I have heard you say will ever leave my lips." Then looking directly at Quintus, he added, "I respect you, Tribune. I respect you as a leader and as a person. I am just a slave, but in my land before then I was a person of importance. I hope you do not think ill of me, but Tribune, you are a great leader." Marcus looked down, somewhat embarrassed in showing his admiration for Quintus, but then he looked up again and said, "You can rely on me, Tribune."

Quintus was somewhat surprised, but pleased. He quietly said, "Thank you, Marcus." Then he left the room.

Quintus left on horseback for the Proconsul's residence accompanied by a guard contingent of Legionaries. At the residence, he was greeted, and escorted to a small dining room where Pontius Pilate awaited him.

* * *

The luncheon was convivial. Quintus was determined to leave Judea without telegraphing his feelings towards and about the Proconsul. Pontius Pilate, however, in his insecurity, sought to penetrate Quintus' reserve to gain some insight of his report to the Emperor. "Do you deem your trip successful Tribune? Will you be able to report conclusively to the Emperor the results of your investigative assignment?" Pontius Pilate asked.

Quintus took a sip of wine. Then he looked directly at Pontius Pilate, "I think so. In fact, I know so." He deliberately stopped and took another sip of wine and sat back waiting for additional questions from Pontius Pilate. He thought it best to keep his replies non-committal and as brief as possible.

Perplexed about how to proceed, Pontius Pilate probed further, "To your satisfaction, Tribune, did you find that everyone in the garrison here, on my staff, and also myself, was cooperative and helpful in your investigation?" Pontius Pilate nervously took a sip as he leaned forward.

"Yes, Proconsul, everyone cooperated." Then he looked once again into the far distance, and sat even further back in his chair as he pushed it back slightly from the table extending his legs. His demeanor and position exuded confidence in himself, and in his leadership. Pontius Pilate on the other hand became even more anxious, adjusting his chair closer to the table and nervously placing his wine goblet on the table. He clasped his hands together, put his elbows on the table, and tried again. "I trust, Quintus, you will relay to the Emperor the difficulties I have had with these people here in Judea." Pilate proceeded, "The Jews are highly intelligent people, unified in their religion, centered around their single god, and with a set of rules that regulate every aspect of their lives. They are governed separately by their own religious leaders, organized as the Sanhedrin, which is dominated by the High Priests, Caiaphas and Annas. With this unity, they are somewhat unruly and governing them with a small occupation force that I have is very difficult. It often becomes necessary for me to exercise restraint in how I use the force I have. As a result, I have always found it useful and necessary to quell any disturbance before it becomes too widespread. I think you understand this, don't you Quintus?"

Quintus looked up and detected signs of fear, uncertainty, and pleading in the countenance and words of Pontius Pilate. His opinion of Pontius Pilate as a poor leader was reinforced. He would have to be replaced as quickly as possible as Proconsul. He kept a totally neutral look as he replied, "I will be very careful and thorough in my report to the Emperor."

The reply did not satisfy Pontius Pilate who, maintained his same position with his elbows on the table, "The situation here is critical and may require armed intervention by Rome. That is the point I am making, Quintus. It is not that critical yet, but it would not take much to reach the stage of requiring another invasion of these people. In fact, if that occurs, I would recommend that their temple be destroyed, since so much of their life is built around their temple, the ceremonies, and the rules by which the people live. Without their temple, they will be easier to rule." Pontius Pilate sat back, and exhaled slowly. He seemed almost defeated as he added, "My position is like walking on eggshells. I do not seek thanks and glorification for having been successful in maintaining the peace here in Judea. I was just completing the assignment given to me when I was sent here."

Quintus was somewhat surprised that Pontius Pilate expected praise for his governorship. On the other hand, he was agreeably surprised at the spark of wisdom and foresight shown by Pontius Pilate concerning a possible future repeat invasion and conquering of Judea. These were exactly the opinions he had formed. He decided to inspire Pontius Pilate with some confidence since he would have to remain as Proconsul at least for now. Quintus was sure that would not be long; he was certain the Emperor would act on the recommendations in his report to recall and remove Pontius Pilate. The alternative was for him to take command immediately, but Quintus had decided that was not a wise course of action. He was reasonably sure that matters would be somewhat stable after he left, at least until Tiberius could act. A little stiffening of the spine for Pontius Pilate seemed in order.

Looking sternly at the Proconsul, Quintus started amiably and then stiffened as he progressed, "Proconsul, you have a difficult assignment. While the people of Judea are not as war-like as some of the barbarians on our northern and eastern borders, they are still difficult to govern because they are unified." Then straightforwardly eye-to-eye with Pontius Pilate, Quintus added, "Jesus might very well have been helpful in pacifying the Jewish people since he was firm in his teachings of 'Render unto Caesar that which is Caesar's and, render unto God's that which is God's.' To a large extent, he preached pacification. He preached goodness, love, remorse, and reward in a future life. He did not preach revolt." Quintus paused for emphasis. "He was, however, a threat to the religious leaders who were concerned about a loss of power and income because of his ideology. So they wanted him removed." Then leaning forward, raising his right hand, and extending his finger directly at Pontius Pilate, who seemed to shrink deeper in his chair, Quintus proclaimed in a thundering voice, "And you listened to them and had Jesus executed! You fool! You cut off your right hand. Do not dare ever to be so foolish again. Never forget that you are a Roman, a Roman Proconsul!" Then in a stern voice, he strongly and with great emphasis virtually shouted, "Govern!"

Abruptly he stood up and once again became a diplomatic Tribune. He waited for the shaken Pontius Pilate to rise from his chair. Then Quintus saluted Pontius Pilate, and was saluted in turn. "I take my leave, Proconsul," said Quintus in his exiting words, "Thank you for your assistance during my stay here."

Before Pontius Pilate could utter a sound, Quintus turned on his heel and walked from the room. He exited the residence, mounted his horse, signaled his guard to accompany him and left for the barracks.

* * *

The next morning, Quintus met with the three Centurions and Marcus. All the documents were signed. One set was placed in a small carrying sack and dispatched to the galley with Aurelius. The second set was sent to Rome via the courier galley.

Quintus then sat with Marcus and went over the contents of all the reports to refresh the matters in his mind so he could prepare his report.

That evening Quintus attended a farewell banquet hosted by Pontius Pilate. Invited guests included Caiaphas, Annas, members of the Sanhedrin, Tribune Lucius, and the Centurions stationed in Jerusalem. Procula, the wife of the Proconsul, was especially gracious throughout. She was the spark of the evening, counteracting a dour Pontius Pilate who drank excessively, and virtually ignored his Guest of Honor. Caiaphas left early with his associates once the mandatory social graces had been observed. Tetrarch Herod sent his regrets at a previous scheduling conflict. None of the followers of Jesus were invited, not even Nicodemus and Joseph of Arimathea. While the banquet was a social success, Quintus would much rather have enjoyed an evening of wine and comradery in the barracks with Lucius and the Legionaries in Jerusalem.

**The Resurrection: A Criminal Investigation of the Mysterious Disappearance of the Body of the Crucified Criminal Jesus of Nazareth**

# Chapter Eleven
# Tiberius

The voyage to Rome was long. An impatient Quintus paced the command deck continually. In his mind he reviewed the approach he would take in making his report to Tiberius. He missed Marcus. It would have been easier for him to deliver his report to the wind, and have Marcus write it down, and then read it back to him. In the absence of Marcus, he did deliver his report to the wind, honing the approach to meet any reaction from Tiberius at any point in the presentation.

After stops for supplies and replacement slaves, they arrived at the docks in Capri. Their approach had been observed, and a chariot awaited Quintus at the dock. In moments he stood before Emperor Tiberius. They were alone in the Council Room. Tiberius was seated at the head of the table, slouched in a chair, pushed back. In his hand was a goblet, and a carafe was on the table before him. He had obviously dropped whatever he was doing to greet Quintus alone.

Quintus was not surprised. He had assumed that he would make a personal report to the Emperor before any report would be made to the Council and others. He had expected to be kept waiting some time while the Emperor rearranged his schedule. Making himself immediately available indicated to Quintus the great importance Tiberius placed on his report; or perhaps he was welcoming back someone he favored? Quintus also noted that no scribe was present. Any documentation of his report would be made afterwards in the event the Emperor wished some part suppressed or even changed for reasons of state, or for that matter for any reason whatsoever. Tiberius was the Emperor.

"Hail Tiberius, Emperor of Rome!" saluted Quintus. Tiberius in turn saluted Quintus and motioned for him to sit beside him. "Welcome home, Quintus! Let me have some refreshments brought in." The Emperor clapped his hands and a steward accompanied by two servants entered with fresh goblets, a fresh carafe of wine, bowls of fruit and pastries. Then they left.

Tiberius waved to the refreshments, handed Quintus a full goblet of wine, and noting that they were again alone, directed a quizzical look at the Tribune, "Quintus, when will you be ready to present your report?"

"Now, Sire," said Quintus. He detected a quick look of surprise and pleasure. Apparently the Emperor expected a short delay after his arrival to become acclimated to land from his long journey. He smiled, raised his goblet to Quintus, and sallied with, "Here's to the resilience of youth. I am pleased since your dispatches have led me to believe you have completed your assignment with distinction. Tell me what you found, and what you conclude from those findings." Tiberius turned his chair outward to face Quintus standing before him. He sat further back in his chair, occasionally sipping his goblet of wine as Quintus made his report.

Quintus brought with him the small shoulder bag with the papyrus rolls prepared by Marcus during the investigation in Judea. He placed this on the table in front of the Emperor, stepped back, and began.

"Sire, you charged me with, as you stated, 'A Criminal Investigation of the Mysterious Disappearance of the Body of the Crucified Criminal Jesus of Nazareth'." Tiberius nodded, sipped his wine, and signaled for Quintus to go on, "Our investigation in Judea was extensive, Sire." Pointing to the papyrus rolls, he added "I have placed at your disposal the papyri prepared by Marcus of our various findings in Judea. These are available for your study as you may wish, Sire. They are a record." Again Quintus stopped. Again Tiberius nodded.

Quintus then outlined to the Emperor the plan he had developed for the study, how he brought Sutonius and Longinus into the study to join Aurelius who had accompanied him, also how various teams of investigators had combed Judea for the facts and of his own interviews and investigations. It had come as a surprise to him that no such study had previously been undertaken by Pontius Pilate or by the High Priest. Here again Tiberius nodded, and even smiled broadly. Quintus thought he heard the Emperor mutter, what he thought sounded like, 'Very foolish of them.'

Quintus proceeded to state that all of these findings, facts and motivational factors became the foundation upon which his discoveries, conclusions, and report were based. Other than the muttered comment, in all of this Tiberius said not a word, but occasionally smiled appreciatively at the thoroughness of the study. There was no doubt in Quintus' mind as he proceeded that the Emperor was greatly pleased at the manner in which he had organized and carried out the study. Inwardly Quintus was relieved. Despite his sense that the Emperor favored him, he was astute and level-headed enough to realize such favor could be fleeting, and must be continually earned and re-earned by performance. Comfortable with his presentation, he continued with the conclusions of his study.

"Sire, you sent me to Rome to investigate the mysterious disappearance of the body of the crucified criminal Jesus of Nazareth. All our evidence points to the fact he was not a criminal, that his body was not stolen, and that there is a very high probability that he did indeed rise from the dead. If he did, then he is a god! If he is a god, then he did not blaspheme as the Jewish religious leaders claimed!"

"Hence, Sire, it comes down to the question: did Jesus of Nazareth rise from the dead or not?"

"The following evidence supports that assertion:

I. Jesus performed numerous miracles before his crucifixion. These included raising three from the dead. All these miracles have been investigated and verified as authentic.
II. As he was being executed, he prayed that his father would forgive his executioners because they did not know what they were doing.
III. Our investigation concluded that he did die, that his corpse was removed from the cross and buried in the tomb.
IV. On the third day, the tomb was found empty.

V. Roman guards placed at the tomb by Pontius Pilate at the request of the High Priest, Caiaphas, told conflicting stories about how the body came to disappear. The initial claim that his disciples overcame them and stole the body, then it was replaced by one that the body walked past them, and the guards fled in terror.

VI. Jesus appeared to at least three of his followers near the tomb stone on the morning of his probable resurrection. Later that day, he appeared to two disciples walking to Emmaus, and dined with them. He was also seen passing through walls and meeting with his closest disciples on more than one occasion. One telling incident concerns one disciple, called Thomas, who actually placed his hands into the five wound locations on the body of Jesus. This provides an interesting factor; his body could pass through walls but was solid enough for this disciple to place his hands into the wounds on the body.

VII. Our investigation determined that hundreds of people at one time or another had seen Jesus of Nazareth after his execution and death.

VIII. His closest disciples were too fearful to challenge the mob organized by Caiaphas, too fearful to object at the trial of Jesus, and too fearful to plead for his release, but these same followers, disciples, or 'Apostles' as they were called, suddenly became strong willed, fearless, devoted exponents of Jesus of Nazareth. They believed he was a deity, risen from the dead, who commanded them to go forth and teach all nations.

IX. Jesus preached and taught honesty, justice, love of neighbor, and righteousness. There was no report whatsoever of any departure by him from that path of obeying the law. Thus his disciples would never be motivated in any way to lie, steal, or cheat. Even their traitor, Judas Iscariot, believed he was not doing Jesus any harm since he believed Jesus could defeat even an army sent against him. As a result, Sire, it is impossible to believe that his disciples stole his body."

"Sire, I am convinced Jesus of Nazareth *did* rise from the dead," said Quintus on his personal opinion, "I am convinced that he was a god. Those convictions come mainly from these conclusions which are the only possible explanation of the facts. I am beginning to see no difficulty in reconciling our belief in many gods into to the concept of a single god. That single god, must of course, have unbelievable power to have created the world and the firmament as we know it. Such power would certainly include all the authority we attribute to each of our gods. I do not understand how it can be so. I do not understand how a god can become a man. I do not understand how a man can exist being God. I do not understand how we can kill the man since we cannot kill a god. But I do accept that Jesus of Nazareth was divine, and I do accept that it is possible for all our gods to be attributes of one god." Quintus continued with his surprising conclusion.

"Sire, I believe that Jesus of Nazareth has begun a movement that will sweep all before it. The conversion of Saul of Tarsus is very significant. Once a bitter enemy, he has now become a vital protagonist. Sire, you were right to sense that something was happening in Judea. But Sire, it is something good. It is a movement that some people are already labeling Christian, since Jesus of Nazareth was considered by his followers to be the Christ, or the promised Messiah. These men and women followers of Jesus, these Christians, are growing in number rapidly. In my opinion, they will continue to grow."

"Sire, I recommend close observation by you and continued investigation beyond my initial findings concerning this sect arising out of Judea. It does not threaten Rome because it cries for justice and goodness and love but, Sire, united with Rome it can enhance Pax Romana."

Quintus paused to give greater emphasis to his next words, "Sire, the results of my investigation lead me to believe that:

I. Jesus was not a criminal but was executed unjustly through the plotting of Caiaphas, the High Priest of the Jews

II. Jesus was truly dead when placed in the tomb; the tomb had no other exit than the one in the front covered by a large stone.

III. No one stole his body from the tomb, attempted to do so, or wished to do so. There were guards at the tomb; his disciples had neither the motivation nor courage to steal the body; and no one else had any motive to do so.

IV. There is no other logical alternative except that Jesus did indeed rise from the dead; he was seen by hundreds afterwards."

The Emperor smiled at each of the four statements. After Quintus delivered the last point, he raised his goblet in salute to Quintus, and said, "Quite thorough, Quintus, but I find it hard to believe that Jesus rose from the dead. Your proof is based on that being the only alternative. You have no proof to the contrary." Tiberius shook his head, "It's a little hard to accept."

"I know, Sire," countered Quintus, "I struggled with that same problem for most of my time in Judea, and even on the trip back. For weeks I wrestled with that conclusion. The only alternatives are that Jesus was not dead when placed in the tomb, or that somebody stole the body. We have ruled out both of those possibilities."

Both remained silent for some time. Tiberius stroked his chin, deep in thought. Then he sighed and focused his gaze on Quintus, "I see the dilemma. I will accept that Jesus was truly dead and that no one could have stolen the body. I also accept that the only other logical alternative is that he rose from the dead. Nothing human can do that. What you are saying, then, is that Jesus was some kind of divine being?"

"Yes," replied Quintus, "that is the only conclusion I could come to." He paused, then carried on, "Sire, there is no solid evidence, but the large and growing number of Christians is testimony that nothing and no one has come forward with any kind of proof that Jesus did not rise from the dead."

This had a marked effect on Tiberius. Again Tiberius stroked his chin. His eyes stared into the far distance. Then once more he turned to Quintus, "Divinity is something we have believed for some time. We have many stories in our history of gods that have visited earth. So I can understand how that can be true." A long silence passed, and then Tiberius went on, "But damn it all, Quintus! It is hard to swallow."

"Yes, Sire. It is. Over one hundred of us spent weeks examining, questioning, searching, and pondering. There is no other logical explanation."

Tiberius let out his breath slowly. Once again he stroked his chin. Then he shook his head as if to clear it, "Let's bypass that for now. I want to hear more of your findings and opinions. What of the political aspects?"

Quintus smiled broadly. He was on much safer ground, "Sire, I anticipated that question. I have three further conclusions and recommendations to my final report." Quintus then proceeded, "And these three points address the political issues directly:

V. The sect of believers loosely called Christians are a force for good, but a force that will sweep the world; Rome might one day ally with them.

VI. The Jews of Judea have the potential for revolt, but not because of Jesus. They seek freedom and will pursue that goal until it is achieved.

VII. Pontius Pilate should be recalled and replaced; the High priest of the Jews, Caiaphas should be replaced; and the Tetrarch Herod of Galilee should be replaced."

Quintus had paused to allow Tiberius to digest it. As each point was made, the Emperor said, "Yes. I see." With the last one, he erupted, "Damn it, I knew that man was an idiot and was being manipulated! Did you threaten to relieve him?"

"No, Sire. I would never threaten. I would just do it if I felt it necessary." Here the Emperor grinned broadly. Quintus went on, "In my mind I kept remembering, even hearing your words, 'All in good time.'"

Here Tiberius burst into delighted laughter. Raising his glass in a toast, he said, "Well done!"

When Quintus added, "I did, however, warn him, and told him to 'Govern!,'" the Emperor sprung up from his chair, put down his wine goblet, walked over to Quintus, braced him on both shoulders with his hands, and looking him straight in the eyes, said, "Well done, Quintus. You have justified my faith in you. Well done!" He grinned broadly in deep appreciation.

Then he clapped his hands, and when the steward appeared, asked if the luncheon was ready. The Steward answered it was ready whenever the Emperor wished. With that, Tiberius took Quintus by the arm and they walked together into a small dining room set for only the two of them.

As they reclined at the table, Tiberius said, "Now, Quintus, tell me more, but tell me especially about the people. It is people who make history. I am especially interested in their motivations." Quintus put down the grapes he was eating and began telling Tiberius about the people,

"Sire, Pontius Pilate lacks the courage and forcefulness to be an effective Proconsul in Judea. This post requires someone who is diplomatic, and will listen to the conflicting opinions and stories presented to him, but will keep his own counsel without deviating from his responsibility to represent the best interest of Rome. Even when appearances are contrived to convince him otherwise, the best approach is to always be independent of the schemes, stratagems and plots of the people he is governing. Pontius Pilate allowed himself to be manipulated by the High Priest, Caiaphas. This manipulation extended also to Caiaphas' father-in-law, the former High Priest, Annas. Seeing the power base threatened, they decided that Jesus, the Carpenter from Nazareth, had to be killed. Because of the popularity of Jesus with many of the Jewish people, they engineered a scenario where the people seemed to demand the crucifixion of Jesus. They did this by causing fear which drove away his supporters, bribery which brought in paid demonstrators, and a hope of reward which brought in the supporters of the criminal. Pontius Pilate mistakenly had Jesus condemned under the fear he would foment an uprising. He condemned an innocent man. Despite his failings, Pontius Pilate is still a Roman and felt some inkling of his error and for that reason, Sire, he went through the ritual of washing his hands."

"Sire, I recommended Pontius Pilate be recalled to Rome, and removed as Proconsul of Judea as quickly as possible because he is a danger to Rome. Incompetence can be tolerated when the stakes are small. In Judea, there are great political problems brewing and I cannot see Pontius Pilate coping with the issues."

Here Quintus sat up and looked directly at the Emperor, "Sire, we may be facing the potential of a serious revolt in Judea."

Quietly the Emperor murmured "Tell me more, Quintus. Why?"

"Because of the leaders - Herod and Caiaphas. I recommend they be removed as quickly as possible. Let me tell you more about my reactions to them from my meetings and findings."

Quintus then summarized his assessment of Herod for the Emperor,

"Herod would sacrifice anything to further his power or wealth. He holds nothing sacred and would stoop to anything. He would allow nothing to stand in the way of his ambition. Rome must be aware at all times that this man will serve the interest of Rome as long as they serve his interests. If the interests of Rome are contrary to his, then he will follow *his* best interests while making it appear that he is working on behalf of Rome. To some extent, he is a much better ruler than Pontius Pilate since he will maintain order. But he is so untrustworthy, and might at anytime turn on Rome if it is in his best interest. He might even engineer a revolt against the Empire, or side with one, if it will enhance or perpetuate his own power no matter what the cost to others. He is a despicable person and the power and nobility of Rome is not enhanced in any way by having such a mean spirit occupy any position of power within any Roman realm. I recommend that he be replaced as quickly as possible."

Tiberius nodded. His appearance became very pensive.

"Sire, I recommend that Pontius Pilate be removed because he is incompetent. I recommend that Herod be removed because he is evil, and is also a threat to Rome. But Caiaphas is worse." Here Tiberius sat up in surprise. Quintus pressed on,

"The High Priest, Caiaphas, is a very cagey adversary. As the religious leader of the Jewish people, he exercises significant power. This is because of his position and because of the rules of behavior which govern the religious and daily life of the Jewish people, a code they call the Mitzvot, or the Mosaic Law. He uses the threat of eternal damnation to keep his people in line. Any High Priest would act the same way as Caiaphas has, or he would not survive for long. Hence, it is in the best interest of Rome to have a weak and irresolute person as High Priest, especially one that is ultra religious and concerned more with adherence to the Mitzvot than to the perpetuation of his own power. That is not the role that Caiaphas has followed. His interest is his position, not the welfare of his people. He would turn on Rome in a second if he felt it served his interests and could be accomplished. Hence, I recommend that he be replaced as quickly as possible with someone who is less corrupt than Caiaphas."

"It was Caiaphas who was responsible for the unjustified execution of Jesus of Nazareth," Quintus declared. "Jesus was innocent of any crime against Rome, and as far as I can determine, free of any crime or transgression against the religion of the Jews. They claimed he blasphemed and as such, had to be executed. But what if he told the truth? What if everything he said was true?"

Tiberius was very quiet. He munched on grapes, sipped wine occasionally. Looking directly at Quintus, he asked "Do you believe there is danger of a revolt in Judea?"

"Sire, there is always danger of a revolt in Judea. The Jews are a hard working, industrious people, educated more than most of our subject peoples. They will always seek to be free of Rome or any other invader. But so long as we allow them the freedom to live their lives and practice their religion as they wish, they will be relatively calm. The Jews are unified. Their daily life revolves around their Temple and the Mitzvot. They follow the religious and behavioral lead of the High priest and the Sanhedrin. But then some new leader will arise and threaten the established order. He will attract followers; finally he will either be crushed by the current leaders, or he will crush them. Then the cycle will start all over again." Quintus went further, "Caiaphas has been too authoritative. The conspiracy to have Jesus executed will stir the followers of Jesus and it will also frighten others who will see through the manipulations of Caiaphas. The basic instability of the current rule of Caiaphas is being challenged, Sire. This instability will increase. That is what Pontius Pilate feared, but he handled it wrong. He should have replaced Caiaphas and not executed Jesus."

Quintus paused, and looking at Tiberius, added, "Those are the bases of the recommendations I made."

Tiberius once more gazed into the far distance, lost in his replaying of Quintus' thoughts. His face darkened with resolve. He let out his breath slowly, and jerked his head up suddenly to stare at Quintus, "You are right, Quintus! I have seen the same cycle happen here in Rome." Again he paused, "I saw it beginning in Rome when I found it necessary to leave to avoid assassins and why I ultimately had Sejanus executed for treason." Then he laughed, "As I said previously and as you quoted me, 'All in good time.'"

Quintus joined Tiberius' laughter with a broad grin, but remained silent. Tiberius continued, "I am intrigued by this Jesus, and his followers. Tell me more about them, and why Rome might benefit from an alliance with them. You called them 'Christians.' Why?"

"Sire, Jesus was considered the Messiah by many, the Savior prophesied to be sent by God to free and lead the Jewish people. Christ is a word denoting 'the anointed' or 'the chosen one.' Hence Jesus has been referred to as 'The Christ,' and his followers as 'Christians.' I believe the term will grow in use."

Tiberius nodded, pursed his lips and softly said, "Yes. Of course." Then he excitedly stated, "Go on, Quintus. Tell me about Jesus and his major followers."

"Sire, I believe his major followers now are three in number. They are Saul of Tarsus., or Paul in his Christian name; Simon bar Jonah, or Peter; and Maryam Magdalene, a woman." He paused for a few seconds.

"Sire, Paul is a remarkable man. He is a tent maker from Tarsus. I met him there on my way to Jerusalem. He is an educated Jew, a Pharisee, as they are called. He could very well be a candidate to become a Priest, even the High Priest. He is a forceful man, driven by his convictions and sincere to the point of zealousness in his espousal of his religious beliefs. Once convinced of the truth and rightness of his beliefs, he will pursue them. He will accomplish what he deems to be right and will stamp out what he believes to be evil. His initial impression concerning Jesus and his followers was that they were Apostates, heretics leading the people into evil ways. While not a violent man, in terms of direct punishment such as stoning, he did condone such actions as necessary and even supported such activity indirectly. After meeting with me in Tarsus, still zealous in his pursuit of the followers of Jesus, he was traveling to Damascus when he underwent conversion with visions of the risen Christ. Struck blind, he was led into Damascus where he lay for three days until cured by a follower of Jesus. Since then he has become an unbelievable tower of strength. I have heard he has gone into the desert to reflect and is expected to meet with Peter and the other Apostles in Jerusalem at some future date."

"Sire, it is significant that a most bitter enemy of this group has now become one of their strongest and staunchest advocates."

Again he paused to give Tiberius time to mentally digest the image of Paul. When the Emperor quietly and thoughtfully said, "I see." Quintus continued,

"Simon bar Jonah is the leader of the sect. Jesus called him Peter, 'the Rock,' on which to build his church." Another pause, then, "Peter was and is a fisherman, but in reality he is a leader. He was called by Jesus to follow him. Peter was a very prosperous fisherman, with numerous hired men and more than one boat. He was also an astute businessman who sought the most favorable income generating locations while minimizing the taxes he would pay. Such is the man who left all to follow Jesus. Prior to his crucifixion, Jesus appointed him the leader of his followers, or the 'Head of his Church.'"

He elaborated more about Peter, "Peter is a man who was at one time was given to almost instantaneous reaction. It was he who jumped out of the boat when he saw Jesus walking across the water, only to sink until supported by the hand of Jesus. It was he who promised eternal support for Jesus but who denied him three times while Jesus was on trial. But it was Peter who was summoned to the grave site after the resurrection of Jesus' body from death. And it was Peter who, on the Jewish feast Pentecost some fifty days after the crucifixion of Jesus became fearless, resolute, outspoken and zealous to the multitudes concerning the teachings of Jesus. In fact, Sire, it was on Pentecost that something happened to firm up the will and resolve of the Apostles. They claim it was the Holy Spirit sent to them by Jesus. This is consistent with all the statements of Jesus and the premise that a single god has many attributes."

"Sire, it is my belief that Peter and Paul, together with the other Apostles, will someday come to Rome. It is further in my prediction, Sire, that their words will bring many to their belief and that these Christians, as they are called, will become a force like an avalanche hurdling down the mountain, sweeping all before its wake."

"Sire, you sent me to Judea to form a criminal investigation of the mysterious disappearance of Jesus of Nazareth. I report to you that Jesus of Nazareth was not a criminal, that he was part of the single god that controls all, and that his body did not disappear mysteriously, but rather rose from the dead."

Tiberius looked very thoughtful, "Quintus, you mentioned a woman. Who is she?"

"Sire, she is Maryam Magdalene. I met with her on two occasions. I was impressed by her forthrightness and her devotion to Jesus. She is the sister of Lazarus, a great friend of Jesus whom he raised from the dead, if you will recall." Tiberius nodded. Quintus proceeded, "Maryam Magdalene followed Jesus on many of his visits to the town of Judea; she followed him to Jerusalem when he made his triumphant entry. Twice she anointed his feet and hands with precious oils, wiping them with her hair; she stood at the cross when he was crucified and watched him die horribly. She was the first person to whom Jesus appeared at the tomb after rising from the dead. She was the one Jesus directed to tell Peter about his resurrection and to summon Peter to follow her to meet with Jesus. She was always with Maryam the mother of Jesus on important occasions in the life, death and resurrection of Jesus of Nazareth. Sire she always seemed to be in the center of important events."

Quintus stopped. He wanted to emphasize his next statements. When Tiberius nodded in understanding of what had been said to that point, he continued,

"She told me she loved Jesus more than life, but that they were not lovers. Maryam, the mother of Jesus, told me the same thing. There are those who would seek to defame Jesus and to deny his divinity by attempting to link the human person of Jesus to Maryam Magdalene in a normal human sexual relationship, perhaps even in marriage. There are some who may even claim Maryam Magdalene was a reformed prostitute, but doing so may be motivated by envy of the esteem in which Jesus held Maryam. Sire, we are all human no matter our position and importance. We are guilty of the human vices that include pride and envy. Some of the bad things said about Maryam Magdalene are no doubt the result of these human failings. But, Sire, women, as we know them in our time, are totally subservient to men. The day may come when they are considered equal, but for now they are not. Hence, any woman who shows qualities of leadership, capability, and intelligence beyond the norm will be frowned upon and attempts will be made to quash her activity. Such efforts will of course be motivated by a common belief of the inferiority of women and their proper role as servants of men; but such are to deny the emergence of remarkable women, and the importance of their impact upon others around them. It is such that I judge Maryam Magdalene. My assessment, Sire, is that Maryam Magdalene is one of the strongest supporters of Jesus, who loved him, admired him, and followed him because of conviction, rather than of sexual desire. I believe that Maryam Magdalene is the forerunner of groups of articulate and skillful women who would devote their lives to the beliefs espoused by Jesus of Nazareth. There is no doubt that her actions and those of her 'sisters' to come will inspire envy amongst many men. Until women are deemed equal to men, which I foresee, then maybe even afterwards, many women with ability will be denied the opportunity to use their gifts fully. Sire, you and I both very well know that the love of an individual need not carry overtones of sex, except in the case of husband and wife. Maryam Magdalene, in my opinion, was a virtuous woman who loved Jesus."

"Thank you, Quintus," said Tiberius, "you have been very thorough in your study and analysis. Now tell me a little more about Jesus and his mother."

Quintus smiled. He had deliberately kept this for last. He firmly believed that her character would provide both understanding and acceptance by Tiberius as it had for him. In intense thought, he pictured her in his mind as he spoke,

"The mother of Jesus is a marvelous woman of spirit. She is full of the best things in life. In her presence I felt peace and attraction to her as I did to my mother when I was a child." He stopped. He wanted to emphasize his next words for Tiberius, "Sire, I am a soldier. I have killed in battle. I have never regretted my actions. But in her presence, I felt different. Battles, killing, glory, the Empire all fell into insignificance as I became engulfed in an unbelievable spirit of peace, calm, and love of Maryam. I felt her love as a blanket that would protect me in anything." He saw the frown on the face of Tiberius, but continued, "Sire, I felt forgiveness." Tiberius' frown deepened. "Sire, I felt I could continue my duties as a soldier but I would not take joy in the killing, but would execute as a necessity to defend Rome and those I loved."

Tiberius' frown was slowly replaced with a look of deep puzzlement. Quietly he said, "And Jesus?"

"Sire", Quintus began, "I never met Jesus but I feel as if I knew him all my life." Tiberius' head jerked up. "Jesus was more than human. He claimed to be eternal. He claimed to be the way of truth and life. He claimed to have been present centuries ago. He transformed himself into a god-like being before Peter and two other disciples, James and John. He performed miracles beyond any claim of trickery. He raised people from the dead, and rose himself after being crucified and killed on the cross. His teachings were of peace, and love of one another and belief in a single God. He preached a complete separation of the religious life from the political life. Essentially, Sire, he preached and taught that men should aspire to the highest order of human behavior. Knowing, however, of the human frailty, he was quick to forgive. He forgave his executioners. He forgave those who taunted and tortured him. And he forgave those who sinned." As he spoke, Quintus became more and more animated. He paused for breath, and slowed his rhetoric, "Sire, this man was part of their unified God."

Quintus reached his conclusion, "He was a man, but he was God. He died as a sacrifice for the sins of mankind to show the way to perfection. He proved it with his resurrection from the dead."

After a few seconds, he added, "Sire, that completes my report."

Tiberius seemed a little puzzled. "Why might Rome consider an alliance with the Christians?" Quintus delved into this point,

"Because Sire, with them we can extend Pax Romana by satisfying the hunger of the people for a purpose in their lives. The teachings of Christ provide a goal for them to permit them to bear the burdens of everyday life. No matter how menial their positions, they can look forward to a future life of reward and equality. Rome, on the other hand, can be the practical partner in this relationship, guaranteeing continuation of their well being, by keeping the public order, and by overcoming the enemies who would destroy all. Sire, Jesus wanted a separation of the religious and political states in function and structure. That is why I think it will happen someday in the distant future. Certainly not now."

Tiberius brightened, "I am beginning to understand." He looked thoughtful for some time, munching on his meal. Quintus too ate slowly, waiting for the obvious next segment of their discussion.

Finally Tiberius opened the matter, "Quintus, I am still not quite ready to accept a divine nature for Jesus, but I can see where many intelligent people can and do, people who know a great deal more than I do at this time, and willing to die for that belief." Tiberius shook his head again. He sighed, and looking directly at Quintus, said, "I can see how you must have struggled with your conclusions. You have done me a great service with your extensive investigation and logical study. Now," he said, after a long pause, "will you accept the position of Proconsul of Judea?"

"Sire," answered Quintus immediately, "I will accept any position you assign me." After a pause, "If that is your will, it is mine."

"Nobly said, Quintus," Tiberius remained silent, deep in thought. Then he looked directly at Quintus, "What if I asked you to continue your investigation of these Christians. What if I asked you to continue in your role as Tribune of the Praetorian, with a special and personal assignment from me to monitor their growth and continually report back to me their activity, their potential threat or potential benefit to Rome?" Then raising a quizzical eyebrow to punctuate his words Tiberius asked again, "Will you accept that assignment?"

Quintus stood at his place, placed his hand over his heart, and without hesitation, answered, "Sire, I am a soldier of Rome. It is my duty," he straightened and at attention, stood even taller, "and it is my privilege to serve you." Then he remained silent.

Tiberius was impressed. What a son he was. He looked at Quintus with eyes that glistened just a trifle.

"Enjoy this meal with me, Quintus." After a moment he submitted, "Your report is superb. Well done." He raised his goblet in salute. "As for the future, I want you in Rome. By my side. Advising me. Protecting me against my enemies, especially those who smile as they plan to kill me. I am the seat of power, Quintus. There are many who seek power. Only a few really know how to exercise it. The best way is never to use it, but have it in abeyance as a threat to be used when necessary. I tolerate my enemies, but if they become too dangerous, I quash them." Then Tiberius raised his hand and clenched his fist savagely, "Like that!"

Looking at Quintus, he said, "Follow the rise of these Christians." Quintus nodded. "They will come to Rome. Watch them." Then he repeated, "They may become a threat, and we will have to suppress them; or they may become a bulwark of support, and we would be wise to ally with them. Does such an assignment please you Quintus?"

"You know my answer, Sire," Then Quintus broke into a broad grin.

The rest of their meal passed pleasantly. Finally Quintus left and Tiberius returned alone to the Consul chamber. He sat in his chair for a long time, thinking over all that he had learned from Quintus. He knew what he had to do. Recall and replace Pontius Pilate; replace Caiaphas and Herod; and watch the Christians until such time when it became obvious whether they were a threat or an ally. That last point would be for a future Emperor. But Quintus would look over them. He might even become Emperor himself. He certainly had the ability.

Then Tiberius suddenly felt tired. He was still puzzled over the so-called divinity of Jesus. But there was no other logical explanation. He shook his head. It was probably true, but still hard to accept. He was increasingly feeling tired by midday and found it necessary to rest before the functions of the evening. He sat further back in his chair, almost falling asleep. Then he did. His last wakeful thought was, 'Would Quintus ultimately become a Christian?' He smiled at the thought. With a start he awoke. The report. He took the papyrus from the packet and looked at the signature page. Quintus had signed it: Q.

# About the Author
# Dr. Rocco Leonard Martino

Dr. Rocco Leonard Martino is Founder and Chairman of the Board of the Cyber Technology Group, Inc. and of CyberFone Technologies, Inc. Most recently he was Founder, Chairman and CEO of XRT, Inc., the world leader in providing complete global treasury, cash and banking relationship management solutions for many of the world's largest corporations and government entities. Treasury systems designed by Dr. Martino are integrated and operate in real-time in a fault-tolerant, on-line environment in over thousands of organizations around the world. Dr. Martino has patented and is the inventor of the CyberFone - the first Smart Phone - and the driving force behind the software systems that unite communication and computer power. The CyberFone provides real-time video, voice and data linkages. in the home or in the office.

Dr. Martino is a pioneer and international authority in the planning and use of computers, and originated many of the methods in use today. Dr. Martino served in various high-level positions prior to XRT and CyberFone Technologies, Inc. He was EVP of Mauchly Associates created in partnership with Dr. John Mauchly, the co-inventor of electronic computers. He allied with Rear Admiral Grace Hopper USN, on Automatic Programming techniques, which were the forerunner of COBOL. As Director of the Computer Division for Adalia Limited, a consulting firm headed by Sir Robert Watson-Watt, the inventor of radar, Dr. Martino participated in the extensive development of wireless navigation systems.

Dr. Martino graduated Summa Cum Laude from the University of Toronto in Mathematics and Finance. He earned a Ph.D. from the Institute of Aerospace Studies for work in the re-entry of Space Vehicles, especially in heat transfer requirements for heat shields. In 1993 he was awarded an honorary Doctor of Science degree from Neumann University for his contributions in Information

Technology. In 2000, he received Honorary Degrees from Chestnut Hill College in Philadelphia and from Gonzaga University in Spokane, Washington. Both degrees were awarded for his humanitarian and charitable activities, as well as for his scientific achievements.

The National Italian American Foundation honored Dr. Martino for Lifetime Achievement in 1992, as did the Monte Jade Society in 1999, and the CYO in 2000. In this latter award he was chosen as a symbol for Youth. In 2011 he was awarded The Order of the Golden Palm by the Equestrian Order of the Holy Sepulchre; and in 2011 the Order of Merit by the Order of Malta.

Dr. Martino served as Professor of Mathematics and Engineering at the University of Waterloo and at New York University. His graduate and senior undergraduate lectures included such topics as Artificial Intelligence, Space Flight, Information Systems, Economics, and Financial Modeling Systems. He continues to lecture at numerous Universities throughout the World.

Dr. Martino has been knighted five times. Most significant is his Papal Knighthood in the Order of St. Gregory the Great awarded by Pope John Paul II in 1991. Dr. Martino has served on various Public Service, Charitable, and Church Organizations. He served as Vice Chair of the Board of the Gregorian University Consortium Foundation and as a member of various public service Boards, including: St. Joseph's University; Equestrian Order of the Holy Sepulchre; Order of Malta; Vatican Observatory Foundation; and Founding Chairman of the MBF Foundation dedicated to applying computer technology for those with severe physical and/or mental handicaps. Dr. Martino has also served on various Corporate Boards over the past fifty years.

Dr. Martino has been a guest speaker at many functions in the United States, Canada, Mexico, Europe and Asia. He has taken part in scores of radio and video broadcasts speaking on Foreign Affairs, Information Technology, Innovation, and National Security. He is a Senior Fellow of the Foreign Policy Research Institute.

Dr. Martino is the author of twenty-one published books, including three novels, as well as scores of papers, and numerous corporate monographs. He is listed in various biographical anthologies.

## Reviews of *The Plot to Cancel Christmas!*

“Rocky Martino is like Rocky Balboa. His book is a punch in the heart and a hug at the same time. So hold on – don’t just read it – pray it!”

***-Jim Murray, Co-Founder, Ronald MacDonald House***

“A timeless tale that speaks volumes...a modern Christmas Carol.”

***-Joe Looby, Voice Actor***

“A book that gives you pause – could this really happen? An engaging story of what greed can lead you to do.”

***-Patricia Parisano, Legal Secretary***

“Rocky gives us a snapshot of how powerful individuals, organizations and institutions can use politicians as pawns and puppets in an attempt to enrich themselves. We are reminded that the ‘Greed is Good’ philosophy needs our vigilance in a world that should care for the needs and rights of the individual. He offers hope in a distressed world.”

***-Jim Fitzsimmons, President, Malvern Retreat***

“Reading this book is an experience in theater. Martino limns his two-dimensional characters with the skill of an artisan bringing them to the third dimension with extraordinary color. They literally dance from the page to the stage.”

***-Sister Marianne Postiglione, RSM, ITEST***

“It’s delightful – a modern day Dickensesque Christmas Carol!”

***-Dr. Joseph Holland, President, Pax Romana***

“This book is a gift that will put your life in perspective.”

***-Tim Flanagan, Founder and Chair, CLI***

“A Classic Battle between might & right!”

***-Jim White, CEO, JJ White, Inc.***

"Martino's story reveals the human spirit and all of its wonderful contradictions through one man's campaign to cancel Christmas. A miser who believes happiness is only found in money just might find true happiness accidentally in his quest for riches & power."

***-Joseph J. McLaughlin, Jr., President, Haverford Trust***

## Reviews of *9-11-11: The Tenth Anniversary Attack*

"Drawing on his vast expertise in national security, defense and the internet, Rocco Martino has done it again. 9/11/11 is a fascinating read that is a product of our time depicting the dangerous world in which we live. I foresee a future big screen Harrison Ford blockbuster!"

***-Rear Admiral Thomas Lynch, United States Navy (Retired)***

"Dr. Martino lays out a credible Al Qaeda sponsored plot to cripple the "American Satan" on the anniversary of 9/11... The theme of the book is apparently that cyber warfare particularly focused on finances is the way we can successfully combat terrorism."

***-Clifford Wilson, Former Member New York Assembly***

"Timely plot, well-developed characters...and a truly engrossing explication of the complexities of international money laundering and the fearsome dangers facing western civilization from fanatics wielding weapons of mass destruction."

***- Dr. Rosalie Pedalino Porter, Author of "American Immigrant: My Life in Three Languages"***

"The story accurately illustrates the complex and abstract world of cyber security and constant vigilance needed for tracking terrorist plots, including their planning, correspondence and financial movements."

***- Dr. James F. Peters, NASA Engineer and Vice President of Technology for Quasar Data Center.***

"The man behind this political thriller is extremely knowledgeable about the world of computers. Dr. Martino wrote the fictional story to stress the need for America to stay vigilant and fight terrorism with Cyber Warfare."

***-Jean-Bernard Hyppolite, Chestnut Hill Local***